Woman of a Hundred Names

a novel

by Jose Sevilla Ho

HydeAway Press

4313 Glenridge St.

Kensington Maryland 20895

U.S.A.

www.hydeawaypress.com

ISBN 978-0-9982971-3-2

To my wife Marie Frail,

and my daughter Nadia

Chapter I

Rosie Tang gazed out of the window above Repulse Bay, her eyes tracing the curve of red cotton trees lining the road twenty floors below her. All around her the hills were studded with lights from towers clinging tenaciously to the slopes. They looked like jewels perched on the back of a fickle, green dragon that slithered up and down the island.

Rosie knew only too well that each speck of radiance represented a fortune wrested from the rock of the place once known as Fragrant Harbour. It was a place so reliant on the sea that temples to *Tin Hau*, the sea goddess, worshipped by fishermen from ancient times, still dotted the coast.

Rosie was the only woman in the gathering at her penthouse on South Bay Road, one of the most select addresses in the former colony. It was a position she knew neither her mother nor any female member of her family could ever have dared aspire to before.

She had grown up in a small ground floor flat in Kowloon that had housed three generations, where the only space she could call her own was the gap between her bunk and the one above it, where her mother slept.

Now her windows looked out on the rest of the territory, as if it were a gigantic set of Christmas lights strung out only for her. It made her feel as if she were in the centre of her own constellation, deciding which way it would spin.

Rosie was the widow of Arthur Tang, founder and CEO of Tang Worldwide holdings, a multi-million conglomerate that owned some of the most profitable enterprises in the territory and overseas. After years of astronomical growth to become one of the most powerful entities in the port city, Arthur's empire had run into trouble.

That trouble stemmed mostly from events on the mainland, which was why more and more, Rosie's thoughts, and of those in her privileged circle, had turned towards the hulking hinterland in the misty distance.

On the far wall of the penthouse were two of her most recent acquisitions, large Rothko-esque works that consisted of oversized black tiger stripes on white backgrounds. Done by one of the most fashionable artists in Hong Kong at the moment, they were bold in execution, so brash they teetered almost on tastelessness, but Rosie liked them. She liked to cultivate a brazen reputation, and they reminded her of her late husband.

She was so fond of them she ordered new carpets that matched the pattern. Her guests commented politely on the recent changes to her home, and they sat dutifully in the large curved sofa facing Rosie's windows.

'Let's start,' she said, and took her seat at the head of the long *Quattro Medaglioni* dining table. Her visitors quickly arranged themselves along the length of the thirteen foot piece, held up by three carved solid wood pedestals, its surface bordered by a black line inlay on briar, polished like a mirror so that it reflected their faces, showing their anxiety or excitement in its delicate grain.

Stanley Wang, uncomfortable in the bowtie Rosie demanded, curled his hands the way he did each time he was about to begin a long bout of *mah jongg*. Like everyone in the former colony, he was addicted to the game, losing all sense of time as he formed the tiles into ragged walls and felt the ridges of the character printed on the tile, plotting his game. In many ways, dealing with Rosie was like playing *mah jongg*, forcing everyone to call on their most acute instincts to see where her whims where taking them, which way her erratic mood was leading the game.

'If there is a bright side to Arthur's passing,' Stanley began, 'it is that the Chinese government seems to have momentarily lost its focus.'

All the faces around the table were turned intently on him.

'Without Arthur they can't link us to what's happening in Anhui.'

Stanley continued. 'If we take advantage of this hiatus, Tang Worldwide can be as strong as it has always been. Maybe stronger.'

There was a ripple of hushed approval from those seated around him, all of them executives of the conglomerate Rosie now ran with the help of her late husband's old partners. Stanley Wang was the most senior of those partners. She was glad he had remained loyal to her, though the company her husband had created was now so vast and complicated Rosie seldom forgot how insecure her position was at the helm.

Like anyone who had clawed her way to where she was, she was conscious of the endless plotting and scheming going on under the surface, the hidden daggers masked by the polite acquiescence and obsequious smiles.

Her husband Arthur had not been immune to such intrigues. In fact, there was a growing suspicion in Rosie's mind that her late husband had been implicated in the huge scandal in mainland China as a result of just such a plot in his own backyard.

Rosie had that Chinese courtier's awareness of the weaknesses in her own position, the ways in which her own vulnerabilities might be used against her. She did not have a background in finance, and her only entry into its intricate realm was through the medium of B-films in which she had danced, cavorted and sung, all to no avail as far as real fame was concerned.

But well enough to highlight her vampish charms and attract the attention of ageing tycoons who started paying court to her. This was, in fact, the real audience Rosie had been aiming for. And she knew she had snagged the prize when she met Arthur Tang, a man to match her ambitions, with an appetite for perverse pleasures that Rosie nurtured.

Now, her protector was gone. But Rosie was tough, as hardy as the flowers that clung to the steep mountainsides of her birthplace. She was accustomed to walking through a field crawling with vipers without missing a dainty step.

Andrew ceded the floor to Andrew Chang, the other senior partner. He was quiet and coldly good-looking in his dark, muted attire. He had sat still as Stanley had spoken, like a shark moving stealthily under the surface, deciphering the incomplete figures he could see from the sea floor, figuring out the best mode of attack.

Andrew went into a discussion of how things stood at Tang Wordwide at the moment. As he went into the details Rosie had tired of hearing, she got up and walked to one of the windows. She heard the word "Anhui" crop up again and again. *Anhui this, Anhui that*, as though it were the name of some new bogeyman that had come to haunt them. She looked out towards where the lights of the territory ended. Beyond that, the dark terrain stretched out into the ageless vastness of China.

There, she thought, *was Anhui*. There, on the reverse side of the stunning vista from the South, was China, behind the wall formed by the hills of Kowloon. China was like the mother that nurtured them all, but whose wrath could destroy this child's edifice they had erected for themselves.

Over the years Arthur Tang had built his fortune on funds provided by backers on the mainland, backers whom he had managed to acquire through the political connections of his first wife, Linda Bo. Linda's grand father had taken part in Mao's Long March and was accorded rewards due to a hero of the Communist Liberation. Bo's fortunes changed, however, when the country turned on its own former leaders during the Cultural Revolution. Once privileged and untouchable, Linda and her family suddenly found themselves hounded and dispossessed, and they survived only through sheer fortitude and luck.

In 1973, towards the end of that disastrous decade, Linda began to pick up the pieces of her life. She married a fellow student Liu Qin, an idealistic Party member who went on to become a prosecutor in his native Chongqing. The marriage was short-lived, however, breaking up in 1980, shortly after the birth of their only child. Linda, abandoned with a newborn child, found herself with few options. Somehow, with the help of her mother's friends, she managed to find her way to Hong Kong. There she found work as a secretary, until she met her future husband Arthur Tang, then working as an investment analyst for Hong Kong and Shanghai Bank.

Linda's life in Hong Kong was the exact opposite of what it had been on the mainland. While her second husband Arthur built up his company, Linda gave birth to a daughter, Julia. By this time, Arthur Tang, thanks to Linda's old ties in China, had become one of the titans of the region.

But misfortune was to strike again. When their daughter was only 23, Linda was diagnosed with breast cancer. She died before her daughter, the heiress to Tang Worldwide, could celebrate her 25th birthday.

Linda left her husband an important legacy however. Her grandfather's links to the Advance Guard of the Chinese Communist Party gave Arthur the enviable inroads that allowed him to harness the growing power of China, just about to come out of its fetters.

Arthur's rivals watched with jealousy as he parlayed his small business into an octopus of an organization that held assets on five continents. But that bond he had to the mainland was always a precarious one.

As his fortune grew, he watched anxiously as unpredictable turns taken by the government in the People's Republic threatened to devour his empire.

Arthur was a believer in the old Chinese saying that those who mounted a tiger could never dismount. His life had proven it to be quite true. His boldness had allowed him to each unimagined heights, but he never forgot the perils of such a reckless ride. This was perhaps why he had chosen the ideogram of the tiger to be his company logo.

In the end, the mythical tiger that had made so many of Arthur's dreams come true lived up to its fearsome reputation.

One morning, news came that Arthur's most important backer, Li Kun Ming, the Deputy Party Secretary of Anhui Province, had been arrested on charges of corruption. At first Arthur and his associates thought the trial would go no further than the borders of the province. But as the official inquiry grew wider, Li Kun Ming's connections to Hong Kong business men like Arthur Tang were probed, and panic began to spread in the boardrooms of the Special Administrative Region. The Party leadership in Beijing seemed intent on making an example of Li Kun Ming, and their edict rattled the highest echelons of Hong Kong society.

Arthur found himself being questioned about deals that went down to the very foundations of his empire. And the once impregnable Tang Worldwide Holdings shook like a paper lantern in a gale.

Rosie looked across the carpet of lights, thinking, *there lies the rest of China.* Beyond the picturesque contours of the eight mountains that gave Kowloon its name, now almost flattened to feed the territory's insatiable hunger for land. So rich in many ways, yet so impoverished in that one resource that made it's existence possible, Rosie's home was like a man with a vast fortune who was trapped on a tiny atoll. There was nowhere to go but up. This land was like Rosie, in her struggle to get herself out of the quagmire into which fate had landed her. From the time she had used her charms to win small parts in Raymond Chow films, to being a weekend girlfriend for the rich men that crossed her path.

For the first time in many months, Rosie thought about Arthur's first wife, Linda, who had unwittingly sown the seeds that a former starlet like Rosie would reap with such extravagance now.

Since her death at the age of 55, it seemed Linda Bo had been erased. When Rosie had married Arthur, he seldom talked about his first wife, whose past remained shrouded in the enigma of that immense hinterland beyond Hong Kong's borders.

For once Rosie wondered if this trouble arising from the Anhui investigation might be some kind of curse. Some kind of vengeance cast by Arthur's wronged wife from beyond the grave. Rosie had been raised to believe that the souls of the departed kept watching over the living, sending down good or bad fortune.

Arthur, after all, was not quite a widower yet when Rosie came into the scene. But she had watched from the sidelines, listened to the gossip, and waited for her chance. Years before Linda's diagnosis, Rosie had learned of Arthur's wandering eye. She plotted for months to get herself invited to the same functions where she knew the tycoon would be present, until at last she managed to catch his eye.

Soon she was spending weekends with him. He told her his wife was dying. She brought him solace, and their relationship became stronger. And at last, as Linda's demise became inevitable, the concubine came out of the shadows little by little. They waited a short period after Linda's death before finally announcing their marriage plans.

Rosie knew even then that though her rival was gone, there remained one obstacle to winning the coveted space in Arthur's heart. There was Arthur's recalcitrant daughter Julia, who seemed to blame Rosie for her own mother's misfortune.

'We really can't afford to let this standstill continue,' Andrew was saying, as if he knew what was going on in Rosie's mind. She was grateful to him for drawing her back to the present, away from her gloomy musings.

'The incident has cost us millions,' Andrew concluded.

The 'incident' was the term everyone had tacitly agreed to use in referring to Arthur's sudden death in a Geneva hotel. And the standstill Andrew meant was the $800 Million deal with the Midas Group to build and operate a natural gas pipeline extension into China. It would have been a huge boost to Tang Worldwide's profits. But since Arthur's unexpected end, everything had been put on hold.

And if that wasn't bad enough, the news about Arthur's demise was followed by gossip that linked him to a high profile corruption trial in China. The back alley channels of the former British colony were buzzing with jittery rumours, fuelling paranoid speculation about the conglomerate. The company stock was sliding downwards each day, inexorably, like the earth on the island's mountains that were being shored up by gargantuan web of steel-reinforced concrete.

'Our problem would be solved,' Stanley Wang interrupted, 'if someone could be found who is formally designated as Arthur's successor.'

Though all eyes turned to Rosie, everyone knew they didn't mean her. Again, no direct reference was made, but Rosie understood what Stanley's omission meant.

He was referring to Arthur's missing daughter, Julia Tang, the one heir whose succession to the leadership of the conglomerate no one would have questioned. Despite all the paperwork, the corporate bylaws and the board meetings, Tang Worldwide, like everything else in the region, was run like a dynasty.

If Julia were around, the Midas Group would not delay one minute longer. The pipeline project would be finished in six months, the gold would start flowing back into the Tang treasury like it always had. And the traders who fought for every inch of space on the trading floor, every fraction of a cent, would cast their vote in droves, and stop Tang Worldwide's slide into the pit of worthlessness, the abyss that Rosie and all the others feared more than any marauding armies from the mainland.

Rosie decided to rejoin the gathering.

'So what if they prove a link between Li Kun Ming and Arthur?' she said as she walked back to her seat. 'What can those poor provincial prosecutors do to us? We're an autonomous region. We're not bound by the laws of the mainland.'

We're as autonomous as a hand is from the rest of the body that owns it,' answered Stanley with a mixture of assertiveness and deference. 'The body can do what it wants with the hand,' he said with an ingratiating smile 'But the hand can't do the same. After all, the body has more than one hand.'

'And no one knows whose pocket the other hand is in,' interjected one of the old partners.

Everyone around the table laughed. The elders of the group eyed Rosie closely to see that she hadn't taken offence.

'Speaking of Julia,' Rosie said. 'What are the chances she'll still turn up?'

It was Andrew who answered, emphasizing his contrary position to Stanley's. 'Well, Tang Worldwide is still a billion dollar entity. Even with the stock prices going the way they are, it's not something you could easily turn your back on.'

'Let's not forget that half of that billion dollars is debt,' pointed out Stanley. 'Debt which looks more and more likely to be called in, the longer this impasse continues.'

'If Julia were to turn up,' Rosie hypothesized, 'would she be liable for the violations her father is accused of?'

Stanley inclined his head in a way that indicated he was about to make a very fine point.

'There was never proof that Arthur helped Li Kun Ming plunder his country's wealth.'

'But why would he commit suicide?'

'He didn't commit suicide!' snapped Rosie, and the man who had spoken sank back into the ranks of his colleagues.

'You all read the Medical Examiner's report,' continued Rosie. 'Arthur's death was a heart attack.'

'But the fact remains,' ventured a board member cautiously, 'that his daughter faces the same legal dilemma if she were to take over her father's position.'

'Which might very well be why we haven't heard anything from her,' said Stanley approvingly.

'That is,' said some underling from Andrew's department, 'assuming Julia Tang is alive.'

Rosie's eyes darted to the man who had said it, and again, like a mollusc sensing danger, the mid-level executive slipped back into the safety of his fellow managers.

Brad Walden, the only American in the group, chose that moment to seize on the notion he'd been mulling over for months. 'There's never been definitive proof whether Julia Tang is dead or alive. And I think we can capitalize on that doubt to save ourselves.'

At that the executives started wrangling among themselves. In the discussion that ensued, the group's greatest fears were aired, their biases and their wishful thinking, against the reasoned, though bleak assessments of those like Brad Walden and Stanley Wang. Rosie sat back and watched them fight it out.

This was how she had conducted these meetings since Arthur had died, throwing in a question as if she were tossing a piece of meat into a pit full of dogs, then watching them tear and claw at each other until some kind of consensus was found.

This was how a former showgirl dealt with men who knew far more than her about the arcane business they were dealing with. This was how she tamed the most hostile of adversaries and found the most useful supporters.

The meeting didn't end until well past midnight. By the time Rosie got up from the table and stretched in that voluptuous way she did in the mornings, she noticed a barrage of text messages waiting on her phone. She had been so wrapped up in the proceedings she hadn't been aware of the device buzzing incessantly.

What's taking you so long?

From the flurry of texts from Jason, she knew he had been fuming, pacing in every direction and cursing at the delay.

She went to the door to signal that the meeting was over. The men filed out into the corridor after saying good night.

When they were gone, she poured herself a small brandy and let out an exhausted sigh. She was going to sit down and pour herself another one, when she suddenly remembered Jason. She got up wearily. Rosie's day wasn't over.

So she made a quick trip to the bathroom and finally headed down to the lobby.

A cool breeze was blowing up from the bay, ruffling the ferns draped along the front in a wild, almost ominous way.

She found Jason standing with his legs apart, looking down on the bay. His tall, lean frame cut a glamorous figure, clad in a black long-sleeved cotton top that showed up his sculpted physique. She shook her head at the sight of his jeans tapering into the fine leather Cowboy boots that he had begun to wear.

She made as much noise as possible as she ran up towards him. That he didn't turn around told her she had some explaining to do. She bowed to his will the way the managers of the company bowed to hers. He was her little emperor, the handsome fruit of her marriage to Arthur, the child who had made a dowager of her. He was her anchor on the Tang fortune, the one son that Arthur's previous marriage had failed to produce.

'Hello, darling.'

When he moved to face her, she put on her most contrite expression. 'Come give mommy a kiss.'

He did as she asked and she smelled the alcohol in his breath.

'Are you drunk?' she asked.

He didn't answer as they made they way down the steps to the waiting Maybach. The chauffeur held the door open and Rosie slid into her seat. Jason slithered in quietly after her.

'Why shouldn't I be drunk?' he finally said with a pout.

Rosie ignored his testiness and lowered the window. The evening breeze blew in.

'What else was I going to do? ' Jason flung his body back against the corner across from her. 'How was I supposed to know you were going to be all night up there!'

'Why didn't you come up?' Rosie bent forward to pat his cheek. 'I was hoping all night you would.'

'Christ, what would I have to talk about with those old men?'

Rosie maintained her jovial, tolerant tone. 'Those old men, as you put it, were talking about your future.'

My future? What's it got to do with me?'

'Well this just happens to be the business that's financing all the things you love. Your cars, your girls, your trips to Macau.'

He glared at her from the opposite seat. 'You talked to them about *that* again?'

'No! Of course not!' said Rosie as the car pulled away and began their descent on South Bay Road. The beach was empty and a few breakers gleamed in the starlight.

In a few minutes they were going through Queen's Road East. The small territory seemed even smaller at this time of night, a make-believe country with its little bridges and hills. The towers of Central, empty now, slipped silently past them.

At last, Victoria Peak came into view, looming above sprawl of high-rises like a luminous iceberg in the night.

'But I mean it,' maintained Rosie to her son. 'You should make it more your business to know what's going on with this company. The board should see more of you now that Arthur's gone. After all, you're my son. The son Arthur never had.'

'Why didn't he appoint me as his successor then?'

We'll never know the reason. But funnily enough that subject did come up.'

What subject?'

The question of Arthur's successor. Where on earth she might be.'

Jason was silent for several moments. The variegated reflections from the neon lights outside passed over his face. 'It's really no mystery,' he snorted. 'She probably knew her father was headed for a fall and that she'd be next. So she either killed herself or faked her own death.'

'I suspect you're right,' said Rosie with a half smile. 'She's probably in Switzerland somewhere or some remote town in France, enjoying her father's millions. Without having to worry about Anhui or any of that nonsense.'

'We'll never find out the truth,' said Jason, sitting back and enjoying the changing scenery.

'Well, I hope not,' replied Rosie.

Jason jerked forward in his seat. 'What do you mean?'

Rosie yawned. 'Oh, I just meant your stepfather. He was such a secretive man. I swear even I don't know everything that was going on in this business. He trusted that damn lawyer Mason more than he trusted me.'

The heavy car made a turn, and at last they got up on the winding road above Mid-Levels. They glided through the narrow path between crowded towers until at last they were halfway up the hill.

Rosie looked down at the buildings below them. They reminded her of the joss paper she and her mother used to throw onto the wishing tree at the Tin Hau temple. It was a tradition that was kept up until now, going to the temple of the sea goddess and writing one's most heartfelt wishes on a piece of joss paper. The paper was then flung onto one of the wishing trees to reach the ears of the gods. It was believed that the higher up on the tree one's wishes landed, the more likely that they would come true.

They felt the engine going into low gear to tackle the steep curves. It was a precipitous, at times dizzying ascent, like the arduous climb from the bowels of penury that Rosie well remembered.

Until at last they reached their home at the island's highest point, once just a promontory called Victoria Hill, now the summit of the world in so many ways. It was so high it felt like the very doorstep to heaven. As they got out of the car Rosie took one last look at the lights below them, looking like so much joss paper dangling from the low branches of the wishing tree.

Chapter II

Sunrise found Rosie in the tower known to locals only as "Two I.F. C.", where she sat in Stanley Wang's office, 70 floors above Man Yiu Street and the Star Ferry Pier. On a large flat screen behind Stanley's desk they could see a red line tracing the unhindered fall of Tang Worldwide's stock, looking like a child's clumsy drawing of a mountain, with one side sinking towards some bottomless chasm in the graph.

'We're in real danger of ending up with a paper empire.' Stanley's manner showed how hard he was trying to keep a grip on himself. 'We'll have all these empty buildings with no one in them, and safes full of worthless stock certificates.'

The thought gave Rosie a feeling like plunging all the 70 floors down to the street below. Everything she had worked for, everything Arthur had built over the years. Reduced to mounds and mounds of worthless paper.

'Yes,' she said staring into space. 'Arthur did warn me about this.'

'Did he say anything about some kind of plan?' Stanley replied quickly. 'In case... anything happened to him?'

Rosie had tossed and turned all night thinking about the exact same question. 'You mean his daughter?'

'Right,' nodded Stanley.

'Well, he didn't have time to tell me anything. If there was a plan, the one who would know about it is that damn Englishman Mason.'

'Yes,' Stanley nodded sagely. 'It would be good to get in touch with him.'

'You'll never find him,' Rosie waved impatiently. 'We shouldn't have let him go so easily.'

'What could we do?' said Stanley. 'We had nothing on him. The authorities cleared him of any connections to the Anhui Secretary. I have to admit, Bernard was always good at protecting his own skin.'

'He must have known something,' insisted Rosie. 'You know Arthur never did anything without Mason's advice. That wily foreign devil! That's why he high-tailed it out of here the first chance he got.'

It got Stanley thinking. 'Hm. He *did* go rather hastily. And quite a while before Arthur made his trip.'

Their eyes locked at a mutual discovery.

'You think Mason knew what was going to happen to Arthur?' Stanley said quietly.

Rosie had never thought about it. But the possibility opened up a host of new prospects. 'I wouldn't put it past him,' she said. 'I never trusted him from the moment I laid eyes on him.'

She picked up her purse and walked towards the window. She had a whole day of shopping ahead of her, and she looked forward to studying the matter more closely. *Could Bernard Mason really have been involved in her husband's death?*

The idea was too tantalizing for Rosie to dismiss. It gave her mind something to chew on. While she left the financial scheming to her money men, Rosie knew her own forte was in divining the intrigues going on behind the scenes.

In a place where it was considered a status symbol among the richest people to have a lawyer for an errand boy, Arthur had surpassed everyone by having even his dry-cleaning done by solicitors. It was joked that he only employed butlers with legal degrees.

But in fact, the personal access he had given to Bernard Mason was unlike anything seen before in Hong Kong. He had allowed the Briton to virtually become like a surrogate father to his only child, Julia, performing all the functions Arthur couldn't do himself. And as Arthur became more absorbed in the conglomerate's business, and his wife yielded more and more to her illness, the lawyer became even more of a proxy parent to the Tang heiress.

It was even said, not without some malice and envy, that the Oxford- educated advocate was responsible for everything from making Julia's tea to correcting her homework.

Of all Arthur's subordinates, only the Englishman was immune to Rosie's attacks. As if Arthur was trying to protect him for something, some crucial part of a plan that Arthur carried to his grave. What could have been Arthur's long term goal? Did Bernard Mason know something that none of them did?

She glanced back at Stanley, who had gotten up from his desk. He stood a respectful two paces behind her, his hands behind his back.

'You know what?' she mused.

Stanley took one step to stand next to her. The sun was shining in its full glory over the stunning landscape now. The vertiginous vista outside the window always gave him a tingling in his loins.

'Yes. Do I know what?" he smiled eagerly.

'I bet Mason's in cahoots with Arthur's daughter,' Rosie gave him that showgirl's pout that had impressed so many of her third-rate film directors. 'This whole thing about her disappearing. It's all some kind of ploy they hatched together.'

Stanley nodded without conviction. Like the master courtier he was, he watched the intrigue play out in Rosie's mind, not committing either way.

Rosie turned away form the view and had another thought. 'If Julia *did* turn up on the other hand,' she said. 'What could we expect?'

'Why, that would be wonderful!' Stanley uttered like an excited schoolboy. 'Our creditors would be happy, knowing Arthur's rightful successor was back in charge!'

After a few moments he stopped pacing and resumed in a more sober tone: 'Of course, we'd have to keep things quiet. Old questions might come up again. Where was she all this time? What did she know of her father's dealings, etcetera?'

As he deluged her with corporate details Rosie couldn't help interrupting him. Something had reached her through the grapevine, and it had gnawed away at her for days. Now she asked him point-blank: 'How true is it that Arthur spirited away half a billion dollars before he died?'

Stanley at first denied any knowledge of the matter, though he, too, had heard the rumours. Rosie wasn't going to be put off that easily. She clamped her hand down on Stanley's shoulder and looked at him squarely. 'Was Arthur putting money aside for something?' she said. 'Someone else I should know about?'

Stanley blinked nervously. He looked for a way out, glancing desperately around the room. His gaze fell upon the graph on the screen. All at once he remembered the news he had heard on the radio that morning. 'Well, we know that Li Kun Ming has been found guilty,' he said, trying to distract her. 'He is facing a possible death sentence unless he reveals more about his shady dealings.'

Rosie knew what that meant. She felt as if an imperceptible tremor had gone through the building.

'The party leadership won't stop until they uncover all the money Li Kun Ming is accused of plundering,' Stanley continued. 'Perhaps Arthur was afraid even his legitimate wealth would become a casualty of the scandal. He was just trying to protect what he could.'

Rosie delayed her departure by a half hour as they went over the implications of the event. They were mostly bad. Rosie momentarily forgot all her other commitments that day: her visit to her tailors', the hour she had hoped to spend at the Happy Valley Race Track watching her horse do the circuits.

This was just another reminder that China was never far away. The past, with all its unanswered questions, was inching ever closer. At last Rosie got up and walked to the door. 'No wonder Arthur's daughter won't show up,' she said. 'If she's alive, she must be watching all this from a safe distance. And she must be laughing.'

Chapter III

Melanie Jane Brooks wanted to laugh. It had all begun as she sat in the restaurant at the Rodeway Inn in Berkeley. She had come for the Tri Island Pursuit Races, not to take part as she used to in earlier years. She was 28 but looked much younger, her long black hair tied in a braid hanging down to her shoulder. The neat appearance was offset by a wayward strand that curved over her eyes, giving the symmetrical Chinese face its hint of vice. The contrasting effect was intriguing.

She had come merely to watch the races, seeing old friends and former students competing in the events she had won for three consecutive years in the past. Now she had bigger problems than winning a sailing competition. She couldn't even buy lunch without worrying about her finances.

So it didn't surprise her when the waiter came back to her table, devoid of his previous eagerness to please. He told her that her credit card had been declined. Melanie didn't react with horror and disbelief as anyone would have done. Instead she calmly thought of ways to extricate herself from the situation, somehow talk herself out of the bind.

She was getting ready to make a discreet exit when a well-dressed man got up from one of the tables and approached the waiter. From their hushed conversation Melanie guessed the man was British, and was baffled to see him take out his billfold and give his own credit card to the waiter with Melanie's bill.

He must have been watching her very closely from the sidelines to know what was going on, because the little drama had unfolded with the utmost discretion. So Melanie, now used to the most improbable contingencies, tried to fathom the man's motives for intervening. Her first thought was that he might be a private investigator, trying to find out if she had other sources of income she had not declared to her creditors. She was not inclined to believe in Good Samaritans or guardian angels, and eyed the man with suspicion as he walked with smug self-assurance towards her table, clutching a light-coloured calf leather portfolio that she found a tad gaudy against his conservative attire.

He looked to be in his early forties, urbane, with a kind of faded blonde charm that was at home in first class lounges and expensive hotels. Not somewhere like the Rodeway Inn.

Stopping a polite distance from her table, he gestured with an effeminate hand at the vacant chair across from her. 'May I?'

Melanie looked up and studied him frankly. His small, boyish mouth was pursed in a way that defied her to refuse. He had a large hooked nose that Melanie knew was supposed to mean he was good at making money.

'I take it you just bought me lunch,' she said to him. 'I guess that earns you the right to join me. Besides, I'd like to know why on earth you'd do such a silly thing.'

She watched him sit down and push the unused plate away, arranging the utensils rather daintily to one side.

'Aside from the usual reasons a man buys a woman lunch,' Melanie added.

The suggestion seemed to horrify him. 'God, no!'

Melanie waited.

'The reasons, I think you will find, are far from usual,' he explained. 'Today, I happen to have great cause for celebration. That's why I'm in such a generous mood.'

'Don't tell me it's your birthday,' Melanie said. 'Or your divorce finally came through.'

The man raised an eyebrow.

'That's so old,' said Melanie. 'But then so are you.'

'No it's not my birthday,' he said. And I've never been married. But the reason I feel like celebrating is because I've just stumbled upon something wonderful.'

'Don't tell me,' Melanie sneered. 'The love of your life.'

'No. Something much better.'

'What could be better than that?'

He leaned forward to give his answer: 'Finding an heiress.'

Melanie laughed out loud. 'I have to admit,' she said. 'I haven't heard that one before. Though I doubt it works very often.'

He took something out of the portfolio and slid it across the table. He said, 'It only has to work once.'

He was pushing a card towards her. Melanie picked it up. It contained a picture of a Cherry Blossom. She gave him a quizzical look.

He smiled as if he had proven a point. 'As you can see,' he smiled, it's not my birthday at all. It's yours. Happy Birthday, Julia.'

'My name is not Julia, ' 'Melanie snapped. 'And it's not my birthday. And furthermore, if there's one thing I'm not, it's definitely an heiress.' After a chuckle she said, 'As you can see from my financial straits.'

She turned the picture over in her hand. 'You think every Chinese person likes Cherry blossoms? You're confusing us with the Japanese.'

'But you will admit that Cherry Blossoms have a particular significance to you,' he replied in a rather pedantic tone. ' In fact your birthday could well be today. After all, the orphanage simply put down your birthday as the day they found you. Under a Cherry Blossom tree as it happens.'

25

She pushed the picture back towards him. 'Who the hell are you?'

'Someone in dire need of locating an heiress.'

'Stop saying that! I already told you. I'm not one. So thank you for lunch, it was nice. Now, goodbye.'

He made no move to leave.

Melanie turned around to look for the waiter. She debated whether to walk out of the restaurant or call the police.

Then, as if reading her mind, he tilted his head towards her with a *tut*, 'I wouldn't call the authorities, my dear. They're more likely to take you for the offender than me. Terrible how they treat people with previous offences.'

She reflected that he was probably right.

'Relax,' he said. 'Why don't you order coffee or something?'

She was tempted, and when a waitress appeared, her hand shot up before she could stop it.

'What the hell,' she shrugged. 'The race doesn't start till 3:00. I've got time to kill. Might as well get a free story out of this. But don't get any ideas. This doesn't mean I'm going to sleep with you.'

He raised his finger in another admonishing gesture. 'No one's going to sleep with anybody. But I assure you, what I have to say will rock your world.'

'You've got five minutes to live up to that promise,' she said.

The coffees were brought and Melanie sat back to savour some deliciously outlandish tale. He said his name was Bernard Mason, and he had been working for a man named Arthur Tang, the founder and chairman of Tang Worldwide, a billion dollar conglomerate in Hong Kong. But recently the tycoon had run into trouble.

'Arthur was under subpoena to testify about his dealings with the Deputy Secretary of Anhui Province,' explained Mason, 'who was being tried for corruption in the PRC. While testifying, Arthur got permission to go to Geneva to take care of some banking matters.'

'And?'

He took a sip of his coffee before continuing. 'Unfortunately, Arthur was found dead in his hotel room in Geneva.'

Melanie sat forward. 'So?'

'So his billion-dollar conglomerate is wasting away. It's like a ship left without a captain, drifting dangerously in the rocky waters of Finance.'

That was the point where Melanie wanted to burst out into a wild bout of giggles. This was the most elaborate attempt at a pick up she had ever experienced. If it was in fact that.

She scooped her purse onto her lap, got ready to leave. 'I still don't see what all this has got to do with me.'

Mason finished his coffee and put down the cup.

'All would be well,' he resumed, 'if there were someone to take over the helm. Arthur happened to have a direct heir, his daughter Julia Tang. But unfortunately she disappeared some time after his death. No one knows what happened to her.'

'Is she dead?'

Mason gave her a resigned shake of the head. 'No one knows.'

The Englishman pulled something out of his portfolio and again pushed it towards Melanie.

'This should answer all your questions,' he said, 'as well as allay any doubts you might have about whether I'm making all of this up.'

Melanie opened the folder and found clippings about Julia Tang. The file contained dozens of articles about events Melanie had been totally unaware of. As if they had happened in a parallel world, separated from Melanie's mundane existence by some unseen barrier. It was a world that had been rocked by powerful tremors, while life went on as normal for people like Melanie. The documents revolved around the disappearance of an heiress to a billion dollar fortune.

The restaurant was half empty by the time she finished reading them all.

'How come I never heard of this?' she asked Mason.

'Ordinary people do all they can to get in the news,' answered the lawyer. 'The most powerful ones use their considerable resources to stay out of it.'

Melanie nodded. She looked through the printouts again and let out a disbelieving sigh. What struck her most of all was her own resemblance to the woman in the pictures. It was as if her own image were staring out at her, snapshots taken from an alternative life she never knew he had.

'My God,' she said. 'I never knew I had a double. It's like looking at myself.'

Mason nodded with self-satisfaction. 'Indeed. Now I trust you understand that I didn't mistake you for Julia Tang simply because all Chinese look alike to a white man like me.'

The folder proved he was right. The more Melanie studied its contents, the less willing she was to walk away. The mystery they weaved about Julia Tang was so compelling, the unexpected parallels with Melanie's own life so tantalizing that she couldn't help letting herself get sucked in.

Apart from the story about the heiress, there was the question of how Mason knew so much about Melanie's own story. How had he come by the details about the orphanage, and the fact she had been found abandoned under a Cherry Blossom tree? Even her adoptive parents didn't know that.

He also knew in great detail how she had struggled with debt for years. He even quoted the dates and names of plaintiffs in the recent lawsuits that had cost Melanie her car, her job, the chance of buying a home, and what had been until then a thrilling vocation as a sailor.

Her situation was undeniably dismal. So not only was his arrival timely, it seemed too good to be true.

'All your troubles will vanish as if by magic,' he said. 'You will become someone else entirely.'

Melanie wanted to believe it, but she knew it could be sheer folly. 'Why would they believe I'm this Julia Tang?'

'Well, apart from the fact that you are, to all intents and purposes, *her*, you will know certain things that only Julia could know.'

'Like what?'

'Account numbers. Passwords, locations. Details from her own life. Intimate memories only Julia herself would possess.'

'And how would I know them?'

That's what I'm here for.'

Her disbelief turned into wariness. 'You know this missing woman's passwords? Her most private thoughts?'

The Englishman spread out his hands. 'For years I was the Tang family's care-taker, butler, nappy changer. Occasional pimp for Arthur. Bodyguard and mentor to Julia, all rolled into one. I knew Julia since she was ten.'

He told her the most minute particulars of the heiress' existence, right down to her preferred drink, her spa, and her favourite jewellers in London. There was so much he wanted to tell her, but the restaurant had already emptied out and Melanie could see it was getting dark outside.

Mason waved for the check and they went out to the lobby.

'We've only scratched the surface,' Mason said at the entrance. 'We'll have to continue this tomorrow.'

The next day he picked her up from Rodeway Inn at 10:00 o'clock, and took her to *La Folie* in Russian Hill. He had booked a table in the airy lounge. They ordered a four-course meal, and the lawyer described the rest of his plan.

Surrounded by the *trompe l'oeil* panels that lined the walls, Melanie felt herself being pulled into an alluring but disconcerting world, where the mind was continually tricked and real objects mingled with illusions.

'But I don't know much about China,' Melanie protested. 'I've lived all my life in America. Who would believe I'm an heiress from Hong Kong?'

As always, Bernard had a response ready. 'Like you, Julia spent most of her life overseas. She practically grew up in Britain and America. One of the first things I did for her family was to arrange for her schooling in England.'

'I might be able to keep up the pretence for a few hours at a time,' said Melanie, 'but I doubt I can fool everybody all of the time.'

'You won't have to be with everybody all the time. You'll only have to be Julia at company gatherings, board meetings, the like.'

'My God! How many people are there in the conglomerate? You think I can deceive hundreds of people all at once?'

Mason raised that fatherly finger again. 'Most people won't even come within a hundred feet of you. Remember, if you're at the top, only a small number of people will have access to you. And only at the times you designate.'

'And who are these people who would, as you say, have access to me?'

'Well, there are Arthur Tang's old partners,' said Mason, 'whose biographies and personal details you will find here.'

He reached under the table and pulled out a thick binder from somewhere. He lay it down in front of her. 'By the time you're done studying these documents, it'll be as if you'd known all these men for decades.'

Melanie flipped through the binder. Her heart sank.

'This is worse than taking five exams,' she said.

'This will be more important than any exam you've ever taken,' said Mason. 'And let's face it,' he added with a smile. 'The rewards are far greater.'

After she was through with the partners, he handed her another file. On top were two 6 x 4 pictures, which Mason spread out on the table. On one of them was an old publicity portrait of a pretty Cantonese actress in a shiny silk cheongsam, her hair tied in girlish buns, staring into the camera with a seductive half smile. The other picture was a glamour portrait of the same woman, now several years older, the playfulness consigned to the corner of her lips now, which curved knowingly at the camera.

'And at last,' said Mason. 'There's Julia's stepmother Rosie. The most important one. If you can convince her, everyone else will fall in line.'

'She doesn't look like Julia at all,' said Melanie.

'Exactly.'

'You think a woman wouldn't be able to know her own stepdaughter?'

'They were never very close,' said Bernard. 'And besides, Julia's been missing for nearly six years. Who knows what she's been through? What she's forgotten? How much she's changed?'

'What about dental records?' held out Melanie. 'And, of course, there's DNA. All they need is to get a sample from me and it's all over.'

He had evidently anticipated such objections. With nary a pause he replied, 'In the kinds of meetings you'll have no one will be asking for DNA. The people you'll encounter will care more about business positions, the terms of a deal, the margins, the percentages. It's not about who you are. It's about who you represent. When millions of dollars are at stake, a few hours' delay could mean a fortune. '

They sat quietly finishing their desert.

After some moments Mason put his plate aside and leaned confidingly towards her. 'Do you know the saying, *The King is dead. Long Live the King*?'

'I've heard it.'

'Well in cases where so many people and so much depends on one person, sometimes it's not that important if the man wearing the crown really *is* the king. It's enough that he's there.'

Despite all the facts he tried to persuade her with, she found it hard to believe the ruse could work. She couldn't imagine how so many people would take her at her word, that she was their missing friend or family member. Despite the uncanny resemblance, and despite parallels she herself found hard to account for.

She knew that the liar would always be aware of her lies, and everyone else would see through her. She remembered once long ago when she had been caught lying in third grade. The punishment was not nearly as unbearable as the whispers and the glances she knew the other children threw her way when her back was turned. *Liar*, their eyes said. *Liar*, said their gestures as they refused to come close enough to touch her.

She vowed never to lie again after that. But as she tried to purge herself of untruths, she found that it was impossible to do totally without them.

Everything about her was based on a fabrication. The birthday she and her parents celebrated every year, when her whole class would sing Happy Birthday, and snacks would be served during recess, it just happened to be the day when the orphanage had found her. And the name they had given her was picked by the staff from a book of flowers intended to be used for every unknown girl they had found.

At last they finished the meal and went outside. She followed him to his car.

'How many people do you think get given a chance like this?' he said. 'Don't you realize it? I've just given you a chance of a lifetime.'

He opened the door and she climbed in. She waited for him to get behind the wheel before she replied.

'I may be many things,' she said. 'But one thing I've never done is steal someone's identity.'

'I'm not asking you to,' he said shutting his door. 'You won't need to falsify anything. You just need to be yourself. For God's sake, you're perfect!'

'Do you say that to every girl?' she taunted.

'No. Only to those who match Julia's qualities exactly. Right down to the sailing.'

Melanie turned to look at him. 'Sailing?'

'Yes. Julia was an avid sailor,' he said. 'As I understand you are.'

'Was,' she corrected. But the mention of sailing made her stop and think. Many of the similarities she could put down to coincidence. But to have the same passion as this woman she'd never met?

She turned to face him. 'So how often did Julia sail?'

'Every chance she got,' said the lawyer. 'In fact that's how she disappeared.'

Melanie waited as he turned the engine and manoeuvred out of the parking lot.

'They found her boat drifting,' he said just before they merged into traffic.

'Did she have an accident?' Melanie asked.

Mason shook his head. 'The boat was clean. No damage that they could find. No evidence of violence or an accident.'

'Could she have just fallen off?' Melanie asked.

'They searched the vicinity for weeks,' said Mason. 'But no body was found.'

'That's odd,' said Melanie. They drove in silence until they were almost at the front of Rodeway Inn again. She prepared to get out.

'How lucky for us,' said Mason as he pulled up at the kerb.

He got out to open her door. He walked with her up to the hotel's entrance.

'Well, thank you for a fabulous meal and the even more fabulous story,' she said.

'It's more than a story,' he said. 'It's real life. Just waiting to be lived.'

'I'll think about it.'

He touched her on the wrist. 'Fate doesn't open a door like this very often,' he said softly. 'You better do something before it shuts again.'

She lay awake all night thinking about the possibilities. But the next morning all the arguments against it came to the fore again. In the clear light of day the pitfalls of Mason's scheme seemed all too clear. There was no way she could convince a stranger's family that she was their missing daughter, or a whole company that she was the child of their late founder. No matter how much the lawyer claimed he knew about the missing heiress, there were scores of details she knew could slip past her guard, little omissions that could lead to disaster.

All morning she went from one extreme to the other, dwelling on why Mason thought it could work, thinking of the reasons such a complex life like Julia Tang's just might allow the subterfuge to succeed. But then she'd see all the ways it could go wrong again.

It wasn't after lunch that she made up her mind. She came back to her room and started packing. She would catch the 2:00 o'clock train back to Chicago. Her best option was to go home. She would resume her ordinary life. come down from this brief flight from sanity.

She picked up the phone to tell the hotel she was checking out. But something made her stop. *It couldn't be worse than the trouble you're already in*, said a rebellious little voice in her head. This voice went on to whisper about the astonishing rewards she was turning her back on. *You've been a gambler all your life. Why not gamble some more?*

In flashes she glimpsed the dizzying plunder. *Even the slight possibility of success justifies the perils. Of course there will be*

35

risks. Isn't there always? At best she would be exposed as a fraud. At worst, she could end up in a Chinese jail.

You can walk into the life of a missing heiress. How many people get that chance?

If she parted the veil, the reality lay starkly in front of her: debts she would probably take years to pay off. Moving back in with her mother, finding a job, rebuilding her life from scratch.

She would keep her head down like she had during all of her childhood, calling on the secret strength she'd built up growing up the only Chinese girl in her white neighbourhood in Austin, hiding the embarrassment of having had a birthday made up for her.

She had no siblings, no one to spend her childhood with. In fact it seemed that her parents' house was built around her room, with its Mother Goose wallpaper filled with cats, pigs and turtles creating her happy universe around her.

But the world outside hadn't turned out to be that pretty at all, or that safe. Her mother said that before they adopted her, their lives had been so lonely. Her father spent long periods away on business, and her mother often went to stay with her sister. But when Melanie came they would spend the weekends together, her father tinkering in the garage, her mother busy in the kitchen.

It wasn't until they had moved to Chicago that Melanie made Chinese friends. Through them she began to find her way. Her adoptive parents made no effort to expose Melanie to the culture she had left behind. They didn't want her to be torn between two worlds, haunted by the same kind of questions that plagued abandoned children like her.

They had paved the way for her to follow them into their middle class American lives. And in many ways Melanie conformed. But the effort left a feeling of emptiness in her, an abiding sense of being an impostor, going through the motions of becoming someone she was not.

This was perhaps what had led to her difficulties. The same school authorities that branded her a trouble-maker lamented her underused intelligence.

No one tried to understand why she found it hard to accept the role her adoptive parents had defined for her. It was only when she discovered sailing that she found a channel for the restlessness that had always felt. Through the sport she made more friends, and, without telling her parents, she started learning Chinese, discovering the ways of the mother who had forsaken her.

Her parents had done their best. The orphanage had given them papers giving the girl's name as Meilin, her real surname unknown. Later on she was given a second name: Jade, and she officially became Meilin Jade Brooks. But over time, Meilin kept being called Melanie, and Jade kept getting mistaken for Jane, and she learned to think of herself as Melanie Jane Brooks.

Perhaps in a way she was like Julia. They were both outcasts in their own world. It was hard to resist the appeal of a parallel life. Julia Tang's existence, after all, sounded like the kind of fantasy life Melanie might have concocted for herself.

Her father's only escape was to spend his weekends remodelling classic cars, but the rest of the week they were like any ordinary family, going about their routines with suburban uniformity. While Melanie chafed under that monotony, halfway across the world, Julia Tang, though younger than Melanie, was dividing her time between London, Los Angeles and Tokyo.

While Melanie bounced from one juvenile program to another, Julia was presiding over meetings that decided contracts worth millions.

They were like the twin faces of one destiny, which had somehow forked into two very different lots in life. But there was one thing that kept tugging at the back of Melanie's mind. Both she and Julia were avid sailors. What were the chances of two strangers having so many things in common, apart from their uncanny resemblance? They both loved the water, and Julia had been lucky enough to be born without the obstacles Melanie had had. And yet she turned her back on it all. Or had she?

It was the questions that kept Melanie from making a final decision. What really happened to Julia Tang? What connection did it have to her? How had Mason known how to find her? What else did he know about Melanie that might shed light to her own unanswered riddles?

In the end, it was too late to take her bags downstairs and try to catch the train. She looked out the window at the setting sun. As shadows chased away the last gilded rays, the thought of going home suddenly seemed dreadful to her. What Mason was proposing might sound insane. But insanity seemed preferable to the drudgery that awaited her. She picked up the phone and dialled Mason's number.

Chapter IV

Less than twenty minutes after checking out she saw a black stretch Mercedes pull up at the front. The chauffeur, a black man about six foot six came into the foyer and stopped in front of her. 'Miss Brooks?'

He lifted her bags effortlessly and loaded them onto the car. In a few minutes she was watching the city lights stream by as she sat facing the rear of the vehicle, seeing the headlights of other cars receding like a movie rewinding behind them.

It was an unusual experience to face away from the road ahead, emphasizing what a strange new world she was entering. They crossed into the Bay Area and she saw only the vista behind them as they turned into Chestnut Street, as if she had relinquished all responsibility as the noiseless car bore her to where chance needed her to be.

Sinuous olive trees drifted by on either side as they climbed the steep slope past sprawling properties. Her heart fluttered a little as they went over the crest and they glided down the other side.

They slowed down until they came to a recess in the vegetation, and the vehicle swung into a concealed entrance. They came out of the leafy arbour to emerge on a circular motor court. The car came to a stop and the chauffeur hurried around to open her door.

She came out and saw the low fountain bubbling quietly away for no one's benefit. In the fading light she studied the travertine paving, leading all the way to the house, its pristine surface seemed to have known little use.

It was a 1930's style Mediterranean villa with a coral stone façade, surrounded by the twisting olive trees, enclosing its hidden world on three lots' worth of prime San Francisco real estate. A gust from the ocean whipped around her.

'Just in time for dinner!' Mason boomed as he came out towards her. He was wearing bright shirt-sleeves that matched his expansive mood.

'Welcome,' he said with his hands outstretched. 'I knew you'd come around.'

'Walter, please?' he glanced at the chauffeur and nodded towards Melanie's bags.

The man grunted and scooped them up in one large hand before following them towards the villa. Mason led her up the bone-white steps into the portico, then through a vestibule with a chequered marble floor and a wood panelled ceiling. She felt like they were going through a tunnel of wonders as they came out into a living room that was several times the size of the lobby at the hotel Melanie had just left.

She took in the casement window with its hillside view, and the French doors on the other side that led out to the patio. The chauffeur put down her luggage by the sofa and disappeared into the back of the property.

Melanie looked around, dazzled. 'This sure is a move up from Rodeway Inn.'

'Nice, isn't it? smiled Mason. 'One of the fringe benefits of being a toady to the rich.'

Melanie looked up the staircase twisting up with its wrought iron railing into the upper floor.' Do you own this place?'

Bernard nodded. 'A gift from Arthur. It's an exact replica of the house he owned in Tuscany,' he said. 'I thought you might as well get used to his grand tastes.'

He led her to the dining room and showed her the rest of the house. She didn't realize it, but her briefing had already begun. He pointed out features of the building, asking her to remember them. On a large table upstairs, he showed her maps of the Tang properties, floor plans and minutely detailed diagrams.

He gave her the particulars about every location, recounting why they were important to Julia Tang and how she was likely to remember them. They did this for over an hour, and when they were finished, Mason got up.

Melanie heaved a sigh of relief and crossed to the window.

'Follow me,' Mason turned and went out.

They moved to the library, where he showed her more photos and videos, enough to give Melanie a clear idea of just how her double moved and talked, what tell-tale mannerisms she had. He even dug out old school notebooks and journals from Julia's schooldays so Melanie would know her handwriting.

She gave him an awed look. 'You've been planning this for a long time haven't you?'

'It was all part of preparing for the unknown,' he said. 'Which you will see is the first prerequisite for this job.'

Melanie leafed through the thick sheaf of documents and asked,

'Does the family even know you have all this?'

Mason shook his head. 'In the kind of work I did, no one told me what I could and couldn't do. No one even defined exactly what you were supposed to do. So it was up to you

to put away anything that might be useful.'

They pored over the material so intensely Melanie forgot the time. When she looked up it was dark. The slew of lights across the bay was twinkling out the West-facing window. She

41

looked at her watch. 'Could your driver take me back to the hotel?'

Mason sat back with a laugh. ' You're not going back down to that place,' he said. 'Once you've made the climb up here, you know you can never go back down.'

Melanie glanced back at the stairs. 'Are you inviting me to stay?'

'Of course!' said Mason. 'We have work to do. There's a lot of ground to cover.'

What Melanie thought would take several hours stretched out into several days. They went about it as though they were in a training camp. A very luxurious one, to be sure, but just as exacting. Mason kept at her like a relentless taskmaster, forever thinking up new ways to test his pupil.

He gave her a family tree of the Tangs. It took days for her to absorb and commit to memory all the complex relations in Julia's life. By that time Melanie could envision the life stories that had brought the disparate paths of Julia Tang's parents together.

Looking at the chart mapping out three generations of a stranger's clan gave her a strange feeling. It was like looking at a maze of connections that she herself never had. Her own history was cut off at birth, and whatever labyrinth connected her to anything or anyone had vanished into the darkness, never to be discovered.

Mason made her repeat the information again and again until it seemed something she had lived through. It went on like this for weeks. The instruction continued from morning till night, whether she was having a leisurely stroll through either of the property's two formal gardens, or lazing in the pool.

In the middle of a casual conversation, Bernard would drop his easy manner and turn stern. 'What was the reason Arthur didn't push through with the agreement with Citicorp?' he would suddenly ask.

'Because one of the co-signatories had an involvement with Liberian diamonds, which would have subjected the deal to a U.S. embargo,' answered Melanie.

Mason nodded his head approvingly, and Melanie relaxed. They finished the meal quietly and Melanie sat back to enjoy the view of the bay.

'That's how it's going to be,' Mason said next to her. 'You never step out of the role. Even when you're at your most relaxed.'

'Do these people ever relax?' Melanie smiled at him.

Bernard gave her a jaded smile. 'They do when they're jetting from one place to another.'

Melanie realized that Mason had chosen the house with good reason. The lavish surroundings helped ease the tedium of her task, taking the pain out of memorizing floor plans and maps, committing to memory the faces of dozens of people she had never met. So that by the end she knew each of them by their titles, their nicknames, their hobbies, and some personal anecdote of Julia's associated with them.

When they were done Melanie knew she had to be able to walk around a building she'd never been in before, and know exactly where the stairs would lead, which doors opened to which rooms.

Mason had all the furniture cleared from the massive living room and watched Melanie move through imaginary offices and homes, while answering Mason's unremitting questions, 'What's right outside the gate of Arthur's house in Severn Road?'

As soon as Melanie gave the answer, Mason fired another one. 'If you go to the West window of Rosie's flat on Repulse bay, what do you see?'

'Stanley Gap,' she'd finally learned to answer after days of grilling. 'And on a clear day, Tau Chau.'

It went on that way, one barrage after another. 'Who's your dentist in Hong Kong? Where do you go most Saturday nights? Who services your BMW? How do you address the chauffeur?'

'Lao Chin.'

'Right. And why do you call him that?'

'because he's been our chauffeur since I was six, and he's like an uncle to me.'

It took her a moment to realize how quickly she had used "I" and "me," unconsciously substituting Julia Tang's biography for her own.

Soon she knew the answers in her sleep. The particulars of Julia's life so permeated her subconscious mind that there were times she woke up not sure who she was. The humdrum facts of her own individuality were subsumed in the more striking, extraordinary life of Julia Tang.

The next day they went back to work until she learned to dress and move exactly like Julia, carrying her purse on the crook of her left arm.

The hardest part was copying Julia's Chinese script.

'Before I got the job with Arthur,' Mason told her, 'I was studying Chinese in Beijing. My Chinese characters are better than yours. Yours look more Japanese or Korean. And stop mixing up your strokes.'

At the end of the second week he seemed satisfied she could pull it off. 'There will be lawyers of course,' he sad, 'which is why you have to be impeccably prepared. But I think you've done enough to convince your stepmother.'

'My stepmother?'

'I mean Julia's. But now she's yours, too. At least for a time.'

Among the things Mason showed her were pictures of the cemetery where Julia's mother Linda was buried. 'Julia visited her mother's grave on the 15th of May every year,' he told her.

Melanie felt an inexplicable sadness looking at the gravestone of a woman she had never known. She began to have her doubts again. It was the one time she was most tempted to walk out of the house and give up on this mad caper.

In the end, it wasn't Mason's entreaties that made her stay. It was a question that had been growing in her mind for a long time. It had been planted there years ago, as she grew up with the feeling that she was in a place she wasn't ever meant to be. Why did she feel that she and this missing woman had somehow changed places?

Since they had begun, Mason had not allowed her to call anyone. Now he relented. He put away their materials and said, 'Let's go.'

'Where?'

'To make your phone call,' of course.'

'Why can't I just call from here?'

'*Tut, tut tut*' he raised that infuriating finger again. 'What have we been learning all these weeks? Everything can be traced. There should be no evidence you were ever briefed.'

'But it's just to my mother!' she protested.

'Nevertheless,' he crossed his arms. 'One little phone call could bring everything down.'

Melanie threw up her hands and went downstairs. They got in the car and sat facing each other without speaking. It wasn't until they had reached Oakland that Mason rummaged in the side compartment and gave her a cell phone to use.

'Remember,' he said. 'No details about where you are or what you're doing.'

Melanie looked at the phone and said to him, 'That's how people disappear.'

'Exactly,' he nodded gravely. 'As we know from Julia's case.'

Melanie got out of the car to talk to her mother. Her mother asked about the race she'd come to see, and inquired if Melanie was ready to work again. 'I've talked to Mary about that supermarket job,' she reported. 'She says you can start as soon you get back...'

Melanie's heart sank. She said goodbye and hung up.

Mason's limo had even more of a gleam as she turned around to walk back towards it. The door opened for her and she was glad she would never have to show up for that cashier's job her mother had lined up for her.

She handed him the phone and he ordered the chauffeur to drive home. While they were on the bridge Mason rolled down his window and flung out the cell phone Melanie had used.

The next morning Mason joined her at breakfast saying, 'How are you feeling today, Julia?'

She was surprised that she no longer felt odd to be called by that name.

'Depends what you've got in store for me,' she replied.

46

'He stretched back and put this hands behind his head. 'Well,' you've been working so hard, I thought it was time to let you play.'

Wonderful!' Melanie smiled dubiously, unsure if it was for real or just another test. 'And what, pray tell, is there to play?'

He looked at her empty cup and plate. 'Well, if you're finished, you can come and see.'

He jumped to his feet. She followed him downstairs to find that he had had the library rearranged yet again. All the curtains were drawn back, and in the middle of the room was a table set with four perfect walls of mah jongg tiles.

'Oh, God,' Melanie shook her head. 'Don't tell me.'

'You're going to Hong Kong,' Mason said pulling a chair. 'It would be like going to Greenland without a coat.'

'I know enough about the game,' Melanie reluctantly took the seat across from him. 'But not enough to win.'

'Who said you needed to win?' Mason smiled. 'You just need to play well enough to lose.'

Melanie looked at the stacked ivory blocks in front of her. 'What's that supposed to mean?'

Mason replied with a sigh. 'Arthur Tang loved the game. He was known for holding eight-hour bouts on his yacht or in his home. *And* he was known as a very good loser.'

Melanie picked up a tile with a frown. 'I don't see how that's something to aspire to.'

'In Arthur's position, losing a game was a way of keeping his guests happy.'

'You mean he played mah jongg just to give money away?'

'Precisely.' Mason nodded. 'It was his way of giving gifts he wasn't supposed to be giving.'

Melanie chuckled. 'Oiling the machinery and having fun doing it.'

'To put it another way, yes.'

He picked up the dice and threw them. He got an eleven.

'Ah!' he scooped them up smugly and handed them to her. She rolled them. Mason peered down to count the dots. 'Seven!' he rejoiced with a guttural laugh.

As with everything, the game had begun before she knew they were starting. He guided her through the rules, and impressed her with his facility with the pastime. He was evidently well trained in the ways of his previous master. After playing a few rounds, Melanie sat back wearily.

'I lost four out of five,' she sighed.

'That's good,' Mason said. 'You're learning to play like a tycoon.'

He pushed all the tiles into one pile in the middle and got up. 'I just need to make a phone call.'

She heard him talking in a low voice in the next room When he was finished he came back to announce, 'Mrs Gu is coming after lunch.'

'Who's Mrs. Gu?'

'She's your new teacher.'

So for the next few weeks Melanie sat in the study with Mrs. Gu, a wiry woman in her mid-sixties, who played the game with ferocious energy and concentration. She trained her in strategies and all the ramifications, including some history, along with the expressions and exclamations that were likely to erupt as the game grew more intense.

At last Mason felt she was ready. He talked about travel arrangements. How he would make an anonymous call to the women's shelter and arrange for them to find her.

'That part about how you got here, you won't recall exactly,' he said. 'No matter how much they quiz you.'

'What if they do tests?' asked Melanie. 'Anyone can see there's no neurological reason for me to forget so much.'

'It might not be that you can't remember. It might simply be that you don't want to talk about it. No one will pressure you.'

'Why not?'

'It's no one's concern where you've been all his time. What you did or can't remember. What matters more is what you know, and what you'll do with it.'

'You're making it sound too easy.'

'It's not,' Mason shook his head. 'But remember, there's a deadline looming over all their heads. They won't waste time asking questions that don't matter.'

Now that we've reached this stage,' said Melanie, sitting down. 'I think it's time you told me more about that deadline you keep talking about.'

And so, with the same thoroughness he had prepared her to become Julia Tang, the lawyer told her about the trial of Li Kun Ming in China.

He recounted the whole complex chain of events, from the time Li was a mere Party functionary at the bottom of the government hierarchy, right up to the time he had clawed his way to being Deputy Party Secretary his native Anhui province.

'Li Kun Ming's old boss,' Mason concluded, was executed for corruption.'

Something dawned on Melanie. 'That's probably why Arthur Tang killed himself.'

'His death was ruled a heart attack,' Mason insisted.

Melanie laughed. 'You don't know the Chinese, Bernard. If someone dies so conveniently, it can't be by natural causes.'

They were silent for a long time. At last, Melanie said, 'Now I know why you made all this so enticing for me. As you say, I'm perfect for it. I'm a sorry loser with no hope. No one's going to miss me if I go to jail in place of this wonderful missing heiress of yours!'

She ran up to her room and started packing. He didn't try to stop her. She walked past him and charged out the front door. At last he ran out to the front steps and said, 'You have no idea what you're walking away from.'

'Yes, ' she answered. 'Spending the rest of my life in a Chinese jail. If not worse.'

'I've been telling you. Julia had no reason to go to jail.'

'Then why isn't she here? Who could walk away from all this?'

'Well, you are, aren't you?'

Melanie looked at the immense house she was leaving. With its twelve rooms and its invisible servants who made the dwelling seem to have a life of its own.

She took one more step across the motor court. 'At least I have my freedom,' she said.

'Go ahead!' Bernard waved his arms towards the road outside. 'There it is. Take your freedom. It's just there!'

Melanie took one last look at the trees and paved walks around her. 'You have to tell me everything,' she said.

'I already have.'

No! Tell me exactly what happened to Julia. Tell me, how did she disappear?'

Mason came down the steps. 'She went out for a weekend sail and vanished off the face of the earth.'

'Was her boat found?'

'Yes, it was drifting about fifty miles from shore,' he said.

'Were there signs of foul play?'

Mason shook his head solemnly. 'No blood or signs of violence on board. The only possibility was that she had fallen overboard and drowned. But no bodies were found in the vicinity.'

'So she could be alive?'

'The chances are remote. But yes. There's been speculation over the years that Julia committed suicide or faked her own death. To date, no evidence either way has been unearthed.'

They had started walking past the olive trees and went towards the back of the property.

'If she did fake her own death,' asked Melanie, 'what would be the reasons?'

'Well, apart from her father's legal troubles, wealth like hers imposes many unwanted burdens. Julia was a very private person. She was known among her friends for long, unexplained absences. Her private life and that of her family was fodder for the Hong Kong rumour mill. It can't be easy if your weekend escapades has an effect on your company stock prices.'

'What kind of escapades?'

'Oh, all the jaunts a single young woman might get up to. But magnified millions of times.'

'Because of her wealth?'

'Yes. That's probably why over the years she developed a mania for privacy. She became so secretive she even had a scrambler on her phone.'

'Did she have a lover?'

'Several,' Mason loped ahead of her towards the swimming pool. 'All across the spectrum, if you know what I mean.'

A look of worry came over Melanie. 'I see. That might be the hardest part for me to fake.'

'You won't need to fake it,' said Mason turned around. 'Once you have the limitless possibilities Julia had, you'd be surprised what you're capable of.'

'Yes, it all sounds quite head-turning,' Melanie said.

Mason gazed into the blue water of the pool for a few moments. 'Yes,' he said. 'And perhaps she paid the price for it.'

'You say her phone had a scrambler,' Melanie said. 'Was her phone was found?'

'No.'

'She didn't take it when she went sailing?

'No.'

'Why would someone sail off without her phone?

'That's just one of Julia's mysteries no one can answer.'

Melanie couldn't deny she was intrigued. After a while Mason sat down on one of the deck chairs, as if he had made his case. He watched her quietly as she stood debating with herself for several moments.

'All right,' she said at last.

'What?' Mason sat forward in disbelief.

'Let's do it,' she said.

He jumped up like schoolboy who had won the Spelling Bee. 'I knew your good sense would prevail!'

They went inside to discuss final details, what clothes she would be wearing, how she would be dropped off at the location where she would be "found."

They celebrated with a sumptuous dinner that night. It was a balmy, beautiful evening, and they dined on the upper terrace, but Mason insisted on sitting with his back to the bay.

'We can't risk being seen together after this point,' he said. 'You are not to call me from Julia's phone or any of the family's homes.'

When they had finished, Mason took something out of his wallet and held it out to her.

'One of Arthur's old calling cards,' he remarked.

Next to Arthur's name Melanie recognized the Chinese ideogram that meant "tiger."

'He chose the "tiger" ideogram to be his personal emblem,' he informed her.

'Why?'

'Because he believed in the Chinese saying, that once you mount a tiger, it's impossible to dismount.'

'It seems to have proven true in his case,' she observed.

'Yes,' said Mason. 'But think of the places you'll get to before the ride ends!'

By that time it was too late for her to back out. She didn't know that she had already mounted the tiger, and had no idea where it would take her.

Chapter V

At about 7:40 on Wednesday morning Stanley Wang got a long distance call. An American voice told him that she was calling from the Safe Haven women's shelter in Los Angeles. His name had been given as the person to contact by someone who had come into their care. When she described the young woman to him, the voice from a continent away sounded almost like it was coming from heaven, telling Stanley that his prayers had been answered.

A burst of optimism surged through him. 'Is her name Julia, by any chance?'

'It might be,' said the woman. 'She hasn't said very much. But when we asked her to write down her name, she just made the letter *J*.'

If it *is* Julia, Stanley mused privately, she might be reluctant to reveal her identity right away.

'Is she okay? he asked nervously.

'She seems outwardly well,' said the woman on the phone. 'But it's hard to estimate the extent of the trauma.'

'Trauma?' Stanley gripped the phone tighter.

'Well, something must have happened for her not to remember anything. She can't say how she got to where we found her. Or even who she is. She had no ID whatsoever when we picked her up. She'd obviously been out of doors for some time.'

Stanley took a moment to digest what the woman was saying. He responded with such excitement that the caller had trouble understanding him.

'Excuse me?' said the lady on the other end.

Stanley tried again. This time, he spaced his words out, enunciating each word distinctly, as he had been taught in grammar school. 'How. How did you find me?'

The woman, too, began to speak a little slower. 'It wasn't easy. The young lady refused to say a word when she was first brought in. We weren't sure she understood English. So we got an interpreter, who gave her a pen and paper. She wrote down your name and number.'

Stanley's first concern was about bad publicity. 'You have told no one about this? No newspapers?'

The woman sounded surprised by the question. 'Certainly not, ' she answered. 'We're aware in such cases that the victim might be trying to flee their abuser. So it's our policy never to contact the press.'

'Good, good,' said Stanley.

He quickly hammered out arrangements with the woman to prepare their patient for travel. They coordinated their schedules and tried to decide the best time for Stanley to come. By they hung up, something came back to the fore of Stanley's mind.

The lady had used the word *victim*. Stanley didn't like that. Had Arthur's daughter been injured in some way? Would she still be in a condition to do what they were all hoping she would?

But on the other hand, violence of some kind might account for her absence all this time. Who was responsible? How had they done it? They would soon find out.

Despite his inner ferment, Stanley knew to be discreet. He called the Travel Department to organize the trip immediately, bypassing his own secretary to avoid dropping hints onto the company grapevine. The fact that it was the

Chief Operating Officer himself making the call told the travel manager how urgent and confidential the matter was.

She asked Stanley what time he wanted to leave.

Stanley looked at the clocks on his wall and calculated the time difference. He was tempted to leave that very day, but knew it would mean arriving in the middle of the night in L.A.

'Let's make it 9:00 tomorrow morning,' he said. It would allow him to arrive in California sometime in the morning and hopefully settle the matter by the end of the day. It also gave him time to think.

He dared not call Rosie with the news. If it turned out to be another false alarm, Stanley might pay the prize for prematurely raising her hopes. So instead he quietly plotted, going through various scenarios in his mind. He went through the day's business without giving an inkling of what was going on in his head.

At last they were going to get a chance to restore some order in their lives. He allowed himself to hope. Could it be that the most elusive piece of Arthur Tang's puzzle had been found?

So many riddles could be solved by this one event! There was even the tantalizing chance that the half billion dollars Arthur Tang was supposed to have spirited away might be found.

If it was all true that this woman in Los Angeles *was* Julia Tang.

By mid-afternoon he could no longer restrain himself. He surprised his secretary by asking her to schedule a board meeting for the coming week. It bothered him how quickly the information travelled through the building. Less then half an hour later he looked up to see his deputy Brad Walden sauntering into the room.

'The meeting's not due for another month,' he said, sitting down in front of the desk. 'Did something new come up?'

Stanley trusted his deputy, but not with something like this. 'I don't know yet,' he replied, lowering his head to avoid meeting the younger man's eyes. 'I just want it out of the way in case we get busy.'

He gathered up his papers, stuffed them into his briefcase and walked briskly out of his office. Brad stared blankly after him as he disappeared around the corner.

Stanley surprised his wife by coming home before 10:00 p.m. He packed for the trip, then they sat down for an unhurried dinner.

The next day he arrived at Chek Lap Kok around 8:40, with plenty of time for the immigration formalities and take off by 9:00. He walked through the half empty lounge to find the pilot waiting for him. The paperwork took about five minutes and they walked out to the plane together.

He settled in for the 13-hour flight. Barring any delays, he figured they would be in Los Angeles just around 7:00 or 8:00 a.m. L.A. Time. He laid out all the papers pertaining to Arthur Tang's missing daughter, including her last passport that had long expired. He looked at the photo in the document, wondering how she would look now, if he would still recognize her. His heart was beating fast as they thundered towards the end of the runway and left the ground.

During the flight, Stanley looked over the plans for the project that had stalled since Arthur's death. He made notes on possible moves to revive it, if his present mission should prove successful. *If!*

Hs mind kept stumbling on the word. That big question loomed over everything he was doing: his plans, this sudden trans-Continental flight. *If.*

It was nearly midnight in Hong Kong when they reached their destination. His body still on Hong Kong time, getting ready to wind down. But in Los Angeles the day was just starting, the bright sun waking him up, making the sudden change in landscape even more of a jolt. The familiar compactness of Hong Kong was displaced by the sprawl of L.A., the heavy traffic telling him he was no longer home.

He sat in the back of the long car, ready to turn around and dismiss another false lead or hoax. There had been so many over the years. That was another reason they had kept the matter strictly confidential. Luckily, Arthur and his partners had cultivated what Stanley thought of as harmonious relations with the Hong Kong Police, and their cooperation had ensured that the story remained strictly in the background.

The car pulled up at the shelter at about 12:20 noon. Stanley knew he should have lunch, but he ignored the needs of his body for the more urgent demands of the moment. *Later*, he told himself. *Later*, he would return to the normal rhythms of life.

It was something he had been doing since Arthur's death. *Later*, he would always cajole himself. Later, life would return to normal and he would go back to the way things were before. But the months had turned into years, and this constant turmoil and uncertainty had become the norm.

The shelter looked to be a mix of rundown apartments and temporary structures. There was a long, unpainted cargo container along one side of the building.

Stanley walked up to the front door. He was met by a young woman with pierced eyebrows and green and purple tattoos from her shoulders to her wrists. She pored over the ID that he handed her.

'Follow me, Mr. Tang,' she said.

'Wang,' she corrected her, but she was already walking briskly ahead of him and didn't seem to hear. She knocked on a door and a female voice ordered them to come in.

Stanley walked into the administrator's office, which doubled as a conference room and venue for what he imagined were many agonizing reunions.

The woman at the far wall got up and walked around her desk to greet him.

'Mr. Wang,' she gave him a warm smile. 'I'm Cristina Moran. We spoke on the phone.'
She was a heavy-set Hispanic woman of about 37, with coiffed reddish hair. After their initial pleasantries, Miss Moran's voice lowered to a near whisper.

'We haven't tried to force her to say anything,' she said with a solemn expression. 'We believe that whatever information she has might come out in dribs and drabs.'
Stanley puzzled over the expression. Then he looked around impatiently. 'Can we see her?'

'Of course!'

Cristina Moran led them down the corridor to the room occupied by the woman they still referred to as "Jane Doe 3". This was to distinguish her from two other women who had ended up in their facility without any identification, both of whom disappeared back into the city after a few days, and had evaded all the shelter's efforts to locate them again.

Cristina Moran explained to Stanley how a concerned citizen had phoned them about young woman wandering in the park by herself after hours, wearing only thin clothing despite the chill. When she was brought to the shelter, the woman was checked for signs of drug use.

'And were there any?' Stanley demanded.

Cristina Moran tilted her head. 'Thankfully, no.'

She knocked on the door. After the longest pause, the door opened a crack and Stanley tried to see over the administrator's shoulder as she had a whispered exchange with whoever was inside.

At last, Cristina held the door open for Stanley. She nodded for him to go in.

Stanley took a few steps. He had to suppress a cringe at the sight of the interior, full of shoddy plastic furnishings, barrack-like, really no more than a cargo container like the one he'd seen outside, just made to look a bit more habitable.

It was the last place he had ever imagined finding Arthur's missing daughter, the young woman he had met in all the most sumptuous surroundings imaginable. He took a few moments to see the small figure seated in the cheap vinyl armchair, looking down on the floor. This kind of avoidance was something Miss Moran had warned him about. 'She might be too distressed to respond normally to anyone,' she had said.

But I'm not just anyone! Stanley thought privately. *I watched her grow up!*

He took a tentative step forward, clasping his hands together, afraid of being too obtrusive.

The girl sat forward and raised her head to look at him. Stanley drew a sharp breath. The young woman's gaze brought back memories of his friend Arthur. Happy recollections flooded back from the days when all was well. When Arthur's world, as well as Stanley's, seemed unshakeable.

'Siew Keng!' he blurted out.

The girl got up from the chair. Stanley noticed a slight hesitation before she took a step towards him. But Cristina had warned him about behaviour like this too.

The slight figure stood before him, peeking up from behind a fringe of hair. He had forgotten how small Arthur's daughter was. *Slightly taller than a school girl*, Stanley thought. Just as he remembered, holding her slender shoulders trembling with sobs at her mother's funeral. Now *here* she *was*. Stanley couldn't believe his eyes.

'My God,' he said softly. 'It's really you!'

She walked towards him and stood on tiptoes to give him an embrace. 'Uncle Stanley,' she said quietly. 'Thank you for coming.'

'Julia!' Stanley said in an impassioned voice, gripping her hands tightly. 'I'm so, so happy to see you!'

Tears had already begun to cloud his eyes. He began talking so fast neither of the women could understand him. Cristina Moran tried to calm him down. She was accustomed to the powerful reactions of friends or family upon reuniting with a missing person. She spoke to him soothingly, reminding him of the things they still needed to do.

'Why don't we go to my office,' she said and stepped back into to the corridor. She let them walk ahead of her, watching discreetly, alert for any signs of deception.

She found none. At least not on the part of Stanley Wang. His relationship with the young woman seemed genuine, though it baffled Cristina how a woman from Hong Kong had ended up in this condition on the streets of Los Angeles.

She opened the door and waved them towards the long conference table. She watched them take their seats. Then she stepped outside again to give them some privacy.

Stanley heard the door closing quietly, but kept his eyes on the flowery tabletop for several moments.

Finally, the girl spoke, 'I guess I won't be sailing for a while.'

Stanley looked up with a big smile.

The girl added, 'I should have listened to your warnings.'

For a moment, Stanley was too overwhelmed to speak. The reminder was an unhappy one, but her mention of it seemed so right. He knew it would have been the first thing Julia would bring up. As if their relationship had only been briefly interrupted. It was so like his recollection of Julia. To pick up where they had left off, as if the interval, no matter how long, was irrelevant to the business at hand.

How like her father Arthur. Stanley mused. He had been right. He had watched the girl pass the hardest tests. He saw how she coped with her mother's death while coming to grips with her new role in her father's conglomerate. Such a person did not give in to pressure easily. Such a woman would not take her own life. Stanley had firmly opposed all speculation that Julia had been too afraid to go on. *Now here was proof!*

'They always said water would be my downfall,' she continued. 'I should always remember how you saved me on the pier when I was small.'

In her mind Melanie was recalling the picture Mason had made her commit to memory. It showed Stanley posing on a pier with Arthur and his family. Mason had recounted how on that day Julia had climbed over the railing to touch a tethered boat with her toe, but her foot had slipped.

Stanley had lunged across the jetty to grab her arms. Julia looked like she was about to cry. But when she realized that the painful grip Stanley had on her was only because he was desperate to save her, she pulled with all her might to get back over the railing.

'Yes!' Stanley mumbled in front of Melanie now. She noticed his eyes were a little moist. 'Yes,' He touched her hand. 'Those were happy times. Even that little accident couldn't ruin it. I often think about it.'

Melanie smiled at him. The image of the snapshot flashed in her mind again. A young family out on a bright day, oblivious to the tragedies that yet lay ahead. She felt a sense of triumph at how successfully she had injected that detail into the conversation. But it was tinged by a sense of loss that puzzled her.

In the next office, separated only by the thinnest wall, Cristina Moran sat with her assistant, listening out for signs of possible trouble coming from her own office. The rest of her staff were busy checking all the information Stanley had given them. Cristina herself was reviewing all the documents he had brought relating to Julia Tang, the details of the disappearance, the dead ends to the investigations that the family had conducted privately. In the last folder Cristina found 4 x 6 photographs of Julia Tang. She compared them to the young woman they had brought to Safe Haven just days before.

At last a complete picture formed in Cristina Moran's mind.

'Very well,' she said. 'Now it's beginning to make *some* sense.'

She got up and walked back to her own office. She knocked softly before coming in. 'Very well, Mr. Wang,' she said. 'We won't hold you anymore.'

She turned to Melanie with a kind smile and said. 'You can go back to your room and collect your things.'

Melanie knew there wasn't much to collect. Just the change of clothes the shelter had given her, a toothbrush and the most basic things. But she knew it would appear strange not to go get them. So she got up and left the room. Cristina nodded to her tattooed assistant to go with Melanie.

When they were alone, Cristina leaned forward to tell Stanley, 'I still can't quite figure out how she had ended up on the streets of Los Angeles. It's a long way from where you said she was last seen.'

Stanley fumbled for something to say.

'But as you say, she's a young woman with vast resources. So I guess the question would be how she went from those circumstances to the ones we found her in.'

'She...was having many, uh, difficulties,' Stanley cagily volunteered.

'Of course it's not our job to inquire into these things,' Cristina said. 'But for the sake of her future recovery, I can only speculate about the possibility of abduction or an abusive relationship. But the most likely explanation might be a mental breakdown of some sort. An emotional collapse brought on by great stress.'

She glanced at the door before she added, 'We found some slight injuries on her. Which led us to think she might have attempted suicide at some point.'

Yes, yes,' Stanley nodded, as if Cristina had cleared the last doubts in his own mind. 'She was under very great stress.'

Her comments were helping him bridge the gap left by six years. Anything was possible in that length of time. But what Miss Moran was saying made sense. This could be why no one could find Julia where they were all searching for her.

Perhaps she had tried to get as far away as she could from them all. L.A. was the one place no one would think to look for her. How she did it and who, if anyone, had helped her, Stanley had no idea. But there would be plenty of time to find out later.

For now, there was no doubt in his mind that he had really found Arthur's daughter. His old friend would have been so proud of him.

Cristina got up and went to her desk. She laid out before Stanley all the forms he needed to sign.

He took off his glasses to go through them. When he finally affixed his signature and got up, Cristina could barely disguise her relief. They had found a solution to the problem of Jane Doe. Though there still remained questions in her mind. She would probably never answer them. But for now it was enough that a vulnerable young woman had been saved.

Stanley excused himself to go to the bathroom. There, he found a quiet corner and called Rosie. His excitement overcame all his misgivings about falsely raising her hopes.

When he came back to Cristina's office Melanie was already there, a small plastic bag with the shelter's blue logo on the table in front of her.

Cristina got up and they all walked to the main entrance.

'Take care, Miss Tang,' she said to the young woman, who seemed taken aback at her use of the name. Cristina leaned forward to give her temporary ward an embrace.

She stood in the doorway, watching the pair uncertainly as they got in the long car and drove away.

As soon as they left, a series of actions followed at dizzying speed. Their first stop was the Hong Kong Consulate. Melanie sat in the Waiting Room as Stanley whispered something to an official and was led through a door into the rear of the office. She glimpsed him briefly through the thick glass behind the counters, as he conferred with a small group behind one of the cubicles. He took out pieces of paper and what appeared to be an old passport and showed it to one of them. The man who had received them turned to give Melanie a probing look through the bullet-proof glass. Melanie looked down to hide her anxiety. This part was out of her hands. Mason warned her it would be one of the most arduous parts of her test.

Stanley came from one of the side doors. 'Please come with me,' he said. She followed him through the maze of cubicles behind the glass, until they reached a small space in the back of the room. She sat on a tall stool and a photographer took her picture. Then Stanley ushered her into the Consul's office.

The elderly Consul gave her a smile and a slight bow, but beckoned only towards the papers on his desk. Stanley went through the forms with her, handing her a handful for her to read. Among them she found Julia's expired passport.

At the bottom of each form was a box where she had to affix her signature. She was almost going to sign her own name, when at the last moment she saw Julia's name. Her hand almost shook as she took the pen from Stanley and lowered it towards the paper.

She knew she was taking the first irreversible step towards damnation. The forms would be forever in these archives, indubitable proof of her claiming to be someone she was not.

Images of punishment flashed in her mind, mixed in with the bustle and noise from the cubicles, along with the memory of Mason's smug reassurances. She became aware that Stanley watching her closely. Another moment's delay might undo everything.

So, calling upon the weeks of training, she leaned down to affix Julia's signature exactly as she had practiced it thousands of times.

She didn't know it then, but it was thanks to the same harmonious relations that Stanley and Arthur had fomented throughout their careers that the whole bureaucratic procedure was over in a matter of hours.

Stanley got up from his seat, draped his jacket over his arm and said, 'Now I can take you home.'

The word *home* resonated in many different ways to Melanie. First, it made her think of her mother's house in Chicago. Then it conjured up the photos and maps Mason had shown her of Julia's home, which were lodged in a compartment in her brain now, like the props, make up and costumes in an actor's dressing room, ready to be picked up before she stepped out on to the stage to play her role.

The last image it conjured up was more vague and mysterious, it contained the subtle promise of return, some solution to the mystery that came before the Cherry Blossom tree, and the fake birthday, and the whole new identity her adoptive parents had given her.

She sat in the back of the chauffeured car, getting unaccustomed to looking away from their direction of travel. She looked back at the traffic they were leaving behind, as if seeing the old life she was leaving.

'Much more traffic than Hong Kong,' Stanley snickered.

'Yes,' said Melanie, leaning her head back tiredly on the headrest. 'It would be nice to be back somewhere smaller.'

She closed her eyes. The tension of the past few days came back to her: Mason dropping her off at the park, then waiting on the bench until the people from Safe Haven came to get her.

Then the drug tests, the nights of silence and refusing to speak. Closing her eyes had been a way of stopping the questions she didn't know how to answer. Now she had to open her eyes.

The car had stopped.

'We're here,' Stanley said with a smile.

They got out and walked into the Executive Terminal. At the lounge, the same pilot that had brought Stanley was waiting for them, nursing a drink, his golf bag by his side.

He got up so shake hands with Melanie, mumbling, 'Good to see you, ma'am.'

Stanley sat next to her while their documents were checked, then, they were let through a door to follow the pilot across the tarmac.

When she saw the plane she almost stopped. It made the whole adventure suddenly real. It stood there, large, white and substantial. It wasn't just a game now. She was *really* flying out to other lands. Her heart pounded like a trapped animal in her chest.

As she forced herself to move forward, she suddenly felt naked. This was first time she was flying anywhere under someone else's name. She was taking nothing of her own, except the clothes on her back, a few papers that weren't really hers, and a mass of lies in her head.

They reached the ramp and she looked up at the aircraft again. Immediately Mason's training kicked in again. She knew it wasn't the plane Julia normally flew in. Stanley turned around to smile at her.

'What happened to the 60?' she said.

Stanley gave an embarrassed shrug. 'Your mother needs it for her trip to London.'

Once again, the word mother made her think of her adoptive mother waiting for her in Chicago. But she suppressed the real memory in favour of the lie.

'Oh, time for the annual fashion spree,' Melanie said, getting into her role. 'How could I forget?'

She climbed up the steps followed by Stanley. The Lear jet 60 had been Mason's favourite. When he made her study the brochures about the jets the Tangs owned, Melanie felt like they were taking part in some idle, impossible fantasy. Now here she was, feeling her heels on sturdy aluminium. Walking up the steps into the cabin she had known only from the literature.

The interior was like a plush cocoon, separated from the reality outside with airtight seals and internal climate control. By entering it Melanie knew she had passed a point of no return. She sat down and strapped herself to a seat by the window. They waited for permission to take off.

At last, as they hurtled down the runway and tilted up to get airborne, Melanie wondered what she had gotten herself into. After several moments the boom of the engine subsided and they eased back into a horizontal glide. They were high in the sky, and the floating feeling made her indifferent to the outcome. For now all that mattered was that she had passed a test she never thought she would.

Chapter VI

Four hours after they took off, Stanley's phone rang. He saw Rosie's number and let out a weary sigh. 20,000 miles above the Pacific and he was just an arm's reach from her. His mind made an automatic calculation and he knew it would be about 11 a.m. in Hong Kong. He could hear the chatter of other people behind her and he knew Rosie was at some restaurant.

'How is she?' she demanded from a continent away. Stanley stole a glance at his fellow passenger, stretched out under a heavy blanket at the other end of the plane.

'She's resting right now,' he said softly into the phone.

'Is she well enough to come home?' Rosie said.

'We *are* coming home.' Stanley looked at his watch. 'We're about eight hours away.'

'No,' said Rosie, 'I mean…'

Stanley knew what she really wanted to know. The same question had been running over and over in his mind since they had boarded the plane. *Is she ready to resume her role?*

'She might still be a little fragile,' Stanley ventured a guess. 'But we can guide her.'

Rosie seemed to like the sound of that.

'Good, good,' she said. 'I'll be at the airport.'

Stanley put his phone away and lay back. He felt like a lucky gambler impatient for the next hand to be dealt. At last he could slap down his cards and claim all his winnings. Like he'd been dying to do all this time.

He looked around the dim, quiet cabin, permeated by the soft hum from the engines. He got up to get a sleeping pill from his case. He gulped it down and lay down to sleep.

After what seemed like a very long time, he was woken up by the pilot's voice on the intercom: 'Madam, sir, we're starting our descent in a few moments.'

Melanie heard it too. She pushed off the blanket and sat up. *So quick,* she thought.

Now that they were about to land, Stanley began to have his doubts. He tried to recall his first impressions of Melanie at the women's shelter. He wondered if she would appear as frail to Rosie and as she had to him at first.

He ran over everything that Cristina Moran had told him. She said that though the young woman had no obvious physical injuries, there was no telling what internal damage she had sustained. It might take some time, she had said, before the young woman recovered completely, if ever, from whatever she had been through.

Stanley wondered if he should confide this information to Rosie or anyone else. Or if he should pretend that everything was alright.

The jet banked and Stanley glanced outside the window. He saw the mass of green and concrete below them, coming closer every second. He felt himself getting more tense as they straightened up and began to nose down. Up ahead he could almost see all the questions that were going to be asked again. Just like the riddles about Arthur they never got to solve.

On the other side of the craft Melanie was facing the window with her eyes closed. Her mind was racing ahead to the next few hours. Dozens of scenarios played out in her mind, what responses she should have for every situation she might encounter. Suddenly a quiver went through the aircraft. They were slowing down for their approach. She sat up and raised her seat. She fastened her seatbelt.

With the precision of a coordinated dance, the landing gear groaned under their feet as it extended fully, adding more drag to their descent. She waited. Seconds passed. Then, the plane dipped into that limbo before touching the ground.

Much sooner than she expected, the wheels touched the tarmac. It made her heart almost burst with dread. They were back on land. Hurtling so fast there was no way to stop or go back. She gripped the armrests tightly as they careered down the runway. If this dream was to succeed or fail, she was about to know.

She knew exactly which door she would walk through once they were in the terminal, which seat she would take on the lounge. She was impatient to begin living out all the imaginary situations Mason had made her go through again and again. Only this time, she would be stepping into an arena where her performance would be judged by the harshest critics, a world away from the life she had been living just a few weeks before. And where Mason wouldn't be around to correct any small errors she might make.

For once she understood why it was always the easiest option to lead an honest life. It was the path of least resistance, the existence that required the least calculation. Life was so much easier when you only had to follow the rules. Now she had embarked on a venture whose rules no one knew. Her old existence was all behind her now. Perhaps for all time.

The jet had come to a full stop. She turned away from the window to find Stanley Wang standing near her. He held out his hands with a big smile: 'Welcome home!'

She got up and followed him through the door.

The heat and the intense light assaulted her as soon as she came out. It was like coming out into a harsh, noisy world after the silky contentment of the womb. She held up her hand against the glare and came down the steps to join Stanley on the tarmac. As they walked the short distance to the terminal, she was aware of how he kept watching her for reactions, and she was glad for the shadow cast by her hand over her face. She hoped it would obscure whatever fleeting expressions might not be up to Stanley's expectations.

The buildings were just a blurred structures ahead of them in the painful brightness, but she felt as if there was a large audience watching her, sitting in a darkened auditorium, making judgements in silence, while everything she did fell under intense scrutiny. In that moment she had an inkling of what Julia Tang's life must have been like.

All at once her clothes felt sticky and heavy on her back. The humidity was something she hadn't been prepared for. Mason undoubtedly knew a lot of things, but he couldn't predict the weather right down to the minute.

Stanley opened the glass door and stood aside to let her through. As she walked gratefully into the cool interior, a thought flashed through her mind: how many other details could Mason have missed?

They reached a frosted glass screen that separated the entrance from the rest of the lounge. Stanley stopped at the desk of an informal - looking official sitting behind a computer. Stanley made small talk with him while he checked their documents, until he finally stamped them. Stanley handed her back her document and she continued past the partition.

Even though Rosie was sitting quietly in the oversized orange armchair, there was still something boisterous about her. Her clothes shouted for attention, her face, the hair, cut in the latest bob from her celebrity stylist at Chater House. Her burnished outfit cut to perfection from head to toe, all of it hinted that something momentous was about to happen. Just her being *there* hinted at something.

As soon as Melanie came into view Rosie jumped to her feet. She stood like an eager poodle too excited to know which way to wag her tail. Melanie had no trouble recognizing her. She knew from her briefings not to be too demonstrative with Julia's stepmother. But Melanie still felt a lump in her throat at seeing a mother rush across the room to put her arms around her. And she was surprised when Rosie held her hand to her cheek, saying softly, 'Oh, don't cry, my little one.'

Melanie was shocked to feel the wetness on her own cheek. Rosie's embrace was tighter than Mason had led her to expect, and her effusiveness gave Melanie a hard time concentrating on the act she knew she had to put on.
As Rosie babbled on merrily, Melanie felt her practiced eye take in everything about her. She worried when Rosie's gaze lingered over her features for the briefest instant. Melanie wondered if it was doubt or disbelief she saw in those eyes.

But by the time they had walked to the chairs and sat across from each other, the misgiving in Rosie's face had given way to approval. As though she were satisfied with Melanie as a specimen, or was deciding she was at least good for something.

'You look tired,' she said, shaking the symmetrical ends of her bob.

'Isn't that my usual state?' Melanie replied. Stanley stood a respectful distance from them. Rosie barely gave him a nod.

Now he took a step towards them with a proud smile, as if waiting for gratitude of some kind.

'She's coming with me,' Rosie told him. He accepted her decision without objection and made his way out of the lounge.

'Let's get some tea,' Rosie said, already raising her hand for unseen minions to come. 'You must be hungry. Are you ready for dim sum?'

'Of course,' said Melanie. 'But not at a terminal.'

Rosie cocked her head for a moment, and Melanie worried. Had she detected something amiss? But the petulant note in Melanie's voice seemed to have struck a familiar chord. 'Certainly not,' Rosie grinned. 'Let's go to Maxim's!'

'No,' said Melanie. 'I've been craving goose. Let's go to Yung Kee.'

Rosie cocked her head again and laughed. 'How could I forget. You and your goose!'

They walked briskly out to find the Maybach parked at the curb, the chauffeur standing like a statue waiting for his masters to snap their fingers and make him come to life. Melanie recognized him from Julia's old family pictures, and stopped briefly in front of him, saying, 'Why, Lao Chin! Good to see you. '

His response was almost inaudible as he bowed with deep emotion and opened the door wide.

Melanie wasn't aware of the awestruck look Rosie gave her from behind. They slid into their seats facing each other. Rosie gave curt orders to the driver and sank back into the leather, her high heels tucked primly under her.

As they sped back towards the city Rosie brought out a stream of news and gossip from her trip to London. Melanie slouched in the manner she had seen in Julia's pictures, and responded now and then to Rosie's comments. She found herself staring at the sheen of Rosie's stockings. Here and there the former starlet would pause in her narrative to stretch or recross her legs. Melanie couldn't help but notice her pointed shoes. Like the witch in any fairy tale, she smiled secretly.

She also noticed that Rosie had very small feet. With horror, she realized that this was perhaps the one area where she might not fully resemble Julia. She pulled her feet back into a corner under her seat, hoping Rosie wouldn't see.

Thankfully, they had reached the city by then, and there were a lot more things to distract Rosie. Outside their windows she the buildings and features Melanie knew only from maps and photographs stretched out all around them, and she struggled to recall everything she knew about them.

'Are Fidelity still on the 17th floor of One IFC?" she said as they drove past the International Finance Centre. 'What happened to the court case between Paribas and The Macquarie Group?'

All Mason's briefings came to her, with a natural flow that made Rosie stop talking and stare at her. Throughout the ride she could feel that Julia's stepmother was studying every pore in her body, and it made her secretly tense, dreading the moment Rosie would turn on her and expose the ruse.

It wasn't until they had passed a few department stores in Central that the imperious widow turned to her. As if the glamorous displays in the store windows had reminded her, Rosie blurted out something she'd been holding back for some time, 'Those are ghastly clothes!'

Melanie hadn't even thought about it. But the sorry state in which she had met Julia's stepmother could only have added to the impression that something terrible had happened to her. It was one of those unforeseen details that worked out to her benefit.

'They're from the women's shelter,' she explained. 'I'd been out in the streets for....'

Rosie's eyes lit up encouragingly, as if hoping for an explanation. But Mason's voice suddenly intruded in Melanie's mind, reminding her to leave some spaces blank. '*Let them fill it in for themselves,*' he had said over and over again. *They'll live with the version that suits them best.*

So Melanie feigned great discomfort and said, 'But I don't want to talk about that right now.'

'Of course!' Rosie reached across to touch Melanie's hand. 'There's no rush, honey. We'll get to everything in good time,'

But she still couldn't abide the garb Melanie had on. 'There's one reason some people become Good Samaritans,' she said. 'They have awful taste! Helping others is all they're good for!'

She fired off a whole new set of instructions to the chauffeur before turning back to Melanie: 'We're going to get you a whole new outfit.'
'But I thought we were going to eat,' Melanie protested.

'One always gets to eat,' Rosie said flippantly over her shoulder. 'Clothes are more important.'

It was another bonus Melanie hadn't counted on. She managed to ignore her fatigue and growing pangs of hunger, as Rosie made the driver scour every corner of the city for clothing shops. She went about it with the seriousness of a tigress hunting for meat.

And she stood by patiently as Melanie tried on various garments in a string of luxury shops. From Prince's Building, to Alexandra house, and The Landmark. They were places Melanie could only have dreamed of entering in her former life.

She thought of Mason as she tried on the most pricey attire, remembering his confidence that Melanie would buy into the scheme. Whatever Rosie was doing now, she was deepening Melanie's involvement in the ruse, making her bite into the irresistible apple, not caring abut the damnation that might or might not come. *Versace, Chanel, Ferragamo, Hermes,* all the brands Mason assured her would be in Julia's wardrobe. Melanie was glad that he had told her even the minutiae of Julia's measurements, so that she knew what size of clothes to take into the fitting rooms.

She found it strange that a family's lawyer would know such intimate details about his employer's daughter. But, seeing how people like the Tangs delegated even their most trivial tasks to their minions, she no longer found it odd.

While they were waiting to pay, Rosie bent down to study the label on one of the garments. 'You're down one size,' she said with surprise. 'My, you've really lost some weight.'

Though she should have taken the discrepancy as good news, Melanie wondered if it was just the first crack in the subterfuge. How many more would Rosie find?

She waited nervously until they reached the cashier, and was surprised to see Julia's stepmother take out her own credit card to pay. She waved al Melanie's protests away.

'Your cards are at home,' Rosie smiled sweetly. 'Don't worry. The accountants will sort it out.'

Thus, with Melanie fully attired in the style befitting her new role, they went off to have lunch.

They drove to Wellington street to Julia's favourite restaurant. Melanie studied the menu and picked out the items she had memorized from Mason's list. Rosie watched with a mixture of familiarity and puzzlement as their dishes were brought, and Melanie did her best to appear delighted with what Mason had told her were Julia's favourite foodstuffs. This was the price of stepping in someone's rather elegant shoes. She ended up having more roasted goose than she had ever eaten in her life. The thought of the Mother Goose wallpaper from her childhood bedroom briefly came back to her and she almost burst out laughing.

Rosie picked at her plate, regaling Melanie with chitchat about goings on at the Asia Society, and the fund-raising dinners she'd had to host. 'I even let Walden organize the last one.'

It was a name Melanie recognized. She called up an image of the American, and hurriedly inserted another well-rehearsed detail: 'How's Brad these days?'

She saw the irritation flash across Rosie's face. 'Oh, he still won't divorce that Hakka slut of his. So I've stopped inviting him to the house.'

Following Mason's advice, Melanie nodded and secretly filed away that fact in her mind.

It was almost 2:00 p.m. by the time they left the restaurant. Melanie looked forward to being by herself for a while. Keeping up the charade was more strenuous than she had imagined, and her long journey was catching up on her.

It wasn't only the distance she had travelled. It was the contrast between the two worlds she had traversed. The disparity was more dizzying than any expanse that separated them. She could have flown three times the span and not experienced the kind of transition she had just gone through.

The whole flight from L.A. seemed unreal now, the details all blurred in her memory, so that it almost felt like the real life she had left behind was the dream, and this new existence as Julia Tang was the reality.

She let Rosie steer her to the car as though she were in a trance. And once they were inside, the lustrous velvet capsule shut out the outside world once more, and they floated to their next destination.

She assumed their next stop would be Julia's house on Severn Road. She closed her eyes to recall Mason's maps. But when she opened her eyes again she immediately knew something was wrong.

'We're not going home?' she asked Rosie.

Rosie tilted her head coyly, 'I've got something to show you.'

Melanie looked out the window. She wondered if she was about to be tested even more. Red blossoms of cotton trees whizzed by above them as the car drove uphill. She glimpsed the sea.

Slowly she recognized the way to South Bay Road. Up ahead a tall glass structure appeared.

When they reached the top of the hill, the Maybach swung left and entered the oval driveway of the building.

The door was opened and she followed Rosie up the steps past the fern-festooned entrance. The stark marble lobby was exactly like in the photo Mason had shown her.

They took the lift to the top floor, its glass sides showing their progress as they rose higher above the trees until they were a dizzying distance above the hillside below. The doors opened on a short, quiet corridor. Rosie stepped out with the excited click-clock of her heels and unlocked the door. She stood back and waved Melanie in.

The luxurious premises were exactly what she was expecting, but she had to feign surprise, 'Wow!'

'Like it?' Rosie grinned with pride. Melanie's gaze fell instantly on the oversized tiger stripes on the wall. Mason had warned Melanie of Rosie's taste in décor. She walked around the large table without comment and stopped at the window.

Rosie joined her.

'Isn't it wonderful?' she lay a hand on Melanie's shoulder. 'I'm so glad you're back.'

Melanie gazed at the cobalt sea below, and understood why it was so important to have Julia Tang back, in whatever shape or form.

Half an hour later, they were in the limo again, travelling towards the city. This time Melanie immediately recognized the upward sweep from Central to Victoria Hill. She watched every turn the driver made and was relieved to confirm they really were heading back to Severn Road. The large car crawled through narrow spaces between buildings that were almost blocked by ancient fig trees clinging miraculously to the walls, their gigantic roots splayed across the masonry like massive hands.

They came out through one of the green shrouded alleys and passed a cemetery, the headstones tilted slightly to follow the slope of the land. Melanie remembered something.

'Oh, have you had a chance to visit my mother's grave?' she said.

The question seemed to take Rosie by surprise. She fumbled for an answer. Oh,' she lowered her head. 'Things have been so hectic.' For once she looked like she was the one being tested.

'That's all right,' Melanie smiled. 'It's up to me anyway.'

Rosie simpered. 'I'm glad you don't mind.'

For the first time, Melanie felt she could relax. She had found, just as Julia must have had, a way to turn the tables on Rosie.

They made the precarious ascent through hairpin turns until they were at the crest. Then the car glided slowly into the *cul de sac* on Severn Road. Rosie shifted in her seat and gave her an expectant look. Melanie got out of the car and found the compact staff of six people standing on either side of the front door to greet her. Two of them surged forward to grab her luggage, and seemed puzzled that she had only the shopping bags from the dress stores. She yielded them and mounted the steps into the house. The beige and ebony tiles inside were so shiny she was afraid of slipping. They stretched out before her towards what seemed like a magical stairway. She walked slowly, and made sure Rosie had caught up with her before she started climbing the steps.

At the top she glanced down at Rosie, who was looking up at her with anticipation, like a spectator in a theatre stall. For her benefit Melanie turned left to follow the hallway that she knew led to Julia's room. She passed the large empty room that she knew Arthur and Rosie used to share. Several feet beyond it she reached the room which hadn't been occupied since Julia had vanished. She took a deep breath before she opened the door.

It was exactly as it was in Mason's floor plan. The Bombay chest of drawers stood untouched except for the endless polishing by the servants. The whole chamber was preserved as if it were some kind of shrine. Melanie felt some trepidation as she stepped in, feeling like an intruder in some holy place. The mirror with its elaborate curves on its corners faced the bed where the missing heiress used to sleep. She put her hand on the gleaming drawer handles that seemed too beautiful for daily use.

She pulled out the top drawer and put her hand in. The interior was lined with embroidered silk. She smiled and looked around. There were no bare surfaces anywhere, nothing that hadn't been buffed to a gloss, nothing that wasn't sumptuous or special. She could tell that even under the bed there were no motes of dust that gathered. Every day dozens of hands reached into every crevice of the chamber, coaxing out errant wisps of dirt that intruded into the Tang's perfect universe.

Even the curtains seemed too heavy for a place that seldom knew freezing temperatures. Their sole purposed seemed to be to shut out the world. She walked around and peered into the en suite bathroom, and giggled with delight to see the round bathtub behind the frosted glass. This was all hers. For how long, she didn't know.

The walk-in closet beckoned to her like a mysterious doorway to even greater wonders. Like a child who had stumbled into Paradise, she entered.

There she found all the missing woman's possessions, stacked like they must have been every day for Julia, now preserved, either in remembrance, or in preparation for her sudden return. All the heiress' possessions were arrayed as if in a museum, bathed in the soft light of unseen lamps.

It gave Melanie an uneasy feeling, knowing that even Mason wasn't exactly sure just what had happened to Julia Tang. She stood there thinking about it. How the room, the whole house, seemed like they were frozen in time. As if they were only waiting for the vanished heiress to walk in at any moment and resume her life.

Melanie's best hope was that everyone would believe she had done just that. Her greatest fear was that the real Julia Tang would suddenly reappear.

Several minutes later, she went downstairs to find Rosie drinking tea in the Waiting Room, with its single sofa set at a right angle to the window looking out on the pool.

Melanie was surprised. It seemed strange for Julia's stepmother to be so self-effacing. She wondered if Mason was right about everything after all.

Rosie got up as soon as she saw Melanie.

'I hope you find everything just as before,' she said, gathering up her purse to leave.

It was another surprise. Melanie had assumed that the home was Rosie's now. But Mason's knowledge only extended up to the time before Arthur died. So Melanie had to guess how circumstances had changed since then.

'Aren't you staying for dinner?' she asked Rosie.

'Oh, I'd love to,' gushed Rosie in reply. 'But I'm meeting Jason.'

Melanie stiffened at the mention of Julia's stepbrother. She found it strange that he hadn't come.

'How is my big brother? ' she asked. 'When is he going to come see me?'

Rosie's face darkened for a moment. 'I'll make him,' she said.

She seemed lost in thought for a brief instant, then she dismissed all her misgivings with a wave of the hand.

'Have a good rest,' she placed her hands on Melanie's shoulders. 'There'll be lots to talk about. But later.'

After giving Melanie a peck on either cheek, Rosie clattered through the marble corridor to the front door. The door slammed shut, and with that Melanie's long test was over. At least for a moment.

She let out a heavy sigh and sank into one of the oversized sofas. All the strain of keeping up the deception came back to her. She felt completely drained. But now here she was, alone in this vast house, like a stranger who had stumbled into a fairy tale castle, pampered but uncertain about the intentions of her hosts.

She pulled herself up and looked around. The wood panels in the walls had a deep rich shine. She knew entire forests had been cut down to produce them. The porcelain jars by the unused fireplace towered over her, and the marble surfaces on the tables reminded her of far Roman quarries where the finest rock was cut out of hillsides to make columns for the emperor.

She felt like congratulating herself. She had done what had seemed so impossible. The gatekeepers had let her in. They had bought her story.

But there was one discordant note. Why hadn't Jason come to welcome her? She sensed there could be a problem. She had rehearsed everything she was supposed to say to Julia's stepbrother, all the remarks about his horse-racing, his love of cars. Melanie had been prepared to dig deep into her own experience, gleaned from her father Joseph's passion for antique vehicles.

She walked up to the windows. The glass extended about twelve feet from floor to ceiling. It seemed too audacious, too grand for ordinary life. There below her was the rest of Hong Kong. Laid out like a shimmering train set built for a very special girl. For once she had an inkling what it would have been like to be Julia Tang. Everything was too outsized, too bold, every act flew in the face of what was normal. To live like that was to go through life without one's feet touching the ground. It meant being permanently suspended between the world of mortals and the overwhelming heights of heaven. Looking down at the lights below her, she wondered what it would feel like to fall from somewhere so high.

Chapter VII

She was someone else. The thought woke her up abruptly. She was in a place far away from where anyone knew her. Where no one could prove who she really was or was not.

She spent her first private moments exploring the upper floor, quiet as a burglar, and, like any intruder, grateful for every moment that she wasn't caught.

Her body was still on L. A. time, where it would be only 2:00 in the afternoon now, the ordinary events of her old life unfolding at their ordinary pace. Meanwhile she was here in this unbelievable world, as if Mason's plan had catapulted her into some secret dimension she'd never known about before.

She reached the top of the stairs and looked down. The house was completely still, with none of the servants around to observe her. She turned around and studied the two doorways that led off from the landing. She decided to walk through the one she had avoided the day before, which she knew led to the opposite end of the floor.

In the dim corridor she passed the rooms that Arthur had used as a work space, their doors half open, suspended like everything else in the mansion. At the end of the hall she found the large airy chamber that had functioned as Arthur's games room, with the four windows facing each cardinal direction, open to the winds Arthur imagined shaped his destiny. Looking at the empty chairs and tables, Melanie could almost hear the echoes of the loud mah-jongg or card games that went in long into the night, a miniature of the wagering that the tycoon did with his business during the day.

She went back to Julia's room and ran herself a bath. She soaked in the soapy warm water and watched the sun rising over the hills, framed in the narrow window next to her. She was too far up for anyone to see her, and the green knoll she could see below her was deserted. The tinkle of the water wrapped around her seemed loud in the stillness, and the seconds passed peacefully. She had no idea how long it would last.

At last she got out and put on one of the bathrobes hanging in the rack. When she caught sight of herself in one of the multiple mirrors she let out a gasp. She looked like a stranger to herself, and for a moment it seemed almost like the real heiress had walked in on her.

She took a deep breath to calm down and walked back into the bedroom. Searching absently through the drawers, she imagined Julia going through her morning rituals. She found the trinkets she wanted and stood in front of the mirror-fronted doors of the walk-in closet. She put on one of the suits she had bought with Rosie the day before.

She felt almost like a little girl again, playing dress-up in her mother's room, trying on dresses that were too big for her. Now the clothes fit her perfectly, and it was a game of dress-up for much higher stakes.

She saw herself transformed into a totally different person. She was no longer the woman with debts and problems with he law, she was an heiress who could do as she wished. Everything was in the trappings. And the trappings certainly were there.

The room seemed to provide everything she needed for the magic to work, giving her all the costumes and accoutrements for the illusion to work. Out of idle curiosity she slid the farthest mirror to one side. It revealed another layer of compartments. Her jaw dropped to see the dozens of handbags in different sizes and colours.

She smiled. So this was what it meant to take over someone's life. She never thought it could be so easy. She picked up a series of purses and tried them against her clothes. They were the kinds she would only have lusted after from the other side of a thick shop window. Now they were hers for the taking.

The one she liked best was a maroon one with a gold clasp and an evanescent sheen. But there were so many others. She couldn't make up her mind. Perhaps she would decide after breakfast.

She buttoned up the blouse and took one final look at herself. At last she felt ready to begin her day as Julia Tang.

When she came down, Rosie was already in the dining room waiting for her. Light was streaming through the house, all the curtains had been drawn. She felt exposed to all the world, the windows sucking in the sunlight as though it were a stage above the earth.

Rosie got up to give her a cheery peck.

'I'm so glad you let yourself sleep today,' she said.

Melanie looked at the clock. It was 7:15. She had forgotten. Mason *had* told her that Julia was always up at five o'clock. So even her Herculean effort to get up before dawn that morning wasn't quite up to her predecessor's rigorous regimen.

'Jet lag,' she shrugged

'I know,' sympathized Rosie. 'You can't have it all. You've got to take the rough with the smooth.'

Melanie sat down and had her first sip of coffee. 'Speaking of rough,' she looked up at Rosie. 'Do you anticipate a tough one today?'

Rosie pressed a finger against her cheek. 'Not easy, I'd say. But no worse than you're used to.'

Over breakfast, served by mute servants who were one uniformed blur to Melanie's tired eyes, Rosie told her about the day's agenda. Melanie knew that when Arthur was alive, this was the morning ritual he would have with his daughter.

It was a new role for Rosie, and she seemed to be groping for the right way. Melanie could sense Rosie looking to her for a little bit of guidance. *Good*, she thought. *We're both novices in this game.*

'The partners all want to see you,' Rosie said.

Melanie expected this, and had prepared for it. She knew it would be in the order of seniority. 'When is Uncle Andrew available?'

'We'll see him first.'

'Then?'

Rosie rattled off the list of people Melanie was scheduled to see, and she made mental notes on them, deciding what to say to each one. It was as awesome as walking a tightrope over a chasm, full of possible places where her foot might slip. Thinking about it only made her anxious. She couldn't wait to get going.

'Oh!' Rosie said, remembering something. 'How could I forget? We'll need gifts for each of them.'

'Why?' asked Melanie.

'Well, it would be unseemly to come without them. It's expected.'

'What's expected?'

Rosie's eyes were stark dots of conviction. 'That someone who's been away should come back with gifts for people. You know the saying, *A swan's feather from a thousand li away.* It's always nice to get a present from somewhere far away.'

'But Rosie,' said Melanie, addressing Julia's stepmother in the way she had discussed with Mason. 'I haven't been anywhere. I've been here all this time.'

Rosie looked up with a delighted gleam in her eye. 'Right! That's true. You've been here all along!'

They finished their coffees and got up to leave. But then Rosie suddenly turned and motioned to someone out of Melanie's view.

A steward came forward, bowed to Melanie without looking her in the eye, whispering something of which Melanie only caught "Siew Keng.'

He placed a box on the table between the two women.

'Stanley told me you had lost everything,' Rosie explained. She nudged the box forward. Melanie rummaged inside. She found a set of keys, as well as a beautiful aquamarine purse.

'That's the one you left on your dresser,' Rosie told her. *The one Julia forgot or left on purpose*, Melanie thought secretly. She knew it meant Rosie had been through its contents, and she doubted whether she should even take it. But when she opened the purse, she found it full of cash. All the cards in it were in Julia's name, current to the last minute.

She wondered. They had kept Julia's accounts going, all the official records of her existence. It must have been terribly important to keep up the impression that Julia Tang was alive. The only alternative explanation was very troubling: that Julia Tang *was* alive, waiting for the right moment to make her own grand entrance.

Melanie closed the purse. It fit perfectly in her left hand. There was just one problem. It didn't match her jacket. She thought of the maroon purse she'd left upstairs.

'I'll go up and get a different one,' she said. She ran up the flight of steps, leaving Rosie shaking her head, 'You never change.'

Andrew Chang received them at his office two floors above Stanley Wang's. His window looked out on the ladder of structures shooting skywards from every corner of the hillside. Melanie kissed his hand and greeted him as her godfather. She walked around the spacious office and stopped in front of the large window. Andrew quietly joined her. 'This view reminds me of the first night I spent on Severn Road,' she said. 'I looked through the glass and couldn't stop myself from crying. It made me think of my mother.'

She turned around to see Andrew standing behind her. He was visibly shaken. He stepped forward and gripped her hands, as if he needed to steady himself. 'Your father said you would take care of everything,' he said softly. 'And I promised him I'd help you in every way.'
From his expression, and the wary glance he cast in Rosie's direction, Melanie understood it was a discussion they would need to have elsewhere.

'Yes, Uncle Andrew,' she said. 'We must have lunch tomorrow.'

'Tomorrow,' he nodded with a slight bow showing he accepted her decision as law, and looked forward to telling her many things. But it would have to wait.

The next few days were filled with rounds of such meetings. There was so little respite between engagements Melanie had to rely on instinct to get her through each encounter. She was glad that Rosie stood at her elbow announcing each well-wisher by name and position. It was her way of declaring ownership of the moment, of staying within the orbit of power, now that Arthur's rightful successor was back.

Melanie wondered if Rosie was aware how she was unwittingly helping Melanie to maintain her ruse. Mason had informed her that Rosie had been a starlet before she married Arthur Tang. Now Melanie glanced at her and wondered who really was the better actress between them.

Everyone they met asked after Melanie's health, expressed sorrow about "her father's demise" and demonstrated great joy at her "return."

Melanie was glad that Julia's prolonged absence made many of them feel they had to fill in some gaps. But after each visit she squirmed at the thought of mistakes she might have made, particulars she hadn't found a way to inject into the conversation.

But the disaster she dreaded did not materialize. For the most part people seemed happy just to see her. They were overjoyed to confirm she was for real, not another wishful rumour that was circulating through their ranks.

Finally, settling back in the limo, Melanie said with an exhausted sigh, 'Now we just have all my father's relatives left to do.'

Rosie waved a dismissive hand. 'You don't have to worry about them.'

Arthur's family, Mason had told Melanie, consisted of uncles, cousins and their children who had found their way into different departments of the company. Most of them owned stocks in the conglomerate, but were nonetheless cowed by Rosie, who had systematically undermined their power while Arthur was still alive.

They were a loose group that met at reunions and made pilgrimages back to their ancestral village. Though they suspected Rosie of being somehow complicit in Arthur's death, they were like a scattered army fighting a partisan war, often the targets of Rosie's most vehement accusations, the scapegoats for all her imagined conspiracies.

Only their power in the board prevented Rosie from cutting them out altogether, so their relationship was one of an uneasy truce.

The one relative of Julia's she looked forward to meeting was Bernadette, the surviving sister of Linda, Arthur's late wife. Mason's description of Arthur's sister-in-law depicted her as perhaps being the only sympathetic character the heiress Julia Tang had known in her life. But it would have to wait.

That night they drove to Rosie's penthouse for dinner. Towards the end of the meal, Rosie mentioned in an off-handed way, 'Stanley wants to know when you would like to see your doctor.'
Melanie nearly dropped her glass. If anyone would know she wasn't Julia Tang, it would be Julia's doctor. She had made up her mind from the very start that she would refuse any medical procedures, or any tests that could belie her claims to be the missing heiress.

'What for?' Melanie protested. 'With everything we've got scheduled. There is really no time!'

'Just a check-up?' Rosie bargained. 'Stanley says the people at the women's shelter mentioned some injuries.'

'What injuries?' said Melanie defensively. But Rosie's disclosure made her nervous. Mason had said nothing about any injuries Julia had had.

'Stanley said they found some cuts on you,' continued Rosie. 'He pondering if you needed some medical attention.'

Melanie realized what cuts Rosie might be talking about. She relaxed.

'They're just old sailing injuries,' she said with a wave of relief. 'You can't be a sailor without getting them once in a while.'

Rosie appeared to relent. 'Of course,' she smiled. 'How could I forget?'

So for the moment, the subject was dropped. Luckily for Melanie, Julia had never been overly concerned about her health, either. She had always considered it secondary to the smooth working of the conglomerate, and only saw a doctor when she absolutely needed to.

As Mason had said, where millions could be lost in a few seconds, no one was going to quibble over simple medical matters. So the matter of seeing a doctor wasn't raised again. Melanie secretly hoped that in time it would be forgotten.
But the next two weeks consisted of gruelling rounds of tests of another kind. As she encountered more of Julia's circle, she lived with the dread of making that one error that would bring everything crashing down.

At night, alone in Julia's oversized bed, she was tempted to call her mother to let her in on her strange adventure. And one day, when she was alone in the house, sitting under the stars by the pool, she dialled her mother's number. It was early afternoon in Chicago, when she knew her mother would be out in her garden.

The phone on the other end had already rung three times when she caught a glimpse of one of the servants walking by upstairs. Melanie was jolted back to her new reality. She suddenly remembered the distance she had travelled. There was no way to make her mother understand the situation. She ended the call before her mother could answer.

'I am Julia Tang,' she said to herself softly. 'My mother is dead.'

At the end of one week, her nerves were frazzled. She longed to retreat to the room on Severn Road and not speak to anyone for days. But even there, she knew she was always being observed. She had no doubt that the servants discreetly noted everything she did. What food she ate, what time she came back at night, what calls she made, or even what clothes she had worn.

Every part of her existence was in the family's control. She was like a bird in a cage she had willingly flown into, and she couldn't stop pretending because there was nowhere to hide.

'We have one more meeting,' Rosie told her on Thursday morning.

Melanie flinched. 'Can't we postpone it for next week?'

'Just one more,' Rosie pleaded. 'Just for dinner and then you're free for the weekend.'

The thought of a break was so enticing Melanie gave in.

So early the next evening Melanie found herself at the dining room of the Marriott. Rosie had booked a table right by the large window looking down on the street sixty floors below. Since her arrival in Hong Kong, she had been taken from one high-rise to another. It was as if she had entered a hidden world, separated not by walls, but by altitude. For people like the Tangs, life seemed to take place in this stratosphere hundreds of feet up in the air, where the people and traffic below seemed toy-like, mere adornment for the few who gazed down from above.

They moved from one place to another on narrow passageways that were like streets of heaven, brushed by the clouds, with breath-taking glimpses of the life below. But being in that world was like standing at a precipice. It was thrilling and scary at the same time. Melanie wanted to leave and she wanted to stay. Like all unreal things it was irresistible.

Right up to the last minute, Melanie wasn't sure the meeting would happen. Rosie kept checking her watch. 'I told him to be here by 7:00,' she muttered. 'I hope he didn't forget. Or get distracted with something.'

Melanie gazed out to the top of the Bank of China building glowing in the night, like an eerie, unearthly head floating in the gloom. Around it was the multicoloured constellation of the harbour district, closer than the stars above, but just as out of reach.

Finally, at around 9:00 Rosie's phone rang. They had finished dinner and were on their second coffees. Rosie answered, and after a brief conversation turned to Melanie brightly, 'He's here!'

Melanie counted the minutes until a tall, slender figure appeared at the entrance of the restaurant. Jason had his mother's movie star looks, though his features showed mainly annoyance at the moment, as he shot an angry glance at Rosie, who evidently had forced him to come.

He stepped forward with a dead expression and looked down at Melanie.

'Well?' prompted Rosie, ever the insistent mother. 'Aren't you going to give your little sister a hug?'

He made no move until Melanie got up to face him. He gazed at her for a few moments, looking like he was about to turn around and leave.

Then for some reason he relaxed. His shoulders slackened and his lips broadened into a smile. He swept forward to grasp her by the arms.

'Am I glad to see you!' he said with laugh.
Aware of playing a role herself, Melanie instantly knew the laugh was genuine, and it puzzled her. He actually seemed pleased to

see her. He put a brotherly arm around her shoulder as she stood on her tiptoes to hug him.

'That's more like it,' Rosie cooed approvingly behind them.

Jason sat down and ordered a Barr Hill gin. He sipped it neat while the two women had their tea. They talked about the days ahead, while Rosie constantly turned to wave to people she knew at other tables. Melanie noticed Jason didn't wear a watch. He seemed to be someone who lived purely by instinct, acting only in accordance with his urges and the needs of the moment. There was another thing she noticed. The more he studied her, the more at ease he seemed to become.

As if his greatest fears hadn't materialized, and for now he could relax. For now they could all play the part of an ordinary family. As ordinary as any family that included an impostor could be.

After another gin Jason was laughing and telling jokes. 'You'll have to come to the Sha Tin Track on Saturday,' he said. 'Gold Flash is running his third race.'

'Yes,' said Melanie, recalling the racing colours Mason had shown her. 'I'll have to see how those chevrons look on your new jockey.'

'Rosie giggled. Melanie kept her gaze on the table, but she caught Rosie exchange meaningful glances with her son. He then turned around to give Melanie a searching look, as if trying to discern who she really was, and what she was trying to achieve.

'I can't believe it,' he said.

'Believe what?' said Melanie.

'You're really back.'

Why?' she said. 'Is that so impossible?'

He seemed lost in thought before he answered. 'I just thought it might take longer.'

'How much longer?' Melanie teased. 'Like, never?'

She wasn't sure it was the right thing to do, but something irresistible compelled her to probe. Jason drew back with a smile. He turned to Rosie and changed the subject. They chatted idly for an hour or so, as the room's patron's slowly dwindled to a handful.

Then, happy to have put in an appearance, Jason got up to go.

'Why don't you stay longer?' coaxed Rosie.

'I have to drive out to Kowloon,' Jason said curtly.

'Kowloon?' Rosie looked at her watch. 'Why? You just got here.'

'Mother,' he said. 'It's almost midnight. Poor little sister has a full day tomorrow.'

Melanie agreed, so Rosie waved for their bill. Jason leaned down to give Melanie another hug. 'It's really hard to believe,' he whispered.

As she watched him walk out of the restaurant, Melanie couldn't help feeling triumphant. The last domino had fallen. Now she just had to keep going. Or hope there weren't any more.

As they got up to go downstairs she kept thinking about Jason's last words. *It's really hard to believe.* It could be understood in many ways. Did he mean he didn't believe her? Or was he just glad she had "come back"?

They stepped out of the building and walked out into the balmy night, but she was still thinking of how Jason had first appeared to her, walking towards them in the restaurant. He seemed almost terrified of something. Then, when he saw her, his tension slowly vanished. He seemed almost relieved. Why?

Did he really believe she was his missing step sister? If not, why pretend? If he knew she was an impostor, he could have exposed her then and there. And yet he didn't. Why?

Chapter VIII

First thing on Monday morning the board members of Tang Worldwide gathered on the 70th floor of 2IFC, on the side overlooking Finance Street in Central. Rosie hadn't told anyone the reason for the gathering, but they all sensed something important was about to happen.

Stanley Wang took his usual place sat at the head of the table. Next to him was an empty seat that was normally occupied by Rosie, on those occasions she chose to sit in on their discussions.

The calm start betrayed no sign of the flurry of activity that had gone on throughout the weekend, Rosie and Stanley phoning up people, confirming their positions on a number of questions. The renewed vigour was in stark contrast to the lassitude that had followed Arthur's death, when they had all stood immobile, like the doomed passengers of a crippled ship drifting towards the reef.

Whatever Rosie and her cohorts were up to, it was a welcome change. That the two men at the top would forget their antagonism for once and unite for whatever purpose sent a powerful message to the group.

They had also noted the extra security measures downstairs, where their guards prowled the lobby in groups of four, looking out particularly for any stray members of the public or the press.

Brad Walden, taking his seat cross the table from Stanley Wang, knew that in this company, keeping things quiet always entailed, ironically, heightened activity.

The members all took their seats and looked through folders placed before them by the slickly efficient staff. But the conglomerate's culture was a strange hybrid of modernity and island tradition. It retained habits going back to the rustic seaside villages from which most of the territory's greatest companies had grown.

Thus, the gathering didn't get down to business right away. As always, tea was served, and an informal chatter began around the long table, rising to one lively babble that evoked a scene from some rural teahouse. Grandchildren were discussed, weekend excursions, the state of one's health or the holiday home.

Then the door opened. A stunned silence fell, as a slight figure clad in a dark blue suit crossed the room to take the empty seat normally occupied by Rosie.

It was the first time any of them realized Arthur's widow wouldn't be joining them that day. In her place was this apparition. The name was on the tip of everyone's tongue, but no one dared utter it for fear of dispelling the illusion.

'Good morning everyone!' she said. 'I'm so glad you could all join me this morning.'

Stanley got up. All the others did the same. The assembly exploded in applause. In a rush, they all surged forward to greet her. And finally the name came out, '*Tang xiao jie!*'

'Siew Keng!'

'Julia!'

They clustered around her to shake her hand, if only to feel that she was real flesh and blood, and not a walking dream for all of them. She moved around the group, shaking hands, murmuring greetings, asking about in-laws and latest acquisitions, hobbies and family outings she had learned about from Mason's voluminous files.

Finally things settled down, and the formal discussion began. Referring to notes she had hammered out with Rosie the night before, she informed the board of her plans to renegotiate or extend present loans. 'If they want to be part of the deal when we conclude the agreement with the Midas Group,' she said, then they'll have to show us some faith.'

There was a murmur of approval.

'That should give us the leverage for the buyback stage.'

'Buy back? She heard her own words being repeated up and down the table, muttered with doubt and unease. She could see she had reached their first impasse. The group behaved like a diffident horse refusing to jump over a barrier, lacking the courage of its rider. She knew that, like a good horseman, she had to calm their fears.

'Andrew,' she said, turning to Chang on her left side. 'Remember what we were discussing last Saturday? How buying back our own stocks will show everyone what value we place on them? It's what we need to drive investor confidence back to the levels they were before.'

'Yes, yes,' Chang took up his cue. 'It's a bold move. And it will announce that Tang Worldwide is back.'

They seemed to like the idea. The zest flowed back into the group. Melanie took back the floor to whip them up some more, 'We've shown our strength through all the storms of the market,' she said, and never in our history have we failed to produce profits or pay back a loan. Now it'll be just like it always was under my father.'

It was her clearest statement that she was there as Arthur Tang's direct representative. And finally having someone to lead them, they were once more a fearless steed under her, ready to burst into a frenzy of speed at her command.

As Melanie presided over the proceedings, she felt the collective's energy sweeping her up, as if someone else were taking over her actions, some unfamiliar spirit moving through her. She could see the faces turned to her reverently, some looking as if to discern the ghost of Julia's father Arthur.

The gathering took all of three hours, and when it was finished everyone got up with a vigour that wasn't there before. As if the jubilant essence of Arthur Tang had somehow returned.

Melanie stood at the door of the conference room as everyone filed out. And when the last ones had left, she crossed to the head of the empty table and sat down. She couldn't help but feel a private triumph. It had been a stupendous test. And she had passed it.

It seemed a pity her mentor wasn't there to see it. But even Mason couldn't have imagined how exhausting it would be. Every breathe she took had to be preceded by careful thought, as if she had to consider every blink of her eye, plan every beat of her heart.

In a flash she remembered what Mason had said. *It doesn't matter if the one wearing the crown really is the monarch, as long as there is someone sitting in the throne.* Knowing what it took to be that person, Melanie wondered how long she would stay there.

Despite the precautions taken to keep her out of the public eye, the results of her arrival were immediate. Overnight Tang Worldwide made millions as their stock soared back to previous heights, and reports spread that the long delayed Midas deal might at last push through. This boosted their holdings even more, so that in less than a week, it seemed as if the conglomerate was back in its heyday, with Arthur at the helm and all their troubles far away.

It was all as Mason had predicted. Melanie didn't need to call him up to tell them that their ruse had worked. His bank balance would give indubitable proof of that. And this, more than an any gift Melanie could give him, would be his reward, his recompense for his meticulous tutelage and planning.

After a while even the things that were once unthinkable became routine. She got used to living alone in the cavernous house on Severn Road. Every morning she got up and put on one of her new outfits and she would be driven to work in one of the fleet at her disposal, no longer having to bother with mundane things like traffic, and coming to think of the hulking tower of 2IFC as her second home.

She knew she had made Bernard Mason even richer than he was before. It had all been worth his impeccable groundwork, his years of kowtowing and secretly building his arsenal.
In the middle of the week Brad Walden was buzzed into her office. He sat down at her desk , saying, 'I've been waiting for a while to give this back.'

She swung her chair around to see him dangling a small key between his fingers. He put it down on the desk.

'What's this?'

'You left it at our place last time we saw you,' explained Brad. 'Biyu called to make sure you got it.'

Melanie searched her memory. *Biyu*. Walden's wife. The "Hakka slut," in Rosie's words. It would be interesting to know the reason for her ire. But Mason hadn't mentioned Julia possibly leaving a key with Walden or his wife.

This was a new and unexpected twist.

'How's your wife?' Melanie said.

'She's in Wuhan at the moment. Visiting her father. But she insists on having you over for dinner when she gets back.'

'When is that?'

'In two weeks.'

'Good!' said Melanie. 'By that time things might have settled down.'

'Let's hope so,' Walden said, getting up again. 'I'll let her know. Be ready for her usual banquet.'

She watched him saunter out of her office. Then she picked up the key. She swung around to face the window once more.

The tall-backed chair had wide wings that hid her from the doorway. It felt like one of those ornate three-fold screens used by actors to change their costumes in, fixing their makeup before coming out onstage again.

She swung around and tried the key on her desk drawers. It didn't fit in any of them. She took out the keys Rosie had given her. This new key didn't match any of them.

She peered at the little metal attachment dangling from its ring. It had a number on one side. The other face was engraved with the name, "Hong Kong Yacht Club". It was a key to some locker.

She summoned her secretary.

Miss Lin came in and she handed her the key. 'Have someone go to the yacht club and bring me what's in the locker.'

She went out for a few hours, and when she came back, a small box was waiting on her desk. She opened it gingerly, unsure whether she was being led into an elaborate trap, or was being made to put her fingerprints on something she shouldn't touch. Inside she found a PDA, worn by use, a repository of secrets no one had suspected.

It had been in a locker all this time. The only reason no one had known to look for it, was because no one knew Walden had the key. Did he know what was in the locker? Did the key end up in his possession by accident? Or did the owner entrust it to him, knowing no one would suspect him of harbouring important information?

She turned on the organizer. The light flickered very briefly before going out again. Her heart sank. The battery was dead from years of inactivity. She hoped it didn't mean the memory in it had been wiped out.

She plugged it into one of the chargers under her desk. About an hour later she tried turning it on again. As soon as the screen came to life, it demanded a password. She tried several obvious combinations, but after dozens of attempts she was back staring at the stubborn screen.

She searched her memory of something Mason might have mentioned, any detail that Julia might have used as a password. She typed in Julia's birthday, but that didn't work. Had she come all this way only to reach a dead end?

She was about to give up when something Mason had told her popped into her head. Cherry Blossom. She keyed in: *ying hua*. It still didn't work.

She did it again, but his time added the year of Julia's birth. But that didn't unlock the PDA either.

Finally she typed in *ying hua*, but this time added the year of her own birth. The result was: "*ying hua* 1982."

To her shock, the gadget came on. She immediately saw the tantalizing first entries on the Contacts List. As she went further down she saw names that were new to her. Afraid that the good fortune would be snatched away from her, she grabbed a pen and copied down as many as she could.

She pressed down on the intercom again, 'Miss Lin, could you send up a company directory?'

The folder was brought in, and Melanie confirmed that several numbers on Julia's list were outside her company. Who were they? This was precisely the grey area in Mason's knowledge of Julia Tang, the kind of associations that heightened the enigma of the heiress. Did they have something to do with her father's illicit dealings? Were they somehow linked to his untimely demise?

The names were like dots that charted out a new direction, an itinerary into Julia Tang's secret life. They were promising but risky destinations.

She put the PDA in the bottom drawer and locked it. She put it out of her mind for the moment, as various functionaries trooped in and out of her office, bearing documents for her signature, contracts for her approval.

As she affixed Julia's signature that had taken her days of practice to master, she understood why it had been so important to resurrect Julia Tang, and why it was imperative to maintain the illusion. The flow of documents from her desk fed the hungry machine that ran on its fuel of paper, the paper that only weeks before Stanley Wang and everyone else had feared was all that would remain of Arthur Tang's empire. Now the empire was back on its feet, and everyone was happy.

But even as she enjoyed the lavish rewards, she never forgot the sword hanging over them all. It was the same threat that had hung over Arthur Tang and his daughter. And now, having taken that daughter's place, Melanie faced the same perils that had made her entry possible.

Everyone around her was anxiously watching the events in China. They pored over every bit of information that filtered through about the widening probe into Li Kun Ming's connections. Julia's father had died trying to stay out of the clutches of the Chinese authorities.

Trying to finish up some business he had in Geneva, was all Mason could say. That was one of the few gaps in Mason's otherwise exceptional briefing. What kind of business exactly was

Arthur dealing with when he died in Geneva? And did it lead to his death? If Mason didn't know, then Melanie was sure no one else in the conglomerate did.

She was sure Rosie didn't know, or she wouldn't have to put up with an impostor like her. So far, Rosie had made a very good show of believing Melanie really was Julia. But was she really convinced? Or was it simply in her interest to play along?

It was all tied up, Melanie knew, with what had really happened to Julia Tang. And that was the great mystery at the heart of it all.

Now part of that puzzle was locked away in Melanie's drawer. She wondered if that was the best place for it. Was it better there or back in Severn Road?

She lost track of the time. The procession of executives to and from her office went on without letup until it was night. She got ready to go home.

As she stared out of the window one last time at the darkness falling over the territory, she thought of Julia's PDA in her bottom drawer. Why had the heiress locked it with a password that meant Cherry Blossom, the name of the tree under which Melanie had been found? And why was part of the password the year of Melanie's birth rather than Julia's own?

As if Julia had anticipated the crossing of their paths, through some prophecy that Melanie had not been aware of, but which the uncannily prescient Mason had stumbled upon.

Sometime before she disappeared, did Julia discover something in the mystical Book of Changes that foresaw this strange entanglement of their fates? The riddle was just one of many that made up the larger enigma that was Julia Tang's life. This charmed but knotty life that Melanie had now taken over.

Chapter IX

Following Tang Worldwide's miraculous resurgence, Rosie remained her charming, seemingly carefree self, flitting in and out of the offices like a happy butterfly, clad in her latest clothes, dropping in for chats with Melanie between shopping trips or afternoons at the race track. Her starlet's exterior never hinted at the high jinks she'd been up to behind the scenes, which she handled with the skill of a virtuoso puppet master, pulling strings and making scene changes without missing a beat.

In the evenings she provided good-natured company for Melanie at Severn Road or at one of her private boxes at the Happy Valley or the Sha Tin Race Tracks. She bet recklessly on horses she liked, jumping up and down in her chair as the chase reached the finish line. At the end of the night she always retreated back to her home on Repulse Bay, so what she got up to after they parted was always a mystery to Melanie.

She spent her nights alone in the cavernous home on the territory's highest peak, looking down on the rest of the island. She wondered if the loneliness she felt right now was Julia's constant state, cut off from the rest of the world in her father's citadel high up in the clouds.

It reminded her of the comment she had made to Andrew Chang on their first meeting. She said that looking out of those windows for the first time had made her cry. Those words had confirmed for Andrew that the woman who had suddenly reappeared really was his godchild, Julia.

He was there at Arthur's house-warming when Julia had stood at the window for a few moments and suddenly burst into tears. She had rushed from the room, leaving everyone puzzled at Arthur's black tie party.

Mason, of course, had told Melanie about the incident. But what prompted Melanie to say the words about Julia's mother was a mystery even to her. She didn't know where it had come from. It was one of those moments when she felt something was acting through her, as if Julia herself were speaking through her lips. As if the words were not about Julia's mother at all, but the sadness Melanie felt for her own.

The effect on Andrew was incalculable. It overcame whatever doubts he might have had. Because only Julia herself could offer an explanation for an incident that had perplexed him and many of Arthur's closest friends. That day in Andrew's office, the normally aloof man had seized Melanie's hands, convinced that here really was his godchild, Arthur's daughter. Returned from one of her frequent disappearances, too haughty to explain herself to anyone.

After weeks, the furore over her return settled down. Tang Worldwide went back to chugging like the well oiled machinery it always was. If anyone still harboured any qualms about Melanie, they didn't voice them out.

To demand answers now would have been like blocking a locomotive that had gotten underway. To demand some verification of her identity could be deemed an unforgivable insult, foolhardy and fruitless.

Their silence was rewarded, as they watched the company stock rise up to the lofty heights where it had always soared, making rich people of all of them.

Every day, the reports that wound up on Melanie's desk told of how the conglomerate was rising from the ashes, flexing its once feeble tentacles across continents again, gobbling up capital, sweeping through the markets of the world.
One day, Melanie couldn't resist the temptation. She took out her new phone and decided to call Mason. She didn't call the

number he had given her. She dialled the one listed in Julia's PDA.

'I thought I'd never hear from you again,' he said as soon as he came on.

'Now, did you take me for that kind of girl?'

'I'm not quite sure,' he replied. 'But do you think it's quite sensible for you to call me?'

'Don't worry,' said Melanie said quietly into the phone, turning her chair to conceal herself behind its wings. 'This will be a test of the best technology money can buy. I asked them to get me the most secure phone. Let's see if they have.'

'How'd you find this number? I don't remember giving it to you.'

'It was listed in the PDA.'

'What PDA?'

'Julia's. She had left it in the Yacht Club locker.'

'And you managed to unlock it?'

'How else would I be calling this number, silly?'

Mason chewed on the information. 'My, my. Aren't you a clever girl.'

'You were lucky to find me.'

'You're doing a marvellous job,' conceded Mason. 'And best of all, you've kept it all quiet. No one's talking about Arthur's daughter being back. But it shows in all the indicators.'

'Like your bank account,' Melanie said.

'Ah, yes. Speaking of bank accounts, I'm glad you called.'

'You want your cut.'

'No, no, no. That's already taken care of. The boost in stocks is more than enough. You've just tripled my assets'

Melanie sighed with relief. 'Well that's one thing less to worry about.'

'Now I'll give you another.'

'What's that?'

'Rosie. Your dear stepmother.'

'What about her?'

'While all this fanfare was going on about the Tangs being back in business, Rosie managed to slip some sixty million dollars out of Hong Kong. If this goes on, it'll haemorrhage the company.'

The amount alone was a shock to Melanie. That it had happened without her knowledge was a big worry. 'I thought I was in charge of this place,' she said.

'There are structures that have been in place long before Julia joined her father's company,' explained Mason.

'What kind of structures?'

'It's the way Arthur operated his business,' Mason explained. 'He had the official structure which everyone could see. And he had the invisible structure, which was where the real business happened. That's how he managed to achieve what he did.'

Melanie's intuition told her that this invisible structure was where many dangers lay. The danger from the mainland authorities, and the danger to Melanie herself. In it may lie the answer to why Julia disappeared.

'How do I find out about this invisible structure?'

She could hear him clucking his tongue on the other end. 'That's something only you are in a position to find out, my dear. Only someone on the inside, and at the very top, has any chance of doing that.' He paused briefly, then added, 'But I have faith in you. You cracked Julia's password. I'm sure you can crack a lot of her other secrets.'

Now Melanie knew why Mason had left out any reference to the so called "invisible structures" when he was briefing her. If she had known about it, she would surely have walked away. Now she looked around her, at the granite ceiling high above her, the glass towers lined up in perfect rows outside her window. She thought, *Too late to back out now.*

Chapter X

On Tuesday morning Melanie was having her tea in the terrace when she heard someone tapping on the glass. She turned around to see Jason standing behind the sliding door. She got up to let him in.

'Why, what a surprise!' she said as he sat down at the chair across from her.

'My mother's seeing her dentist,' he said by way of explanation.

'I understand,' Melanie said, pouring him some tea. 'She doesn't have to run around looking after me.'

They sat in silence for a moment, while Jason took a sip of his drink.

'You didn't expect me to come back, did you?' Melanie said suddenly.

He put his cup down slowly, his eyes wary. 'But I'm glad you did,' he said at length.

Over the rail behind him, she could see the pool, a shimmering blue like the sky above them.' So am I,' she smiled.

After a thoughtful pause he asked, 'Why *did* you come back?'

'What an odd question,' Melanie said. 'This is my home.'

'You didn't seem to think so before,' he said. 'This was just one of many places you could be. You spent more time in Tokyo or London. You only came back for the board meetings. '

'Well,' Melanie said with a shrug. 'That was quite a while ago. I'm a different person now.'

He took another sip of his tea, nodding thoughtfully. 'Were you in some kind of trouble?'

'Do I have to be in trouble to come home?'

He shifted in his chair to lean one arm on the rail, stretching out. 'Well, you sure chose a strange time to return.'

'Why do you say that?'

'Nobody jumps back on a sinking ship.'

'Tang Worldwide isn't a sinking ship. Didn't you see the news? We're riding high again.'

'Again.' He sounded unconvinced. 'For how long?'

'That's something no one can predict,' Melanie answered. 'That's why we go to work every day.'

His face darkened at that, and they fell silent again. She wondered why he had really come to see her. She was sure it was all orchestrated by Rosie, just as she was sure the "visit to the dentist" was a disguise for something else. She wondered if it was Rosie's way of showing her displeasure.

Every morning since Melanie had arrived, Rosie had made an effort to visit or call her. Now her sudden absence was a sure sign that something wrong. It was the first crack in what had seemed a cordial relationship. And Melanie had a good idea what had brought it about.

She recalled the last time she had spoken to Mason. After the call, she had summoned Andrew Chang. She gave him categorical instructions not to allow any more fund transfers without her approval. This decision was sure to impact Rosie, and sure enough, she was suddenly too busy to see her precious "stepdaughter."

Now, Melanie thought, I'm *really being like Julia*. If Rosie hadn't been convinced that her stubborn stepdaughter had returned, Melanie felt sure that by now she must be. And here was Jason in her place, being all charming and interested for a change.

'What brought you here so early in the morning? ' she said.

;Oh, I'm meeting Feng at the library today,' he replied. 'I thought I'd swing by before that.'

'The library?' she raised an eyebrow. Then she remembered that he must mean the Whiskey Library at *Man Hing* Building.

'Jason,' she said mockingly. 'How nice of you to spare a thought for me on such a busy day.'

'It's the least I can do,' he said. 'Seeing how hard you're working. In fact, I came to invite you somewhere.'

'Oh?' Melanie answered with creeping wariness. To where?'

He turned around to see how she would react, 'How about a quick trip to Macau this evening?'

'What's happening there?' She asked.

'Nothing,' he shrugged. 'Does there have to be a reason to show my little sister around?'

'It's just that Macau doesn't really hold much for me,' said Melanie.

'You don't remember gambling there all night on my last birthday?' he leaned forward to quiz her.

She paused for a moment, then shook her head. 'No, I don't remember that at all.'

His face fell, as though he had been foiled. 'No,' he leaned back, smiling to conceal his disappointment. 'I guess not.'

After they finished tea, Jason left. She was driven to work, wondering what the evening had in store for her.

During the day she used operational questions to summon one executive after another, scoping them out, trying to gauge what they knew of what Mason called the conglomerate's 'invisible structure.' She asked leading questions about unseen hierarchies working in the shadows of the company. But they all stuck to the version that Tang Worldwide had only one structure, and that was the one described in all the company papers.

Melanie wasn't sure if this was a result of the typical corporate culture of fear. Or if it was the product of Arthur Tang's policy of keeping his subordinates in the dark about how he really ran his business.

Her last meeting was with Brad Walden. She wondered if he was another Bernard Mason, busily squirreling away information that might prove important later on. As they engaged in aimless banter, she felt sure Brad wasn't under Rosie's thumb, unlike most of the Chinese executives.

At a break in the conversation, she asked him pointedly, 'How did Rosie manage to move out $60 million without my knowledge?'

Walden looked doubtful for a moment, as if she were testing him.

'She managed to find out about the holding company,' he answered with some relief. 'With a little coaching from Stanley, she's learned how to slip money through that.'

He was obviously referring to something Julia must have known about. That put her in a delicate position. She didn't want to ask for information Julia would already have.

'How did Rosie find out about the holding company?' she ventured. She had her accountants go through all the old memos,' Brad explained. 'She found one from you that mentioned S. A. Kura. Unfortunately that was before you ordered all references to S. A. Kura expunged from company records.'

Melanie tried a tack that she thought might elicit more information. 'Has Rosie tried to interfere with the holding company?'

Brad shook his head. 'She doesn't have the authority to. So it remains as it was when your father was still alive. With the accounts in Geneva and all the other holdings.'

Melanie's ears perked up. Brad had just confirmed that this holding company was connected to Arthur's last trip to Switzerland. This entity must be the "invisible structure" Mason had been referring to.

'Is the holding company's phone number still in the directory?' she asked with veiled hope.

'No,' said Brad. 'It was deleted on your orders, and their number and location were known only to you and your father.'

No wonder even Mason didn't know much about it, reflected Melanie. That meant she would have to dig up all the information herself. She discreetly scribbled the name Brad had just mentioned.

'S. A. Kura,' she said softly. 'With a *C* or a *K*?'

Walden looked a little confused. '*K*, as in the flower, I think. You never did explain why you chose that name.'

Like getting a slap on the face, Melanie realized her mistake. She had been asking him about something Julia had set up herself! This was the error she had been dreading all this time. It had come too fast.

She rubbed her head, feeling genuinely dazed. 'There's been so much on my mind....'

I understand,' he said. 'It's been a terrible time for everyone. Especially for you. It's hard to focus on everything at times like these.'

Melanie felt genuinely thankful. She smiled at him, 'Yes, thank you Brad.'

He got up to leave. At the door he turned to say, 'In certain kinds of climate, it's actually convenient to forget a few things.'

She shut the door and went back to her seat. She had found what she was looking for. The holding company was the invisible structure Mason had been talking about. It was the thing that had allowed Arthur Tang to get away with possible wrongdoing. Perhaps her hunch was right: this was the urgent business Arthur had been trying to attend to when he died in Geneva.

And possibly it held proof that could have brought down Arthur's whole empire. Maybe the conglomerate really had reason to fear the results of the trial in China. In which case Melanie was now at the top of a glass house that was about to come crashing down. She thought of her gaffe with Walden, and couldn't help feeling a crack was already beginning to show.

It took Jason's arrival to extricate Melanie from the massive workload. After weeks of immersing herself in the company's operations, she had learned to find its details absorbing, a rare peek into the workings of a complex giant that straddled several legal systems.

Julia's stepbrother bounded in and slid into the chair in front of her desk, dressed in slacks and a light jacket. He brought in the whiff of the outdoors, looking stifled and awkward in the highly functional workplace. It was just after eight o' clock, and most of the staff had left.

'Why this is a pleasant surprise,' Melanie said. 'Twice in one day.'

'Good things come in pairs,' he said with a charming smile. 'That's why you've got me and my mother.'

She locked away Julia's PDA and put the more

important papers in her drawer.' Do you want to sail or to fly?' he asked her.

'Fly where?' she glanced at her watch. 'Isn't it a bit short notice to go on a trip?'

'It's the best time to go,' he urged her. 'We can have our dinner there.'

'Where?'

'Macau. Remember? I told you this morning.'

'Oh.' The invitation had seemed so casual, she had barely given it another thought. But once more she was reminded that for people like the Tangs, the most casual whim became an immediate possibility, the most airy fancy could easily be made real.

In less time than it took to drive around a city block, Miss Lin had arranged the helicopter and chirpily announced, 'It's ready!'

Melanie and Jason rode the elevator up to the roof. When the doors opened they were buffeted by the vigorous gusts blowing above the building tops. They crossed the helipad's rough surface marked by gigantic rings and straight lines stretching out to the edge of the roof. They walked slanting against the powerful wash of the rotors, which made the exposed flatness above the other towers feel even more vertiginous. She covered her ears against the noise, until they were in the chopper's glass bubble, and the din dwindled into a muffled *thump-thump-thump*. With a surge of the engine, they were heaved up so quickly the circles and lines on the platform skewed at crazy angles and shrank to little figures as they climbed higher.

They soared above the night lights of the city just coming alive, sparkling like burnished gemstones in a jeweller's velvet case. She felt again the unreality of Julia's life, ascending

123

at will to the sphere of angels, always outside the bounds of ordinary existence.

She wondered if this was why Julia had found it so easy to leave it all behind. None of it seemed real. It was like a dream from which one could wake up at any moment. For Melanie it was like an unbelievable fairy tale that she was living only because Julia's family had chosen to accept her deception. Why did they let her get away with it? How far would they let it go?

The air pressure made conversation impossible, so she let herself be hypnotized by the sights below them. Sampans and ferries crossing the harbour looked frozen with their bone-white wakes in the darkening sea.

The skyline of Hong Kong became smaller behind them and in a few minutes the chopper zeroed in on a brightly-lit spot that resolved itself into the heliport in Macau. They pitched this way and that until finally the skids touched the ground and they levelled off.

Jason helped her climb out and led her into the elevator. As they descended to the ground floor she slowly adjusted to her surroundings. In the lobby Jason whipped out his phone and made a barrage of calls. She understood restaurants were being arranged, drivers assigned, their return being organized. Melanie was surprised. Despite his happy-go-lucky manner, Jason seemed no less a puppet master then his mother.

At last they went out through the glass doors, and a gleaming black sports car pulled up in front of them. The driver got out and opened the passenger door for Melanie, making a slight bow before disappearing back into the crowds.

Jason got in the driver's seat and shut the door. 'Now,' he said with a boyish gleam in his eyes. 'How hungry are you?'

She was ready to eat, but not quite as desperate as Jason seemed from the way he revved the engine. Despite the light traffic, he made the car leap into every gap that appeared   in front of them, roaring up and down the slopes like he wanted the car to fly.

'Slow down!' she snapped at him. 'We're not in such a hurry.'

He shot her a petulant look and shifted the engine down to a rumbling purr. 'What's the use of a car like this if you can't go fast?'

For once she felt as though he really was acting like a brother towards her, full of the normal frictions between siblings.

Melanie was glad when they finally got to Cotai. Jason parked and they walked into a restaurant. As soon as they crossed the threshold half a dozen waiters rushed forward to greet them. They cleared the way for them to get to a private room with a large round table.

'Is anyone joining us? Melanie asked.

'Of course not,' he shook his head with a smile. 'We're having a private chat.'

'Then why do we need such a big table?'

'This is their place of honour,' he told her. The size of a table reflects the importance of a guest, remember?'

'I know that,' but we don't have to take what we're given.'

He looked at her like they'd had these kinds of arguments many times before. 'They've never known me to settle for anything less,' he said. 'I've got my reputation to maintain.'

They sat down, and a procession of dishes was laid before them. Again, like the table, it was less about what they wanted and more about their standing. A man like Jason was never supposed to have a simple meal. He was acting grandly, living up to expectations.

Since they crossed the border from Hong Kong he had entered his own role. It showed in the way he boasted about the attractions of Macau, comparing various establishments and the best gaming rooms in each one.

She could tell this was his stamping ground, the place where he could best express himself. He acted like a schoolboy deigning to show his little sister his secret haunts, his manner wavering between chumminess and suspicion, as though he was daring her to convince him, but then also approving when she did or said the right thing.

It made her tense. She still remembered her earlier gaff with Brad Walden, and was careful of making any more mistakes. Of everyone she had encountered, Jason seemed to be the only one least swayed by her. He appeared to know something no one else did, but for some reason he chose not to expose her. It puzzled her even more now that he seemed to be trying to win her over.

Since their uneasy first encounter, something seemed to have changed. For whatever reason Jason seemed more prepared to let Melanie get away with her ruse. She found him perplexing and somewhat threatening, the one rogue card in the deck Mason had dealt her.

After dinner he drove her to Taipa on the other end of the causeway. The road was a thin ribbon of light stretching out over the dark sea. They turned into Avenida Marginal Flor, drenched in variegated swathes of light that made it seem wider and much longer than it actually was. They passed a profusion of gleaming hotels before they stopped in front of the Grand Waldo. Its hypnotic bands of purple light reflected on the fountains in the front.

"So what do you say?' Jason grinned at her from behind the wheel. 'Care to try your luck at the tables? They have poker, baccarat, or even *fan tan*.'

The sight was enticing, and for a moment she almost said yes. But every minute of the day since she had arrived had been a wager, a hazard played quietly with losses or gains that no one was aware of but her. She was in no mood to take any more chances than she had to.

'No thanks,' she shook her head. 'You know I've never been much into gambling.'

'Yes,' he said with a nod. 'You do your gambling in the stock exchange.'

This was how Mason had described Julia's family get-togethers. Tit for tat about who did this or that, competing over who did worse or had spent more money, whose hobby horse had been a greater drain on their wealth. It was an ordinary family in certain ways, only with access to phenomenal resources, making them prey to extraordinary pitfalls and temptations. 'Come into the bar at least,' he pleaded.

Melanie unfastened her seat belt and opened the door. 'Okay.'

He celebrated with a jaunty walk into the lobby. He got the same kind of welcome as they entered the Rain restaurant, the waiters and maitre d' rushing forward to do their bidding.

Out of long established habit, the maitre d' led them to the table right in front of the band, but Melanie pulled back.

'Let's go somewhere quieter,' she said.

So they ended up at a corner furthest away from the stage, where Jason kept gazing longingly at the front seat he normally occupied. It was after their second round of drinks that Melanie gleaned the whole purpose of the evening.

'Mother says you're being too strict with her,' Jason said in his attempt at a brotherly tone. 'She feels stifled.'

Melanie wanted to laugh. If being strict with Rosie meant not allowing her to move millions from one account to another, she wondered what Rosie would think about having her credit cards declined, having to move from place to place to elude debt collectors. Involuntarily Melanie reflected on the life she had been living before Mason stumbled upon her.

She had crossed from one extreme of life to the other. Now here she was, toying with the fortunes of one of the richest families in the world. It was as unbelievable as the mirage of lights around her, the promise of great fortune that awaited every hopeless gambler that walked through the casinos' doors.

She finished the last of her drink and put the glass down. 'No,' she said firmly. 'I'm doing this for the good of the company. Now is not the time to go on spending sprees. Now is the time to put our acorns away.'

He looked like he didn't understand her, and she wondered briefly if she had used the wrong expression. But perhaps it was also because he simply didn't understand being turned down.

At some point in the evening, three men stopped at their table to chat with Jason. One of them was a rough-looking man in his late 50's, with gold teeth, a large elaborate tattoo up the side of his neck, and an expensive gold watch on his wrist. The white faced Omega Deville looked stark against the man's dark skin, and seemed to have the same gleam as the gold in his teeth. Melanie smiled politely, but knew they were part of the shady cast of characters her mentor Bernard Mason had never encountered.

As the evening wore on, more and more of the patrons left. Until finally the band performed its last song and said goodnight. Melanie waved for the bill. She signed for it and got up. 'Well, come on,' she motioned with her head. 'I'd like to get back before midnight.'

When she returned to work the next day, she found a reminder she had written to herself. 'S. A. Kura,' it said. The name of the holding company Brad Walden had told her about. The secretive entity within the company that only Julia and her father knew the details of. She had been about to do some digging when Jason had shown up the night before.

Now she picked up where she had left off. She spent the first half of the morning searching through Julia's archived files, hoping to find the number of the holding company that might have escaped the mass deletion Julia had ordered. After hours of searching, she came across an old email to Julia from a senior partner named Ho Kinseng. It mentioned transactions in Geneva, but nothing more.

Hoping to supplement the meagre information, she picked up the phone to speak to Andrew Chang.

'Have you heard anything from Ho Kinseng?' she asked.

He seemed taken aback at the question. He cleared his throat and said, 'No. I haven't been in touch with him since he, uh, left the company.'

From the date on Julia's email, Melanie deduced that this sudden departure of a senior partner would have been after Arthur's death. She saw the hand of Rosie. As soon as she finished talking to Andrew, she took out Julia's PDA from her bottom drawer. She searched the contacts list and found two numbers listed for a "Kin Ho."

She dialled the first one. After a few rings, a chirpy female voice said, 'S.A. Kura Holdings!'

After explaining where she was calling from, Melanie was transferred to frail-sounding man who came alive when she identified herself as Julia Tang. He hurriedly gave her directions to his workplace, and Melanie left her office without telling anyone where she was going, and drove herself to Kowloon.

Half an hour later she was in Room 814 in the Evergreen Building. It was the exact opposite of her own office across the water. It was cramped and a little unkempt, the chairs of peeling faux leather, with rusting metal filing cabinets covering most of one wall.

The elusive Ho Kinseng, Arthur's disgraced partner and now administrator of S.A. Kura, was in his late 60's, wiry and more energetic in person than he had sounded on the phone. He had served as Arthur's accountant from the start of the tycoon's career, and was in his inner circle right up to the time of Arthur's death. But soon after that he became one of the first to taste Rosie's wrath, the first to learn the lesson of daring to stand up to Arthur's widow.

For his efforts to adhere to the founder's policies, Kin Ho had suffered the fate of all those before him who had stood in the way of imperial whims, and Rosie was glad to be able to make an example of him.

Despite a record of commendable service Kin Ho found himself stripped of his powers and chased out of the conglomerate he had helped to build. His name was purged from the company records, leaving him forever under the cloud of suspicion. That was why Melanie didn't find it easy to track him down. If not for that stray email in Julia's PDA, she might never have found him.

She found the drab workplace an unlikely site for a holding company that had links to one of the biggest concerns in the region. Its position, looking away from the majesty of 2IFC across the harbour, seemed to symbolize its murky role. Like a mistress hidden away in a dingy neighbourhood, out of sight from her patron's legitimate family and respectable enterprise. That was why Melanie sensed she could probably learn more from this backdoor segment of Tang Worldwide. Having come through the back door herself, she sensed this was probably where much of the real action went on.

For his part, Kin Ho, seeing the woman he believed to be Arthur's daughter, beamed like a drowning man who has just seen a passing ship turn around and make its way towards him. At last all his fortitude was paying off.

He had always believed in burying himself behind those he considered more powerful or more capable than he. Accepting that he himself was perhaps not destined for greatness, he contented himself with being allowed to survive, being able to weather the great storms that brought down men like Arthur Tang.

He believed in the security of being invisible, refusing to be drawn into a public battle with someone as powerful as Rosie and her cohorts. Through their onslaught, he had remained calm and polite, while secretly seeking ways to endure and further his own ends. He believed in the silent strength of stones, which survived cyclones and forest fires while the mightiest trees were annihilated.

'So tell me about the gambling debts,' Melanie said to him.

Kin Ho stood up and brought down the books from the steel shelf. He laid them out on his desk like a warrior solemnly laying out his weapons. These were his tools, the instruments by which he would bring down his foes.

He went through every item in the ledgers, showing Arthur's daughter how things really stood in the company, what happened to the money that came in, how it was fed to the hungry apparatus, how it was squandered.

'From this day on,' Melanie said, 'no more payments will be made through you. Everything will go out the front way.'

Kin Ho nodded. At last he felt that a sense of order was returning. He looked at her gratefully. Then, as if he had finally come to a decision about her, he said, 'Do you want your father's book?'

Melanie was taken aback. 'My father's book?'

'Yes,' Kin Ho said eagerly, as if waiting for this moment for so long. 'I've kept it here. I took it with me when I left.'

He got up again and crossed the room to walk behind a waist-high bookshelf. He took out a key and bent down to insert it. She saw him open a black metal door and reach in.

Melanie knew she had now entered territory beyond Mason's knowledge, the new lay of the land that took shape after the lawyer's departure, which had resulted from the clandestine manoeuvrings that had begun long before Arthur's unexpected demise.

The old book keeper walked around to his desk again and lay down a black leather volume.

'There was no one to give it to,' he handled it with almost religious reverence. 'But now you are here. It's yours.'

Melanie looked at it. Inside were secrets so important Arthur Tang didn't breathe a word of it to his trusted lawyer Bernard Mason. And now it was hers to take. Each piece of the puzzle she found was moving her further and further away from Mason's plan, into a course she was charting out for herself, creating new risks she would have to find her own ways to face.

She pulled the tome towards her, wondering where it would be safest to keep. She thought of her room back in Severn Road, but a thought suddenly flashed through her mind. She had found Julia's PDA in a locker at the yacht club. Evidently Julia hadn't felt that her most private possessions were safe in her own home.

'I'll have to find a secure place for it first,' she pushed back the journal towards him. "Make me a copy of the pages. 'But keep this here for now.'

The old book keeper went to do as she had asked.

Soon the copies were bound in the most ordinary-looking folder, without even a label to indicate what was inside. Melanie clutched the folder tightly as she went down to her car, thinking ahead to where she would put it as she drove back to the granite tower that was 2IFC.

Chapter XI

The pages Kin Ho had copied from Arthur's book showed how faithfully Arthur had observed the anniversary of his wife's death on the 15th of May every year. The entries showed that he had kept it a private affair between himself and his daughter. The only other person invited on those occasions was Linda's surviving sister, Bernadette. One of the last pictures Mason took before Arthur died showed the tycoon and his daughter standing with Bernadette at Linda's gravesite.

Mason had told her Bernadette's relations with Arthur were never the best, and they turned for the worse after Linda died. Rosie's entry into the picture seemed too abrupt, and her hostility pushed Bernadette further away from Arthur's circles.

Julia's aunt had never married, and relocated to Malaysia soon after her sister's death. But one of Linda's last acts was to ensure that Bernadette got a large share of stocks in the conglomerate, and she found herself in a constant tug of war with Arthur's new wife for her share of the Tang wealth.

Their battles became fodder for the Hong Kong rumour mill. Twice it erupted in court cases, when Arthur had to intercede to keep the family's quarrels out of the public eye.

Despite the strained relations with Rosie, however, Bernadette maintained a close bond with her niece Julia, who used to make frequent trips to Malaysia to see her aunt.

'Julia's pet name for her aunt Bernadette was *Tamago*,' Mason had told Melanie.

'What does that mean?'

'Well, it's a Japanese term of endearment.'

'Why Japanese?'

'Julia once had a Japanese nanny, who kept calling her *tamago gata no kao*. Which means someone with an egg-shaped face, which is considered very pretty by the Japanese. And the joke between Bernadette and Linda was that Bernadette was the egg-head of family. Hence Julia christened her *Tamago*.'

As the anniversary approached, Melanie grew more and more nervous about meeting Bernadette. She seemed to have been the closest person to Julia. If anyone could tell the difference between the missing heiress and an impostor, it was Bernadette.

Melanie prepared obsessively for the encounter. But she knew that no amount of rehearsal could accurately replicate the relationship between two people. She could memorize all the details she wanted, but there were still countless random gestures, spontaneous responses that might come out false.

And so May the 15th finally came, and she got up earlier than usual, too anxious to sleep, bracing herself for everything that could go wrong. But the reality was still more surprising than she'd expected.

When she came out to go downstairs, the first thing she saw was the luggage by the sofa. She walked down the steps slowly, trying to decide what her facial expression should be. Then she saw the slight figure by the window, who spun around with a gasp. She gaped up at Melanie like someone seeing a ghost.

Melanie recognized Bernadette from all the pictures she had studied. But she was surprised at her own emotions. It was as if her old wish to meet someone from her real family were suddenly coming true. It was as if she were meeting her own closest kin, someone with whom she had to be completely honest. That was the reason she took the last few steps at the bottom of the stairs with a sense that the charade was about to stop, that she wouldn't be able to carry on with the deception.

Bernadette ran forward and wrapped her arms around her. As she felt the affection she knew was meant for the woman he was impersonating, Melanie knew it wouldn't be that easy to break out of the deception. There was too much at stake for everyone involved. Bernadette leaned back to look at her. 'I came as soon as I heard you were back,' she said. 'I had to come see for myself.'

She gave Melanie a probing look. 'I was so afraid it would turn out to be another lie.'

But it is! cried a voice in Melanie's head. She began to hate herself.

'But now I've seen it with my own eyes,' Bernadette continued with an awed look. 'It's so good to know your worst fears haven't come to pass. And on this day of all days. On this day your mother would have shared...'

It was clear Bernadette's late sister was still very present in her mind. Perhaps in the same manner, she projected cherished memories of her missing niece on Melanie. Melanie put her hand on the older woman's shoulder. 'Sit down, Tamago.'

A smile broke on Bernadette's face and her eyes shone at the word. Her eyes welled up with tears, and she let Melanie guide her to the sofa. Melanie raised her hand for one of the servants she knew was always watching.

She ordered for tea to be brought. When the tray came, Melanie took care to pour from the teapot with her left hand as she knew Julia did, and Bernadette gazed at her with more astonishment and disbelief. She cupped the hot drink in her hands, as if treasuring the moment, and dreading the instant she would wake up from a wonderful dream.

But while they sat and talked, Melanie began to notice Bernadette's uneasiness in the house. She kept glancing towards the stairs as if expecting someone to come down.

'Isn't your stepmother here?' she inquired at length.

Melanie remembered the hostility between Rosie and Bernadette.

'She hasn't been for a while,' Melanie assured her. 'Forget about her. You're here to see me.'

'And your mother,' said Bernadette, touching Melanie's hand.

'Of course,' Melanie put down her cup. With the old woman's touch she felt herself pulled back into Mason's charade, unable to extricate herself from the lark she herself had begun. Julia's aunt seemed so full of joy at seeing her that Melanie didn't have the heart to pull away and tell her the awful truth. That her missing niece hadn't really come back and probably never would.

She found herself being forced by circumstances, like a swimmer forced by an overpowering current, to go in a direction she had never intended. As if by some kind of muscle memory, Mason's training kicked in and once again, and Melanie knew exactly what she had to say and do.

They chatted for a while longer, then Melanie had the tea set cleared and ordered Bernadette's bags taken into the guest room. The elderly lady watched as her belongings were taken away, taken aback by the young woman's presumption she would stay.

'You're not just going to pop in and out like you always do, Tamago,' Melanie declared in the clipped tones of Julia Tang she had heard countless times on Mason's videos.

Bernadette looked at here probingly, then threw up her hands in submission.

In a quarter of an hour they were driving to the cemetery to visit Linda's grave. The car took the route Mason had shown her on satellite maps, which were accurate right down to the shrubbery overflowing out of window boxes high above the street, and the banyan trees that shaded the drive. Bernadette sat serenely watching the scenery go by, her hand on Melanie's. She didn't feel for one moment as if a stranger's hand were touching hers. It had nothing to do with Mason's training, but seemed to arise from something innately right. Almost as if she'd found a connection she'd always been longing for.

And when they finally arrived at the burial ground, she silently thanked Mason again for his thoroughness. It enabled her to pick her way through the bewildering junction of footways snaking through the jumble of memorials and tombs.

In death, too, the former colony showed an irrepressible impulse to ascend. The headstones were arranged in tiers along the steep incline of the hill, like the sides of an arena for the dearly departed to look down on the spectacle of the living. It reinforced the belief that one's ancestors were still there, observing everything.

Melanie climbed the stairs she knew would take them to a curving path, which ended in a small gate. Mason's voice echoed in her ears as she slid the bolt back and pushed through. She followed the half circle between the upper tiers that offered a stunning view of the sea. At last they arrived at Linda's tomb, breathless from the precipitous climb.

The pictures she had studied, the maps and diagrams somehow turned into this guiding force that seemed to take over her actions. She didn't know if it was the same force that induced a deep sadness when she bent down to run her fingers on Linda's name on the stone.

She didn't know what exactly came over her, but she suddenly burst into tears, as if she were crying for some loss of her own, some separation to which she had never put a name.

Her body shook with grief for several moments as she stood at this grave of a woman she had never known. A life cut short, a mother lost, leaving a gap in someone's heart, like the one Melanie had known all her life.

Bernadette put a gentle hand on her shoulder.

'It's all right,' she said softly. 'Now you are here. It'll be like she's still here, too.'

Bernadette had come with her usual offerings, like on that day when Mason had snapped that picture Melanie remembered from their briefings. He had had the image enlarged and told Melanie what the items in the bowls were, to be left that day as gifts at Linda's crypt.

So Melanie wasn't surprised when Bernadette took out container of cherries and placed them in a bowl. The stories about them had been a vivid part of Melanie's training.

'So that cherry tree is still alive?' she asked.

Bernadette nodded with a smile. 'Still in the spot where our grandmother planted it when your mother and I were children. It's almost a miracle. Even if they've built roads and new towns around it, the tree is still there. I flew home this year just to gather this fruit. Now your mother can enjoy them.'

Melanie sat down next to her. 'It'll be like all those years when you sent her the fruit.'

'This time I even managed to bring some blossoms,' Bernadette said, reaching into her bag for another container. Melanie was taken aback by the cherry blossoms Julia's aunt scattered in front of the tombstone.

140

This was something Mason hadn't prepared her for. Looking at the flowers and the fruit in their bowls, she felt something tug at her heart. But she had no idea what it meant.

Next, the elderly woman produced a bottle of liquid. She dusted a spot on the granite before laying down the bottle. Then she fished out three small glasses and laid them out in a circle. Melanie recognized the bottle of *baijiu*, and understood immediately.

'Nothing could deprive your mother of her pleasures,' said Bernadette. 'We can't let this little separation do that now.'

They sat down and Bernadette poured the clear liquid into the glasses. For each round they drank, Bernadette poured a glass for Linda. By the time they finished, Melanie's head swam from the powerful liquor.

'We've got to leave the rest for her,' Bernadette said with a laugh.

They drank their last shots and Bernadette capped the bottle.

'This is the best way to remember your mother,' giggled Bernadette. 'She would have done exactly the same if she were still here.'

She motioned to the attendant watching them from the end of the path. He came towards them and stopped with a slight bow. Bernadette gestured simply to the granite and the man understood. He bent down to move the tomb's lid. Some cool, moss-scented air escaped and Bernadette thanked him. He left.

Then she and Melanie knelt down to gaze into the cavity, where years of gifts, mementos, and wishes for the afterlife had accumulated. Melanie glimpsed pictures from Julia's holidays like the ones Mason had shown her. She even espied a newspaper announcing Arthur's sudden death. Bernadette took out cards and letters from her bag, and laid it down amongst her other presents to her departed sister.

'That way she knows everything that's going on in our lives,' she said. 'She won't have missed anything when we meet again.'

Melanie planned the rest of the day so that they would spend as little time as possible in the Severn Road house. She wanted to minimize the chances of an encounter between Rosie and Bernadette.

They spent the afternoon paying calls on people Bernadette knew. Stanley basked in the glory of having "rescued" Arthur's daughter, while Bernadette thanked him profusely. They glanced at Melanie and congratulated each other on "Julia's" return.

Then they were at a café in Causeway Bay, Melanie's phone rang. She immediately recognized Rosie's number.

'Hello Rosie,' she said, catching the look of distaste on Bernadette's face at the mere mention of the name. Rosie babbled her apologies for not having visited on this day, offering her best wishes on the sad anniversary.

'That's okay,' Melanie said, cutting the conversation short. 'I'll see you the day after tomorrow. I'm busy with the arrangements.'

She hoped Rosie would take the hint and stay away.

'Now,' she said putting down her phone. 'We can have a quiet night at home.'

Bernadette chuckled. 'If you can guarantee *her* not showing up.'

'I can order the staff to lock the gate.'

Bernadette laughed. Privately, Melanie had no doubt Rosie knew Bernadette was here. For sure the former starlet would be dying to know what information Julia's aunt had imparted to Melanie.

'But seriously,' Bernadette gave her a lingering gaze. 'I've got meetings scheduled for tomorrow afternoon.'

'I understand,' Melanie said. 'It's the same for me.'

'But we have all night,' Bernadette waved expansively.

'Yes! A nice relaxed dinner without unwanted guests.' Bernadette raised her cup to that.

As they drove home Melanie was secretly ecstatic. Not only because of the treasure trove of knowledge Julia's aunt represented. But because the elderly woman was the first person she had met since her arrival who gave her a genuine feeling of warmth.

But she was also aware of the dangers in this. She had entered this arrangement with a clear purpose, and she didn't want old childhood aches to cloud her judgement.

When they got back to Severn Road, Melanie looked at Bernadette with concern. 'You look tired,' she said. 'Why don't you go for a rest?'

Bernadette mulled it over for a moment. To Melanie's relief she nodded, 'Maybe I will. Just for a few minutes.'

'Take your time, Tamago,' Melanie walked with her to the stairs. 'There's no hurry. I'm not going anywhere.'

Bernadette turned around with a laugh. 'I hope so.'

Melanie watched her go up wearily to the guest room, wondering what those words had meant, dreading what mistakes she might have made to arouse suspicion.

But when the old lady disappeared into her room, Melanie felt a wave of relief. The break bought her some time to gather herself, to go over how she should act in the time she had left with Bernadette. She hoped Julia's aunt would rest as long as possible. It would cut down the time she had to evade difficult questions she couldn't answer.

While she waited, she got the urge to escape again, to take what she could and run before she was unmasked.

It was almost dusk when Bernadette came out of her room, looking refreshed. Her kind expression gave Melanie confidence again. She ordered for drinks to be brought to the poolside. They sat by the water's edge, watching the sun go down over the hillside. Bernadette gazed at the hypnotic shimmer of the water.

'Aren't you going in?' she suggested with a smile. 'It looks so inviting.'

Melanie wondered whether she should. Whether the remark was a test about something Julia would have done in the situation. But she was afraid, in case Julia had any physical characteristics Mason hadn't known about, but which might be obvious to Bernadette.

'I think I'll wait till after for dinner,' she said at last.

After a few more drinks they went in for dinner. Throughout the meal Melanie could sense Bernadette wanting to ask her something. But for some reason she held back. Melanie was careful to steer the conversation away from questions she might not be able to answer. She feigned distress whenever she sensed such questions coming up. But Bernadette took her by surprise.

'Have you kept your mother's letter?' she suddenly asked.

Melanie froze. She was thrown from the conviviality into the cold reality of her situation again. She couldn't disguise the look of panic in her eyes as she searched her mind for an answer. But there was none. She put her head in her hands just to avoid Bernadette's gaze.

Bernadette reached over to touch her. 'I know it's painful to remember,' she softly stroked Melanie's hair.

'There are so many things I can't remember,' Melanie wanted to cry.

'It's all right,' soothed the old woman.

'I don't know where the letter is,' Melanie lied. 'I don't know if I even showed it to you.'

'You didn't,' Bernadette continued stroking her hair. 'But I knew what was in it. It was I who urged your mother to write it.'

'Why?' Melanie asked.

'Because you had to know the truth before she died,' answered Bernadette gently. 'I wanted it to come from her.'

This was all part of the things to which Mason had not been privy. He had known nothing about the letter Bernadette was referring to. If that letter still existed, Melanie knew she had to find it.

But for now she felt like a tightrope walker who had suddenly glimpsed the chasm below her. And how far away from either end of the rope she was.

She buried her head in her hands, afraid to go further.

'It's all been so hard,' she moaned. Though the words were not from her role as Julia, but from her true feelings as an impostor, Bernadette responded to the plea. She got up and squeezed Melanie's shoulder.

'I understand,' she cooed. 'Sometimes it's easier to forget. It couldn't have been easy to do what she asked you to do.'

Melanie waited. She tried to think of something but her mind was a blank. All of Mason's tutelage was useless now. She knew she was about to be unmasked. Bernadette would find one untruth after another and her whole house of cards would come down.

Melanie looked out at the lights on the hills. Perhaps it was just fitting. Julia's aunt was the one person who deserved the truth. Melanie wondered how she would break it to her.

'It must have been such a shock to you,' The elderly woman took her other hand. 'To find out something like that just as your mother was dying.'

Melanie was speechless. She was sure Bernadette had realized she was an impostor. She wanted to stand up and confess. She would leave that very night, pack her things quietly and disappear from this fairy tale world.

But the old woman was looking at her with a wistful look. Melanie could tell she was thinking about her dead sister Linda, seeing things as they were before, rather than as they were now. She was relishing some sweeter version of the past, accepting an impostor to make the illusion seem more real.

'It couldn't have been easy,' Bernadette said. 'Trying to find someone you've never known.'

And once again Melanie was pulled back in. She wasn't going to end this masquerade just yet. Perhaps she had no choice but to see it through to the end.

After a silence, Bernadette resumed, 'That's why your mother chose not to tell you until you were old enough.'

For the rest of the evening Bernadette made occasional remarks about the places Linda had loved, sharing reminiscences about Julia's late mother. She was unwittingly filling in gaps in Melanie's knowledge of Julia's life. Through it all Melanie tried to avoid the one subject that made her feel vulnerable.

At last the elderly woman pushed back her chair and looked upstairs. 'Maybe I better turn in.'

Melanie prepared to get up. But then Bernadette suddenly asked the one question Melanie had been dreading all night. 'Why didn't you write? I was so worried what had happened to you.'

It was the one weakness even Mason acknowledged in his plan. There was no way to account for Julia's silence before she suddenly reappeared as Melanie. If their ruse was to work, Melanie had to find a way to make up for this one fatal flaw.

'I'm so sorry,' Melanie said helplessly, drawing from the truth of her own life as much as Julia's, 'I was in such a terrible state. There were times I felt it would have been better if I never came back at all.'

Bernadette was quiet for a long time. She picked at the threads of the mat in front of her. At last, she tilted her head and looked towards the window. 'Did you enjoy being anonymous?' she asked.

Melanie wondered if Julia's aunt was toying with her. After a long hesitation, she dug deep into her own memories to find an answer.

'It was like starting all over again,' she said. In her mind she was thinking of the day she had met Mason and he had made that outlandish proposal to her.

'I could go anywhere and not be known,' she continued.

In truth she was thinking of the simple ordinary life she had been living before she had taken on this charmed but thorny existence.

Bernadette leaned forward to touch her hand.

'I understand,' said softly. 'It must have been so awful for you. Your mother dying so early. Then things going so terribly wrong with your father. And all the burden you suddenly had to bear on your own.'

Her eyes caught the light when she smiled, 'There have been times when I've felt the same way. Go away and never come back.'

Melanie's answer was more certain. 'But I did come back.'

Bernadette's face broke into a big smile, 'And I'm so glad you did.' She suddenly sat forward as if she'd remembered something. 'Before I forget. There's something I've been wanting to give you for a long time.'

She got up and went to the stairs. 'I'll go get it.'

Melanie waited tensely until Julia's aunt reappeared, carrying a pale-coloured calf leather portfolio.

The excited look on Bernadette's face told her she should feign delight.

'You left this at my house on your last visit,' Bernadette said.

Melanie stood up to receive it.

'I've been wanting to give it back to you,' Bernadette bit her lip and looked at her with glistening eyes. 'I didn't know if I'd ever get the chance.'

'Why thank you, Tamago,' gushed Melanie and embraced Julia's aunt.

Chapter XII

The night after Bernadette's visit, Melanie found a quiet moment to look through Julia's portfolio that Bernadette had left. She searched through the bag's plush pockets, musing on whether she had really succeeded in convincing Julia's aunt. Did Bernadette really believe her missing niece had returned?

She probed through the inner recesses of the leather case, which were probably last touched by Julia's hands. Had Julia left it with her aunt on purpose? For safe keeping, perhaps? The same way she had left the locker key with the Waldens? Was there a reason the heiress didn't feel safe about leaving such things in her own home?

Melanie looked around her at the spacious chamber. It was a lavish cage to be sure, but a cage all the same. She was completely in their control. From the food she ate, the water she drank, and the clothes she wore.

She felt like the performer in some mysterious play who was being allowed to put on all the rich costumes and finery for an audience she couldn't see.

It was like being the character in *The Beauty and the Beast*, who walked into an empty house and found the most sumptuous food laid out for her, the most comfortable bed waiting for her to lie down in. Melanie remembered the conclusion of that particular tale: how the young woman finally met the unseen host who had been so generous to her, and she was appalled. The monstrosity that had been hiding in the shadows while she enjoyed his largesse came out in the end and forced her to make an awful choice.

Melanie slowly put down the calf-leather case. For a moment the allure of her surroundings faded. The pool below her window, the incomparable views, all laid out to lock her into some devil's bargain. Was a similar monstrosity waiting for her? Would she be forced to make a choice she couldn't bear to make?

As she was mulling over the possibilities, she heard a light rap on her door.

She almost jumped. She had to take a deep breathe to dispel the frightening parallel of the airy tale.

'Come in,' she called out. The door opened slightly and she saw Jason standing there. She looked at the clock. It was past 11:00.

'Jason?' she said partly getting up. 'What an unusual surprise. Why the late visit? Did something happen?'

He stayed in the doorway, leaning his elbow on the side. 'This the best time for some things.'

She didn't return his smile. 'Like what?'

He must have sensed her tension. He put on his jovial manner and cajoled her,

'Come on. You'll see when you come outside.'

'Now?' she said.

'Why not?' he continued in his mock-brotherly tone, 'You didn't come back so you could go on being an old maid. Stop sitting in your room by yourself every night.'

She could see his impatience to leave, his restless energy roiling against the confinement of four walls. Part of her knew it would be pointless to refuse. Another part of her wanted to see where all his was going, if this visit would bring about some kind of turning point.

'Give me a minute to change,' she said. He stepped back into the hall.

'I'll be downstairs,' he said over his shoulder as he walked off.

Melanie was tempted to stay in her room, but she didn't want to delay whatever lay in store. She stepped out into the balcony to check the temperature. There was a slight chill to the air, so she went in to put on a light jacket. She wondered whether to bring her purse or not.

She was still mulling it over when she came down. Jason pulled himself up from the sofa and sprinted out the door.

'I hear you didn't come to work yesterday,' he said as they walked down the steps to the front. 'I wondered if something was wrong.'

'There was nothing wrong,' Melanie said. 'I just decided to take the day off.'

She thought about Bernadette's brief visit, and wondered what Rosie had been doing behind the scenes. It was clear she had sent Jason to fish for information.

She followed him across the quiet street and they stopped in front of a yellow car parked on the kerb. It was an Aston Martin DBS V12.

'This is what was so urgent,' he gestured towards it proudly. 'It doesn't look half as spectacular in daylight.'

He opened the driver's side.

She waited for him to get in, but realized he was holding the door open for her. 'What are you waiting for?' he sneered. 'You scared?'

She looked at the handsome machine, and found the offer difficult to turn down.

'You still know the way to my old flat, don't you?' he said.

It was another thing she wasn't prepared to decline. She wondered what he would think if she showed him how she knew every turn and intersection to get to his place.

'How could I forget?' she said, sliding in behind the wheel. Only then did she notice a second car a few feet away from them.

'Aren't you coming?' she said up to him.

'No,' he said, nodding towards the other car. 'I'm going to ride with Feng. He doesn't know the way as well as you.'

He walked away. Melanie turned the engine on. The roar of the machine sent a shudder through her. The steering wheel felt almost too light as she pressed cautiously on the accelerator and pulled out. The vehicle glided softly and crossed the distance too quickly. Without meaning to, she found herself hurtling down the dark mountain road towards Central. For a while, she enjoyed it too much to slow down.

She knew Jason would be watching, noting not just the direction she was taking, but her habits at the wheel. How soon her brake lights came on as she approached a corner, and how quickly the motor would roar again after rounding the bend.

She found herself engrossed in the automobile, wrapped tightly like a protective glove around her, responding to her every wish with hair-trigger quickness and the power of a small jet.

After she left the causeway she heard a rumble rising behind her. And suddenly, the rear lights of the other car were in front of her. This was part of Jason's challenge. She knew she had to catch up. As the lights of the little traffic left on the roads blurred into streaks, she tried to get a glimpse of the other vehicle. As if to make matters worse, the found the way closed off ahead.

This new detour hadn't been in the maps Mason had shown her, now she saw she had been going down a completely different route than she should have done. She had been failing the test without knowing it. She quickly turned around and tried to find her way back.

As the dark streets branched out in front of her, the green glow of the instrumentations shone tauntingly at her.

Then she saw Feng's car again. She aimed the Aston at it and gunned the motor. The gap between them was closed in less than four seconds and she was about to veer left to pass Feng when she felt something strange with the wheel.

She met resistance each time she tried to turn to either side. Her instincts told her to hit the brakes. She had slowed down to almost half her speed when she felt the impact on her right. Part of the railing hurtled through the window and glass bits sprayed on her. She hit her head on the side as the vehicle came to a stop.

She woke up in the hospital to find Rosie sitting next to the bed. She stood up and leaned over as soon as she saw Melanie stir.

'What happened?' Melanie said.

'It's nothing,' Rosie said soothingly. 'They just wanted to make sure you had no serious injuries.'

She weighed the implications of that statement for some moments. Then she gingerly asked, 'And do I?'

Rosie was quick to answer. 'No. Thank God it was the side away from you.'

Melanie tried to feel her limbs. There was no obvious damage that she could detect. She was relieved. But suddenly she realized something horrible. It was almost worse than the thought of dying in a car crash: *she was in a hospital!*

By now they would have had all the samples they needed to confirm who she was. Or at least who she wasn't. She wondered if Rosie already knew. Or everyone in the hospital who had treated at her.

She closed her eyes until her heart had stopped racing. She turned contritely to Rosie. 'Did I smash Jason's car?'

Rosie puffed her cheeks and looked up at the ceiling. 'Don't worry. He's used to it. He's done it many times himself.'

'There was something wrong with the steering wheel,' Melanie tried to explain.

'I know. Jason had been complaining about it for weeks.'

And yet he let me…' Melanie didn't finish her sentence. She knew it was useless. Jason had let her get behind the wheel of a faulty machine. And he had encouraged her to go faster than it would have been safe even in the most ordinary of cars. Melanie knew she wouldn't get her answers from Rosie. And she realized the charade had reached a new stage.

Jason was perhaps rethinking his acceptance of Melanie, reconsidering her usefulness now that the conglomerate had been pulled back from the abyss.

'Speaking of Jason,' Melanie said. 'Where is he?'

'He stayed for as long as he could,' Rosie replied. 'But he didn't want to attract too much attention. If he had stayed, people might start wondering. Then there would be talk among the staff. And before we know it the press would be outside.'

Melanie closed her eyes. 'Did anyone recognize me?'

'No. I called Dr. Chow as soon as I heard. He made sure everything was kept extremely private. Even your nurses were hand-picked by him.'

'So, no word about this to anyone?' Melanie asked.

Rosie shook her head. 'It was all kept very quiet.'

As quiet as Julia's disappearance had been, reflected Melanie.

Now she knew it wasn't so easy to be a princess. Standing guard at a great fortune wasn't safe for anyone. She lifted herself up and suddenly felt afraid. Had Jason really intended to kill her? Or was this just a warning?

Another hour or so passed before the door opened and Dr. Chow, bald, frail-looking man came in. Rosie stayed in the room as he checked Melanie's limbs, tested her vision, then asked her probing questions about her recollection of events.

Melanie didn't know what they had given her while she was unconscious, but now she found that her memories were a mix of her own life and Julia's.

'Do you know what today's date is?' Dr. Chow demanded.

Melanie told him.

'And what date was yesterday?'

Melanie knew it was only a medical procedure, but the question worried her. She realized she wasn't sure. Was everything as she remembered? Was something done to her between the last moment she remembered in the car and waking up in this hospital bed?

Her panic mounted as the doctor kept probing. Her only relief came when the doctor left the room to confer with his colleagues. She lay back on the pillow and pretended to sleep. She pictured the layout of the room, calculating the distance to the window, trying to glean the length of the corridor outside from what she had glimpsed of it through the door. She knew she had to escape. But she had no idea where she was. Mason's plan had never included a trip to the hospital.

At last the door opened and Dr. Chow reappeared. Melanie braced herself for the moment he would divulge his findings. That her medical profile or DNA did not match Julia

Tang's. Rosie watched closely as he elderly physician read through the chart.

'It looks like you've come out of this pretty well, young lady,' he bent down to smile at Melanie. 'This time you were very lucky.'

Rosie was elated. 'Now we'll get you home!' she jumped up.

Melanie winced at how dreadful the word "home" sounded coming from Rosie's lips. Now she knew what Julia must have felt. She looked up at the ceiling while Rosie ran around processing her discharge papers. After an interminable pause she returned with an attendant pushing a wheel chair. He tried to help Melanie out of the bed, but she insisted on walking.

She knew that, despite everything, she was expected to carry on as normal, because Julia would have done so. Melanie was finding that she certainly had big shoes to fill, and now they had just proven to be dangerous as well.

Though she was relieved that the hospital hadn't done the DNA checks she so dreaded, she found that her ruse had become harder. Because on top of everything else, now had to deal with flashbacks of the crash, occasional dizzy spells, a weakening in her knees when she was behind the wheel.

It made her reassess her surroundings. What had seemed like victories at first might not be that after all. And it became even more urgent for her to find out the truth about Julia. She thought of finding a hiding place for the portfolio Bernadette had left behind. She recalled that she had been looking through it when Jason had made his unexpected appearance. Suddenly she stopped.

Did Jason know about Julia's portfolio? Did he know Melanie was about to stumble upon crucial information they couldn't allow her to have?

She laid out the contents of the case on the desk. There were two calling cards. She put them aside for the moment. In another pocket were letters from various organizations, which included a number of charities. There was a brochure for a non-profit group called "Traffic Jam." Another envelope contained a letter of thanks from an aid organization called "Shelter Trust," describing their efforts to battle human trafficking in Asia and Eastern Europe. The papers painted a noble picture of Julia. They showed her to be a benevolent, high minded person who wanted to help others. She did not sound like someone who deserved to vanish without a trace.

Whatever really happened to Julia, Melanie felt good for once about being an impostor. It put her in a position to conclude whatever unfinished business the heiress might have had, and to right whatever wrong might have occurred with no one the wiser.

She looked at the calling cards. The first was for a Chad Northam, with Hong Kong Yacht Club in fine print under the name. The second card had the name blacked out, with only part of the company name peeking out: "Pan."

Melanie dialled the number, aware that she was now venturing without any guideposts into Julia's secret world. From now on she would be without a roadmap, without the safety of Mason's guidance. She would be just as vulnerable as the heiress had been.

After two rings, a female voice answered. 'Hello?'

Melanie detected some unfamiliar accent. She didn't know enough about the person at the other end to pass herself off as Julia. So she decided to try a different tack. She introduced herself by her real name, saying she was an old friend of Julia's.

'Any friend of Julia Tang's is a friend of mine,' said the woman.

'Your name is blacked out on Julia's card.'

The woman was silent for a moment. Then she laughed. 'Oh, that card! Well, that's Julia for you. Paranoid as always. But my name is Estelle.'

She sounded eager to meet anyone connected to Julia.

Melanie ventured an invitation. 'Are you free for lunch?'

'Lunch?' the woman repeated after a coy pause.

'Well, it's a beautiful day, she gushed. 'Just the kind of day Julia would always drag me out for a sail.'

'Sail?'

The word sent a sudden spike of pleasure through Melanie. It brought back something she had pushed to the back of her mind.

"Becoming" Julia Tang had been so arduous, the task of wresting control of the conglomerate had consumed so much of her energies that everything else had to be put on hold.

But in her spare moments, her thoughts always wandered back to the prize, to the reason she had come in the first place. More than Julia's homes, her cars, her riches, Melanie coveted the sailing life that had been denied to her. She had often wondered when she would be able to inspect those marvellous toys. Those possessions of Arthur Tang's that meant most to her.

Like a dreamer obsessed, she knew the layout of the family's yacht, the feel of its controls, the sound of its engine purring under her feet. Mason's briefing had only added to her own knowledge of pleasure craft. It strengthened her desire for things that would always be out of her reach, turning into a waking dream she couldn't wait to bring to life.

Now, unexpectedly, the moment had come.

'Why don't we go for a sail then?' Melanie said. 'Make it like it was with Julia, as much as possible.'

'Very well,' said Estelle. 'I can meet you at the yacht club café at 10:00.'

Melanie put down the phone and dialled her secretary. 'Miss Lin, could you call Causeway Bay marina? Tell them to get *Sea Tiger* ready.'

At 10:00 she was at the yacht club, looking out the window at the forest of white masts in the harbour. Estelle had been right. It was a perfect day for sailing.

Half an hour later, she caught sight of a chic, dark-haired woman coming towards her.

Melanie had no doubt it was Estelle. The bob with the pixie curl over her forehead, the sensuous pout and the swaying gait were the embodiment of the sensuous voice she had heard on the phone.

'My Gosh,' said Estelle, her French accent more pronounced in person. 'I thought I was seeing a ghost.'

Melanie got up to greet her, but Estelle's arms wrapped instinctively around her, like a gesture repeated too many times to be unlearned.

They sat down and Estelle looked squarely at her.

'Has anyone ever told you? you're a complete dead ringer for Julia.'

Her eyes had flecks of purple or green, an evanescent colour that was as ambivalent as her gaze. From one moment to the next Melanie couldn't be sure if Estelle was teasing or judging her with those eyes.

'So why are you looking through Julia's calling cards?'

Melanie leaned closed and said softly. 'I'm helping the family find out about her.'

Estelle nodded with a smile. Melanie wasn't sure if she believed her or not.

'But Julia never mentioned you,' she said. 'She never told me she had a double.'

Estelle tilted her head whimsically at her. 'It's a shame. It would have been something to see you side by side.'

'Yes,' agreed Melanie. 'I'm sure it would have been quite disconcerting.'

'Did she meet you through Chad?' asked Estelle.

The name rang a bell. *Chad Northam. The Hong Kong Yacht Club.* It all made sense to Melanie now. She said, 'Yes, in fact she did.'

Privately Melanie wondered if Julia had been aware of Mason harvesting information about her. Information that was now helping Melanie play her part.

The menus were brought and they sat back to decide. Melanie could feel Estelle's eyes studying her over the list. The place was filling up and Melanie became anxious about being seen. She knew the sight of "Julia Tang" was likely to cause talk among the island's elite. She turned her chair to face away from the rest if the room.

'I'll have the lobster and black truffle pasta,' she declared.

Estelle gave her a lingering gaze. 'You're more like Julia than you realize.'

Melanie laughed. 'I take that as a compliment.'

'She would have ordered the exact same dish,' Estelle remarked.

'I don't blame her,' Melanie said. 'It's the best on the menu.'

'Of course,' Estelle brought her glass to her lips and laughed. Estelle ordered wine, as if from long habit, and they watched as it was poured.

'To having nothing but the best,' Melanie raised her glass.

'To the best that gets better,' Estelle responded with a meaningful gaze.

During the meal Melanie kept glancing out towards the boats in the harbour. Estelle couldn't help but notice. 'You look impatient to get going.'

'I'm just worried the weather might change,' Melanie replied.

'Oh, don't worry about that,' Estelle grinned. 'It already has.'

Melanie paused for a moment to get her meaning, but Estelle laughed and got up, 'Well, let's go catch some of those rays, then!'

They left the café and headed out to the jetty. Oddly, as they passed a dozen or so yachts, Melanie found herself getting nervous. As they walked out towards the larger vessels, she felt like she was about to come face to face with a dream.

Suddenly the *Sea Tiger* loomed before them, and she thought about every aspect of the craft, which she only knew from the brochures and photos Mason had shown her. The diagrams were from the manufacturer, but Melanie made the vessel her own, adding her own knowledge of it from stolen moments on other people's yachts, precious fragments that would make up for the missing whole. She didn't know if Estelle was an experienced sailor who would be watching her with a critical eye.

They reached the vessel and stopped. The sight of it took her breath away. There it was, gleaming in the sun. This was the hook by which Mason had induced her to sell her soul. And seeing it here before her now, she felt no regret for the pound of flesh it would cost her.

Its bow was emblazoned with Arthur's personal emblem, the ideogram that stood for tiger, the ferocious beast which Arthur felt best symbolized him and his life. Melanie remembered Mason's words before they started this caper.

They climbed aboard and Melanie thought, *I am mounting the tiger.*

She familiarized herself with the vessel while Estelle went up and down peeking into every compartment. Amid shouts from harbour personnel going back forth over the water, they were untied and Melanie started the engine, feeling the eighty-foot vessel shudder to life underneath her. The pilot approached to haul them out. The tugboat eased them out of the slip and through the narrow, jagged channel between moored vessels until they were out of the harbour. The Sea Tiger moved under her control with the weight and stateliness of her dreams coming true.

She steered towards Victoria Harbour in a leisurely sweep, watching their wake curl like a lacy ribbon behind them before it slowly disappeared. It vanished in the dark ripples at their stern like her old life, while she stood at the helm of this lavish craft, her feet planted firmly on its humming floor.

They followed a steady course close to the coast until they passed North Point on their right. Then she eased up on the throttle. Their progress slowed to a crawl. After several minutes she killed the engine and let the large craft glide. They reached a quiet spot just off Quarry Bay. The hills and skyscrapers loomed on either side of them.

The two halves of the metropolis looked serene across the water, their noise muffled over the misty stretch of sea. They were in the city without being inside its flurry. It was like a cocoon invisible to most people, where life could go on behind an unseen shield.

She walked around the main compartment. There was, of course, Arthur's foldaway gaming table, and several sets of mah-jongg tiles in the drawers, which must have allowed the tycoon to spend hours away from his normal pressures, while never losing touch with his business. The vessel was a virtual floating command centre, with complete communications and office equipment, all hidden away in closets to maintain the craft's relaxed atmosphere.

Real tiger's fur covered the seats, and the wood panelled state room held a king size bed. The vessel carried all the plush accoutrements befitting a man of Arthur's status and tastes. It was exorbitant and intoxicating, and it gave new meaning to Arthur's ethos of riding a beast. This kind of luxury did not come without its hazards. Almost as if Arthur didn't want to forget that his audacious life was never without its perils.

Melanie imagined him or his daughter Julia spending days on board, drifting off the territory but never cut off from their empire, getting up-to-the-minute information from their laptops and the small TV.

She went out and joined Estelle, feeling relaxed for the first time in a long while. Out here she felt far away from the constant tests, the ever changing demands of the situation she had let herself into.

Estelle was stretched out face down on a deckchair, her shoes on the floor near her feet.

'Funny you should stop here,' she said to Melanie. She struggled to raise herself to a sitting position. The imprint of the chair's surface showed on her cheek.

'Why?' asked Melanie.

'This is exactly the spot Julia and I used to stop,' Estelle revealed, looking around and inhaling the sea air hungrily.

'She loved it here,' Estelle continued. 'It was like being here and not here. She could still make her phone calls and pretend she was somewhere no one could find. Our own little magic bubble.'

The words resonated in Melanie's mind: *Here and not here*. Was Julia ostensibly not here, but watching them from somewhere close by?

She sat down next to Estelle, who turned halfway to give her a searching gaze.

'It's uncanny,' she said. 'You not only look like Julia. You do things the way she would have done.'

Melanie smiled.

'Are you sure you're not a long lost relative or something?' teased Estelle.

Melanie looked up and saw her ambiguous smile. Estelle was the most complex person she had encountered thus far. Her tests didn't feel like tests.

Melanie shrugged, 'I wouldn't know.'

A puzzled look flitted across Estelle's eyes. She looked away, the smile still playing on her lips.

'Ah!' she stretched out contentedly. 'I never thought I'd be doing this again.'

'Did you used to do it often?' Melanie asked.

'Almost every week when Julia was in town.'

They sat silently for several moments, transfixed by the hazy skyline in front of them.

'Was this the last place you were with Julia?'

Estelle laughed. 'I've tried to erase it from my mind.'

Melanie sat up a little. 'Why?'

Estelle turned her face up to the sky with her eyes closed, letting the sun bear down on her cheeks.

'I remember,' she suddenly opened her eyes. 'Because she was in quite a bad mood.'

'Did she tell you why?'

'She said she'd had a big row with her father.'

'About what?'

'Seems he found out about something Julia had set up in Geneva.'

Melanie quietly made a connection in her mind. Was that the urgent business Arthur had seen to before he died?

Estelle got up to lean out over the rail. Melanie backed off and left her to her thoughts for a while. There were dozens of questions screaming in her head now, but she held back until the right moment came.

At last she sensed Estelle coming out of her reverie. She got up to join her.

'When exactly was the last time you went on this yacht with Julia?'

Estelle turned to look at her. Her eyes caught some glints off the water. After a few moments she said, 'You know that's a funny thing. I know the exact date.'

She took a step towards the wheelhouse.

'Let me get my purse,' she said. Melanie walked back to one of the deck chairs to wait.

After a few minutes Estelle came back holding her phone.

She sat down next to Melanie and played with the buttons of the device.

'I'll never forget the last time I sailed with Julia,' she said, 'because it was the day before I got this picture.'

She handed Melanie the phone. The screen showed the image of some kind of rocky trail, going past a lone tree in some arid setting. It was a strange location. The tree stood on a small patch of greenery, fighting or life on some barren knoll. Beyond it the sea was visible, and in the distance, some kind of tall landmark.

'Where is this?'

'I have no idea.'

'Who took it?'

'Julia did. She snapped it with her phone somewhere then sent it to me.'

'When?'

Estelle reached over and tapped on the keys. 'There.'

The date at the bottom of the image told Melanie the picture was sent just before Julia disappeared.

'Does anyone know you have this picture?'

Estelle shook her head. 'Apart from you.'

Melanie moved her chair closer to Estelle's. 'Can you give me a copy of it?'

'Sure. Give me your number.'

Melanie told her. With a few strokes from Estelle, the phone in Melanie's pocket buzzed. The strange image had been transferred,

'And you have no idea where this might be?' she said.

Estelle tilted her head sadly. 'This is one time Julia's own precautions worked against her,' she said. 'She was so paranoid she disabled the GPS tracking on her phone.'

Melanie mulled it over for a second. 'Sounds like she had reason to be paranoid.'

Estelle nodded and looked away. In the silence that followed, Melanie realized the stupendous thing that had just happened. With no traceable means, she had just gotten hold of information Mason would have killed for.

Chapter XIII

On her first day back at the office Melanie got a visit from Stanley Wang. He gave her an update on the deal with the Midas Group. The first phase of the agreement, he said, was now in motion.

'They're just making final checks on the pipeline,' Stanley proudly disclosed. 'In a few months we'll be able to begin operations.'

Seeing Stanley in her office took her back to that day in the women's shelter in Los Angeles. It seemed as if a whole lifetime had passed since then, and Stanley, the man who had rescued her from anonymity that day, looked at her smugly, as though she were somehow his responsibility, some protégé of his that had grown into everything he had hoped for.

Her own gamble had gone beyond her wildest expectations. Every day she still looked around her, unable to believe all this was true, wondering when her stupendous flight would end, and how it would feel to plummet back to earth.

That dreaded moment hadn't yet come, and her reality for the moment was this: playing her role to ensure that this massive enterprise continued, and the funds needed for it kept pouring in.

Each time a document was brought in for her to sign, she affixed the signature she had mastered from weeks of studying Julia's handwriting obsessively. It was almost automatic for her now. So ingrained was it in her muscles she found it harder to write her own signature.

'There's just one hiccup,' Stanley intruded into her thoughts.

'What's that?' she looked up.

'The Chinese authorities insist on one thing.'

'Which is?'

'That we hand over all records pertaining to your father's dealings with Li Kun Ming.'

This was one of the things that Melanie had always feared. She tried not to show her alarm. 'But we already told them,' she mustered all her self-assurance. 'Those documents don't exist. Because my father had no dealings with Li.'

Stanley nodded his head sadly. 'But they insist those records *do* exist. Li Kun Ming apparently confessed to handing them over to your father. And if we can't produce them, then the project cannot proceed.'

She was caught in a bind. Refusing to comply would mean the collapse of the one venture that was shoring up Tang Worldwide's fortunes.

If, on the other hand, there was proof that Arthur had assisted in Li Kun Ming's embezzlement, then handing the records over could signal the end of the conglomerate. In one way or another, Melanie knew her position wouldn't remain stable for long.

All at once she understood why someone like Julia Tang would want to disappear. Why she would leave a space vacant for an impostor to fill.

A thought flashed in her mind: that book of Arthur's she had asked Kin Ho to hide in his safe. Could that hold the explosive information the Chinese authorities were seeking? Was there some part of it she could give up to the Chinese government in exchange for the Midas deal?

Hoping it would not come to that, she and Stanley spent the morning thinking up alternative solutions.

'Very well,' Stanley got up when they were done. He was perspiring from the effort, his neatly pomaded hair slightly dishevelled. 'We'll see how these counter-proposals work.'

He walked jauntily out the door.

She had a few minutes' respite before her secretary buzzed her: 'Mr. Walden to see you, ma'am.'

'Let him in.'

The door opened and Brad Walden strode in. 'Ready for some unfinished business?' he said with a hesitant smile.

The term "unfinished business" put her on guard. Mason had mentioned no such thing, so she knew she was drifting into uncharted waters again.

'You mean unfinished company business,' she asked gingerly. 'Or personal?'

He inclined his head with sympathy. 'Family.'

'Go ahead,' Melanie said and he sat down. He laid out two folders in front of her. Several Excel sheets detailed Rosie's spending: travel, Club fees, upkeep of horses, staff wages, jockeys' wages. Another set of sheets plotted out the money trail left by Jason's seemingly free and easy ways. One detail jumped out at her: it was an invoice for $16,000 for a gold Omega watch. She found it odd because she knew Jason didn't wear a watch.

As Brad was explaining some of the figures to her, a memory flashed in her mind. It was of the tattooed, rough-looking man she had met in Macau with Jason. The one with the gold teeth and the expensive watch on his wrist. She had never forgotten the peculiar detail of how the gleaming watch seemed at odds with his coarse appearance. Now something clicked.

That man was obviously one of those Triad enforcers who collected on debts from hapless gamblers. They were always

169

around Macau, lounging around the bars into the small hours, waiting for their menacing services to be called on.

Seeing the invoice for the watch now gave her an inkling into Jason's hidden life. He seemed to have the habit of using his stepfather's company to pay off large personal debts.

The sheets Walden was showing her represented large strains on the conglomerate. But such was the scale of Arthur's fortune that even the excesses of his widow and stepson seemed fairly tolerable. But as a seasoned sailor she knew only too well how even the smallest leaks could eventually bring down the mightiest of vessels.

'That's why you decided on a rearrangement,' Brad was saying, 'before...'

The thing he didn't put into words was whatever had happened to Julia that left these "unfinished matters" that Melanie now had to conclude.

She understood. In the shifting environment of Arthur's corporation, the truth had to be carefully handled. One had to check what others were thinking before expressing one's opinion. Even if the facts were obvious.

And so Julia's disappearance hadn't been spoken about, the same way there had never been much official speculation about Arthur's sudden death. There was so much more to speculate about, but her mind was drawn back to the business at hand.

'Help me refresh my memory on the particulars,' she said.

'This first point was about your stepmother's allowance,' Brad pointed to the items in a six-page list. 'After your father passed away, the board granted your stepmother's request to raise it.'

Seeing the figures Brad had amassed, Melanie felt she was right in comparing the expenditures with the leaks on a sinking ship. Rosie had been exceptionally good at hiding the extent of her extravagance.

'I want you to set a limit of $40,000 for her,' said Melanie.

Brad looked up with a hint of surprise. 'A month?'

'Yes.'

He nodded impassively, but the curl on his lip hinted at his relief at her firmness. 'She's not going to like that,' he said.

'I'm sure,' replied Melanie. 'But neither would she like bankruptcy.'

Brad's smile widened and he let out a laugh. 'No. Not our Rosie.'

Melanie laughed, too, already envisioning Rosie's furious reaction. 'And what's next on your list?'

'The second question is about your stepbrother.'

Though Melanie was aware she was only playing a role, she couldn't help but flinch at the thought of having Jason for a sibling. Even if only a step-sibling. She knew it couldn't have been pleasant for Julia, either.

'What about my wonderful brother?' she said.

'Well, it seems you finally came to some kind of an agreement about his plans. There was some headway on this question before…er, the interruption. And it seemed clear which you were heading.'

The interruption, she thought. So that was how Julia's disappearance had been rationalized. It didn't cause too much disruption, and it kept the possibility for business to go on as usual. No wonder Mason had been so confident every one would accept an impostor like Melanie.

'Where exactly did we leave it?' she asked.

'Well, Jason had always expressed a desire to move to London. He had looked at some properties there, and had made an offer on a place in Knightsbridge.'

'And?'

'It just needed your approval. In addition to…'

'In addition to what?'

'His allowance,' said Brad. He tried to continue with a straight face, 'Jason had demanded a monthly stipend of $50,000. But your father had agreed only to 10,000 a month.'

'So my father had decided on this?'

'Yes. He had turned it down outright. But Jason was lobbying for a reconsideration.'

This would have been the pressing matter at the time Julia disappeared, thought Melanie.

Brad pushed a sheet of paper towards her. 'These are the details of what it would cost to let him purchase that apartment in London, and the allowance necessary to let him set up there for good.'

Melanie looked at the neatly printed rows of figures. She thought back briefly on the accident with Jason's car. It occurred to her that perhaps letting Jason have his wish was the safer option. With him far away, she could go on without having to worry about what he might be plotting.

Perhaps this was the bargaining chip Jason had been counting on. The reason he hadn't come out and exposed her outright as a fraud.

'Of course with the allowance,' Brad resumed. 'That would mean that even from a distance you will retain control.'

He betrayed a more intimate understanding of Julia's family than he let on. Melanie had been right. Brad Walden was another Mason.

'It's settled then,' she said. 'Let Jason get his place in Knightsbridge. And give him his allowance.'

It was a fair price to pay to be left in peace to fully become Julia Tang.

'Good!' said Brad with undisguised relief. It seemed clear many others had been hoping for the decision Melanie had just made.

He gathered up his papers and lingered near her desk.

'Oh, by the way,' he said. 'Biyu is back from Wuhan. She was wondering if you could come for that dinner she's been planning for weeks.'

The casual invitation required a great deal of preparation for Melanie. She had an idea how close Brad's wife had been to Julia . This made her wary of any more slip ups that could lead to her exposure.

Thankfully, she had a new source of information in Estelle. The Frenchwoman was quite obliging. It seemed she had been waiting to find an ally for a long time. She had quietly nurtured her suspicions about what really happened to Julia Tang. Now she pinned her last hopes on Melanie.

So in the course of several dinners, she imparted intimate information Julia had never shared with anyone else. Only then did Melanie feel ready to accept Walden's invitation.

'I'll be gone for a few days,' Estelle said as they parted. 'Some business in Tokyo I need to take care of.'

So two nights later, Melanie showed up at the Waldens' flat in Mid-Levels, bringing flowers and champagne that Estelle had told her Julia never came without. She had already made excuses to make the evening as brief as possible.

Thankfully, news of Melanie's "return" from the women's shelter had already trickled through to Biyu. She was solicitous and careful, knowing not to press their guest on certain subjects.

Though Biyu clearly wanted to know what had happened to her friend, she avoided painful topics, and never referred directly to the "disappearance."

Melanie for her part dropped hints of traumas that made it distressing to remember certain things. Thus she allowed herself space to harvest information without being subjected to too many questions herself.

She was alert to any hints about Julia's life that cropped up in their conversation. Within the first hour, for instance, she managed to glean that Julia used to stay over with the Waldens, and was not shy about confiding some of her family troubles to them.

'Is your stepmother still angry about the charities?' Biyu said, picking up some interrupted conversation with Julia.

Melanie was unprepared for the question. She played with her food to disguise the effort of having to think of an answer. She thought back on everything she had learned in recent weeks. Suddenly she remembered the letters she had found in Julia's portfolio. The names of two charities popped into her mind.

'She seems to find "Traffic Jam" and "Shelter Trust" the most objectionable,' Melanie bluffed.

'I'm not surprised,' Biyu laughed. 'Rosie comes from a milieu that still believes women's feet should be bound. So she probably wouldn't understand why her stepdaughter would commit millions to saving women from human trafficking.'

'And she thinks of shelter as something you buy in Monte Carlo,' Brad added, 'So it's probably beyond her why her

174

husband's sole heir would care so much about building homes for orphans in India.'

All at once Melanie knew she was now many steps ahead of Mason, privy to disputes he had had no inkling of.

The evening helped her put answers to a lot of questions. For instance she understood why Julia's locker key had been with Brad Walden. Julia had left it in the flat on one of those nights she had stayed with them.

'Thanks for sending back my key,' Melanie said to Biyu. 'It had completely slipped my mind.'

'This was probably the safest place for it,' Biyu answered with a vague shrug. She seemed to look for some kind of reaction. Melanie looked down to hide her lack of one.

To break the uncomfortable silence, she volunteered: 'My aunt Bernadette was just here.'

The couple obviously knew that the death anniversary of Julia's mother was the reason Bernadette had come.

'She must have been so happy to see you,' Biyu placed her hand on Melanie's. Melanie remembered the question Bernadette had planted in her mind. It was the one about the letter from Julia's dying mother.

Melanie took one more risk, 'She asked me if I still have my mother's letter.'

'Letter?' Biyu's expression was blank. It was clearly not something Julia felt comfortable confiding in even her closest friends. It must have been of enormous importance to the heiress. Which made it even more urgent for Melanie to find that letter. But where?

She had scoured every inch of Julia's room and found nothing. She would have to keep looking.

She stole a glance at her watch. To her surprise, she had stayed far longer than she had planned. Her brain was brimming with so much new information, she just wanted to get everything down on paper.

'I'd best be going,' she said.

Biyu leaned against her husband. 'You don't know how good it feels to see you,' she breathed. Brad smiled his agreement.

Melanie got ready to leave. She gazed around the dining room and said, 'I hope I haven't left any more of my clutter here.'

It was a pure fishing expedition on her part. But she was astounded when Biyu got up. 'As a matter of fact I think you have.'

She went into the bedroom and came back holding a thick envelope.

'It was probably providential that you left this here,' Biyu smiled as she handed it back.

Melanie sat down again to look at its contents. They were half-finished forms and other documents. She recognized Julia's signature on most of them, along with another she found hard to read. But stapled to the corner of the last document was a calling card.

She looked up to see Biyu watching her closely. 'I hope I was right to keep it,' she said with concern.

'Of course you were,' assured Melanie. 'Why wouldn't you be?'

'Well, I remember you saying it was these papers that caused the row between you and your father,' Biyu said. 'I wasn't sure you still wanted them, after he...passed away.'

Mention of the row Julia had with her father brought back something Estelle had said.

'Anyway,' Melanie slid the envelope to her lap. 'Thank you so much for keeping them.'

Neither she nor the couple really knew just how much they had helped her.

She got up and gave each of them a warm hug.

'It's been stupendous!' she said, using one of Julia's favourite expressions. 'We should have less of these long interruptions.'

They accompanied her to the door. Biyu stepped out into the hall with her. Melanie gave her another peck on the cheek and whispered, 'I'll call you soon.'

Biyu touched her hand as she turned around and walked away. She looked after Melanie with an ambiguous expression, as if wondering if and when they would see each other again.

She got in the lift and rode down clutching the envelope tightly in her hand. When the doors opened in the basement, she crossed the parking lot briskly to get in her car. She locked the doors and, like a huntress clutching a valuable prize, took out the forms for a better look. They appeared to be papers for setting up companies and bank accounts. The accounts appeared to be in Geneva.

Again Estelle's words came back to her: how something Julia had set up in Geneva had caused the rift with her father. Melanie sat back and looked around the dark, empty cars around her. Did these papers hold the secret to Arthur's sudden death? Were they the missing pieces that would solve the puzzle of Julia Tang?

She took out the form with the calling card stapled to the corner. It was from a lawyer named Jennifer Maynard. Now why would Julia need another lawyer when she had an army of them in her own company?

The next night was set aside for Rosie and Arthur's old partners. They gathered at Rosie's private box in the Happy Valley Race Track.

In the presence of Stanley, Brad and Andrew Chang, Rosie and Jason made a fuss of Melanie. They thanked her for her generosity, and complimented her on her firm handling of the company. There was a lot of optimistic talk about the future. At the end, Stanley got up to propose a toast.

'To Arthur Tang's successor!' he raised his glass. 'Who is taking on all her father's obligations, as well as her own. To Julia!'

'To Julia!'

'To Julia!'

'To Julia!'

The words echoed around the table and in that solemn moment it almost seemed to Melanie as if they were toasting the ghost that she was representing. Her own identity had been subsumed in that ghost. Her glance wandered warily towards Jason, who said loud enough for her to hear, 'To Julia. My sister!'

She was struck by the apparent sincerity in his face.

There followed a lull in which the talk around the table diffused into dozens of separate conversations. Rosie divided her attention between her guests and the races being shown on the large screens. Until at length the partners got up one by one to leave.

'I'll walk them downstairs,' Rosie announced and rose to usher the last ones out of the box.

Melanie sensed that this moment had come about by some arrangement, and she braced herself.

Jason started by apologizing about the mishap with the car. 'I thought they'd really fixed the problem,' he said.

'I'm sorry, too,' Melanie replied. 'I never intended to total your precious Aston.'

He waved her regrets away.

'I just thought you could still handle those machines,' he said. 'I didn't expect you to forget those things.'

She wasn't sure if he was still testing her, but her natural defensiveness arose before she could stop it. 'I didn't forget. I just wasn't very familiar with this one.'

He gave her a mock punch on the shoulder. 'I know, I know,' he grinned. 'You know how I like teasing you.'

Melanie relaxed.

'Anyway,' he said, 'thank you for the generous offer.'

'My pleasure.'

'I'm sure.'

Melanie looked up. 'Excuse me?'

'Of course it's all for your pleasure. Or convenience, rather.'

His expression had darkened and his voice was cold.

Melanie's smile faded. 'I thought that was what you wanted.'

'Yes,' he crossed his arms. 'But that's not as important as what *you* want, is it?'

Melanie wasn't sure if his anger was towards her or towards the woman she was replacing. 'What do you mean? I thought you'd be happy.'

'Not as happy as you would be,' he spat. 'Jason packed off to England somewhere. Given his allowance to keep him quiet. Just like a schoolboy being sent off to boarding school.'

'But that is what you always wanted,' said Melanie.

'No. That's the second thing I wanted.'

'What's the first?'

'To get what's mine by right,' hissed Jason through gritted teeth. 'I am Arthur Tang's true successor. I am his *only* male heir. His poor first wife tried twice and failed. Giving the poor man nothing but two daughters. And now *you*! What kind of world is this? That they'd rather have an impostor take the place of the son!'

'I am not an impostor!' she said, forcing herself to keep her voice down. 'And you were just my father's step son.'

'He wasn't your father! No more than he was mine. I don't know who the hell you are, but you're not going to send me off to London so you can have free rein to take over what should be mine!'

They were quiet for a moment.

At length Melanie said, 'So what do you want?'

He didn't answer right away. 'I want more than what you gave me. And I want it to be controlled by my mother. Not you!'

'You know what you're asking is impossible.'

'What's impossible?' he spread out his hands. 'How is it possible that some unknown scam artist like you can come along claiming to be my missing half sister? And everyone believes you! Now, *that's* impossible. But that is *just* what *happened*!'

There was another silence, and Melanie broke it by saying, 'If you never believed I was Julia, then why did you welcome me? Why did you pretend to be convinced I was really her?'

'Because she had her uses!' he snickered. 'If she weren't around, the whole thing would collapse! So it's better to have her around. Even if it's only someone who seems to be her.'

Melanie understood everything at last. 'I see.'

'From the moment I laid eyes on you,' Jason said through his teeth, 'I knew there was no way you could be my step sister. I'll have to admit I'm still amazed how you managed it. There are even times I *do* wonder if, by some weird set of circumstances, you really *are* her. But I'm the only one you'll never fool. And that's my weapon. No matter how far away you send me, I'll be the one in control.'

Melanie knew that he had laid down his challenge. It was the first time anyone had put all his cards on the table. Now they would see how the other cards played out.

Chapter XIV

The fact that Stanley arrived flanked by Walden and three of his other aides told Melanie something very urgent was up.

'The Midas Group are threatening to pull out,' he stated as delicately as he could. 'Unless we give the Chinese government what they want, this whole deal will fall through.'

He sank into the chair in front of her. 'We'll be back where we started.'

Melanie knew that it could mean the end of the glass house that was standing all around her, the whole charade, from Stanley's "rescue" of her from the women's shelter in L.A., to the change in the company's fortunes since she had arrived.

'What can we give them?' Melanie asked.

By signals so subtle Melanie almost missed them, Stanley indicated to his aides he wanted them to leave, and Brad knew from their abrupt rise that he had to exit with them.

'We have to give them something,' Melanie said. 'Does it have to be about my father?'

Stanley shook his head. 'I think they're more concerned about Li Kun Ming. They want anything that shows he had undisclosed activities outside China. And someone was helping him. They want to know who.'

Melanie thought immediately of Kin Ho, though she didn't mention it to Stanley. She knew that in that drab back office across the water, Arthur Tang's trusty old accountant might have something that would save the conglomerate yet again.

'I'll have it by the end of today,' Melanie promised. 'It'll be on your desk in the morning.'

Her certainty was feigned, but it made Stanley get up with a big smile. Though she wasn't sure she could keep her promise, watching Stanley strut out into the corridor gave her a surge of reassurance as well.

As soon as he was out of sight she noticed Brad Walden lingering just outside her door.

'Come in, Brad.'

His smile told her he was on a personal mission. He sidled up to her desk with a hand in his pocket.

'An old friend of yours is in town.'

'Who?'

'Jennifer Maynard,' he said softly.

Melanie busied herself with the papers on her desk while she searched her mind for the name. Then she remembered the forms Biyu had given her a few nights before. *Jennifer Maynard. Julia's secret lawyer.*

'Why, yes!' Melanie looked up. 'How is Jennifer?'

'She's in town for a few days ,' Walden replied. 'She's been trying to call you for months. She's wondering if you changed your number.'

Melanie thought ahead a few steps. First she had the Midas deal to worry about. But the chance to meet a confidential associate of Julia's was too good to pass up. 'Give her my number on Severn Road,' she said.

'Will do,' Brad nodded and sauntered out.

Melanie took a deep breath. She would need time to prepare for Jennifer Maynard. But Kin Ho was the one she had to see first. Her best hope was that Arthur's old friend could come up with just the right documents to satisfy the Chinese government, without also giving them a reason to bring down Arthur's company.

She left instructions with her secretary and got up to leave.

Half an hour later she was explaining her dilemma to the elderly book keeper. He sat and pondered silently for a moment. Then he got up with a sigh of resignation, as if he'd always known this moment would come.

He searched meticulously through his crammed shelves for the information she wanted. He walked back to his desk and sat down with a mystified look.

'You're sure they're not with you?'

Melanie sat forward. 'Why would they be with me?'

'They weren't there when I opened your father's safe.'

Melanie was taken aback. 'You opened his safe?'

Kin Ho nodded sadly. 'It was after he passed away. I tried to reach you, but...'

'And they weren't in the safe?' Melanie probed.

'There was only your father's book,' said Kin Ho, 'which I showed you.'

'Did anyone else know you had it?'

'Well, somehow your stepmother got wind of it,' said Kin Ho. 'She demanded I hand it over to her.'

'Did you?'

Kin shook his head. 'I refused. That's why I...'

He waved his hand across the water, summing up the events that had driven him out of the company he had started with Arthur.

Melanie sat back and clasped her hands. 'So where could those other papers be?'

She glanced out the small window behind Kin. The little light that seeped through the small gaps between the buildings made the hour seem later than it was. It made her feel that time was slipping away fast.

'Uncle, tell me,' she said to the old man, 'What happened after I...left? Didn't they try to look for me?'

The accountant ran through events in his mind before answering. 'Well, your stepmother refused to report you as a missing person. She was sure you had just gone away for a while and you would be back.' He paused for a moment before adding, 'You know how something like that could affect the company.'

'I understand. So the police didn't investigate at all?'

'The Marine Police gathered information. Then they searched around the area where your boat was found. But before a more thorough search could be started, your stepmother called them and said you had gotten in touch with her. She said you were safe, so the search was called off.'

Melanie got a picture of the manoeuvrings that created the conditions for Mason's ruse to work. Had Rosie known what had actually happened to Julia? Was she covering up the truth?

'But what did people say in private?' Melanie pressed Kin. 'What did you hear?'

'Everyone knew how hard it was for you. First, your father's death. Then, the investigation about your father's ties to Party officials in China...'

'I see,' Melanie gave a nod. She appreciated the dilemma Julia must have been in. It was very similar to the one she was in now.

In Julia's case, those in her father's conglomerate resigned themselves to whatever the circumstances were. They were happy to look the other way if they thought it would keep the company going.

If Julia *had* decided to fake her own death, then they would go along. If that was the only way the heiress could escape the consequences of her father's misdeeds, then so be it. It was precisely that collusion of silence that allowed Melanie to come in and step into Julia's shoes.

Now she would have to face the consequences her predecessor had managed to escape. That was the real price of the deception. She had to pay it if she was to continue living the dream. She looked up at Kin. 'Is there any record of the initial inquiry?'

'Of course,' answered Kin, getting up again to fetch some papers. He lay them before her. 'I have developed good relations with the responding officers. They've been most helpful.'

Kin Ho's specialty seemed to be cultivating such "good relations," and she was glad to have him on her side.

She opened the document and began to read. It stated that the last contact anyone had with Julia Tang was on the morning of Friday February 20, 2004. That day workers at the Causeway Bay marina reported seeing her as she set off by herself on her sail boat. It was a clear day with calm conditions, with light traffic around the harbour.

She was known to spend whole days at sea or on one of the islands, and kept irregular hours, so no one was concerned when she did not return to her Severn Road home that night. In addition, Julia was known to make sudden, impromptu flights to Macau or other destinations, so it came as no surprise when she didn't show up for work on Monday morning.

It wasn't until her boat was found drifting about thirty miles off the coast that the alarm was raised. Even then, the family did so in the most discrete way possible. They used private resources to conduct a low-key search without involving the authorities. Given Julia's position in Tang Worldwide, information about her disappearance was kept to a minimum.

While the consortium went about its multi-million dollar business, rumours flew about the young woman who was at her company's helm. The corporate hierarchy closed ranks, and refused to give out information about what was really going on. To all outward appearances, everything in the corporation was going on as normal.

But Julia's friends wondered about her sudden silence. Her close friend Estelle Gagneux came back from a trip to Japan to find a picture on her phone that Julia had sent to her. It was perhaps the heiress' last communication with anyone before she vanished off the face of the earth. But given the paranoid atmosphere in the company at the time, Estelle probably had good reason not to mention the picture to anyone.

'Where's my boat now?' Melanie asked Kin.

He was gazing dreamily out the window. He turned his chair to her and said, 'It's back in the marina.'

'Did the police take any pictures at the time it was found?'

'Yes. They did thorough forensic tests.'

'And?'

'They found nothing.'

Melanie nodded. Mason had told her that the absence of any clues only bolstered suspicions that Julia had staged her own death.

'Have you seen the pictures?' Melanie demanded.

Kin Ho gave a sad shake of the head. 'The police want to keep them sealed,' he said. 'They're hoping that if there was a culprit, that they'll reveal themselves if they don't know what the police know.'

'So there's no way of seeing them?'

The accountant rubbed his temple. 'Officially, no. But we can keep trying.'

There was at least a small window, thought Melanie. It gave her hope.

She went back to reading the rest of the report. It described police interviews with associates of Julia. Many of them said that Julia seemed distraught about her father's sudden death. Others held the opinion that the heiress was under a great deal of pressure from her father's alleged dealings with a disgraced Chinese official. Stanley Wang, however, dismissed speculations about suicide. He stated that Julia was saddened by her father's death, but not suicidal.

"I'll take these with me,' Melanie put the report in her bag. Kin Ho nodded and she got up to leave.

Back at her own office, she made prudent inquiries and managed to locate Julia's boat. Miss Lin was trained in Julia's secretive ways and did it with utmost discretion.

At last Melanie understood the significance of the second calling card she had found in Julia's portfolio. The man named Chad Northam turned out to be a professional sailor hired by the family to maintain their sail craft, in particular Julia's boats. He had worked as skipper on the family yacht on longer outings and had also served as Julia's sailing instructor. She called the number. She did her best to copy Julia's accent when she introduced herself as Arthur's daughter over the phone.

'You caught me just at the right time,' he said eagerly. 'I was just preparing to go on a long cruise.'

'Lucky you,' Melanie bantered. 'I wish I could do the same.'

'No, you wouldn't,' laughed Chad from the other end. 'This is purely work for me. I'm taking a retired couple to the Caribbean.'

'I didn't know you were also into elderly care.'

'I take care of the vessel,' he laughed. 'They take care of themselves.'

They arranged to meet at the yacht club. On the way there, Melanie went over what she had read in the report about Julia's disappearance.

She found Chad Northam to be a trim, tanned man in his late 30's, clad in an all white outfit, nursing a cocktail at the bar when she came in. Melanie found his expression hard to read as he crossed the room to greet her.

'What long time it's been,' he said, gripping both her hands. She gave him a hug, calculated to mimic Julia's level of intimacy with him, and they sat down at a table. While they were having coffee Melanie steered the conversation towards Julia's boat.

'I was going to ask you to check my dinghy,' she remarked.

'I already did,' he said smugly.

'You did?'

'Yes,' he smiled. 'It's exactly as it was when I decommissioned it for storage.'

Melanie privately wondered who had been giving Chad instructions in Julia's absence. But the image of a giant clock came back to her, a multitude of gears turning from some unseen spring, all the parts functioning without orders coming from anyone. It was almost as if the missing heiress were controlling everything from beyond the grave. If that was indeed where she was.

He waited for her to finish her drink and dusted off his hands. 'Come on, then. I'll show you.' Melanie signed the bill and they went out to the storage facility.

The manager recognized them both and walked them straight to Julia's recovered vessel. Melanie's heart sank.

The dinghy looked like new. She couldn't even be sure it was the same craft Julia had taken out on the day she vanished. Perhaps the efficiency of everyone working for the family was not such a good thing after all. Whoever had taken care of the decommissioning for storage had done one through job. Frays had been repaired, tracks lubricated, and damaged slugs replaced.

And because the family had said nothing about potential evidence, the boatyard workers had performed their function without taking care to preserve dings or dents that might prove useful to any investigator. If the police had missed anything, there was little chance of finding it now. This was one instance where the family's extreme discretion proved a real disservice. Melanie wondered if it was intentional.

She knew Chad was watching her as she reunited with the craft on which she supposedly learned to sail. Melanie felt a diffidence approaching the fibreglass body. As though it had some unlucky emanation that she was afraid to touch.

'I hope there wasn't too much damage,' she said.

'No, just a few broken things here and there.'

Melanie didn't want give herself away by asking what things. 'Blame it on my bad sailing,' she said.

'Oh, there wasn't anything outside. Everything on the exterior was fine. Just…'

'Just what?'

Chad searched his memory. At length he shook his head. 'Just minor dents here and there. Nothing out of the ordinary.'

Melanie remembered the police report: No signs of a struggle inside. She was sure Chad hadn't been privy to the documents Kin Ho had shown her. But she wasn't certain if he was in fact one of those people the police were trying to catch out by withholding information. She made a mental note to get Kin Ho to get hold of those pictures the police had taken of Julia's boat.

They spent about an hour in the dry dock.

Then they walked back to the club house. Chad stopped to chat briefly with one of the dock supervisors. Then he rejoined her and they walked back to the club entrance.

'Well, good luck on your journey,' she leaned forward to give him a hug.

He crossed the street and hailed a cab.

Whatever Stanley and his deputies had concocted, they managed to stave off disaster for another week. It allowed Melanie to put the matter of Arthur's missing papers temporarily out of her mind.

The company resumed its routine. Melanie busied herself with the work of her predecessor. She was aware of how the mere sight of her through the glass walls of her office sent a buzz of reassurance through the building. Everything was in its place and all was well.

Mason was right about the monarch on his throne. The wing-backed leather chair was her throne. Her kingdom was a dominion so vast she only glimpsed a small part of it. But she got inklings of its life through the documents that passed through her desk.

Everyday she was learning more about Arthur Tang's creation. What had been structures of bewildering complexity to her before were becoming familiar. The apparatus in which she was an important cog was revealing more of its inner workings to her.

She may have come as an impostor, but she was teaching herself to become indispensable.

Then out of the blue she got a call from Estelle. She had just flown back from Tokyo and was eager to meet.

The next day they met at the Yacht Club. They had a quick breakfast and set off out of the harbour.

'Did you have a good time in Japan?' Melanie asked as she steered the Sea Tiger out of the port.

'I wasn't there to have a good time,' answered Estelle. 'But to make sure others did.'

There was a half-smile on her lips that dared Melanie to read between the lines. She remembered the calling card in which she had first seen Estelle's number. 'Did you go to Pan?'

Estelle seemed to flinch a little in surprise. She looked at Melanie a little more closely.

'Julia had your calling card,' Melanie explained. 'It said "Pan".'

'Oh, of course,' laughed Estelle, relaxing.

'That's where I met Julia in fact,' she said. 'She didn't go anywhere else when she was in Japan.'

The cable cars of Wong Chuk Hang loomed into view to their right. Estelle turned around to look at them.

Do you go to Japan often?' Melanie asked.

Estelle fished out a pack of cigarettes from her purse. She lit one before she answered. 'Only when I need money.'

'Did Julia used to go with you?'

She smiled thoughtfully through the haze curling out of her lips, 'Often I was the reason she went there.'

They were quiet for a moment. Melanie watched Estelle's lips massage her cigarette sensuously, sucking on the filter until the tip smouldered brightly in the sun. The charred bouquet of the smoke that at first had repelled Melanie was now beginning to draw her. 'Did you work a lot?' she asked.

'No more than usual,' shrugged Estelle. 'I even managed to catch a film.'

'Was it good?'

'It was an old one, but I enjoyed watching it again.'

'What was it called?'

'It's called *Kagemusha*. Ever seen it?'

Melanie shook her head.

'You should. It's quite good.'

'What's it about?'

'It's about a dying *samurai* whose family employ a thief to impersonate him.'

Melanie suddenly grew wary. She didn't know if Estelle, in her own playful way, was setting a trap for her. This was the unknown territory that she had reached on her own, where she had to make things up as she went along.

After a pause, Melanie said, 'Estelle, the last time you saw Julia. Did she tell you anything?'

Melanie thought she wasn't going to get an answer. Estelle took three or four drags on her cigarette before she replied. 'I just know she was preparing to go on a trip.'

'Where?'

'To L. A., I think.'

Melanie was struck by the coincidence. 'L.A.? Why?'

'Because a private investigator told her to,' blurted out Estelle.

Melanie didn't want to lose the moment. But she knew better than to rush Estelle.

So she killed the engine and they drifted for a while, suspended between the poles of land on either side of them. Swaying in the middle, they were temporarily immune to its pressures and norms.

When enough time had passed, she probed gently, 'Did Julia explain why she hired a private investigator?'

Estelle was thoughtful for several moments. She gave a shrug. 'All I know is that this was when the Li Kun Ming trial in China was just starting. Julia never quite went into detail about it. I just remember her saying how angry her father was.'

'What was he angry about?'

'It seems he found out about the companies Julia was setting up without telling him.'

Melanie remembered the name on the calling card: Jennifer Maynard. Julia's lawyer on the side

'Those companies,' Melanie said. 'You think Julia was setting them up to distance herself from her father? To protect herself from the Chinese government?'

'Maybe,' Estelle shrugged again. 'She never got the chance to explain.'

Melanie let more minutes pass, letting the relaxed surroundings do their work on Estelle. 'Did Julia ever tell you the name of the private investigator?' she gently probed.

Estelle searched her memory for some moments

'The agency was called Wolverton Services,' she revealed. 'They specialized in due diligence research, making discrete inquiries.'

'Discrete inquiries about whom, in particular?'

'It was something to do with her parents,' Estelle replied. 'Something her mother did when she was still in China.'

The words reminded Melanie of Bernadette. The question about the letter from Julia's dying mother. Strange that finding out something about her mother's past would be one of the last things the missing heiress ever did.

They ended up staying in the same spot for nearly two hours. The sun was getting more intense, and Melanie checked her watch. 'You want to move somewhere a bit cooler?'

Estelle pursed her lips and thought about it.

'Sure,' she raised a shoulder. 'Can we go south from here?'

Melanie was surprised. She got up to turn the engine back on. 'Anywhere in particular?'

'Go through the West Lamma Channel,' proposed Estelle. 'That's the route Julia always used to take.'

Melanie felt like she was on the verge of some new revelation, and her heart beat a little faster as she steered the vessel excitedly through the channel, finding a gap between the criss-crossing sampans going to and from the outlying islands. She looked to Estelle for further directions.

Keep going until you reach Dadong Bay,' Estelle instructed.

Melanie did as she asked, and after about twenty minutes they had left behind the busy waters of the territory. Ahead of them lay the last chain of islands before the expanse of the South China Sea.

'This is where Julia liked to go,' said Estelle. They looked out at the emptiness extending towards the horizon. Melanie cut the engine and let the vessel drift.

Estelle lay back down on her deck chair. Melanie joined her. They gazed out at the calm stretch of sea around them.

'Julia asked me to go with her on that last trip,' Estelle suddenly revealed. But I didn't.'

196

'Why not?'

'She liked to go to the most out-of-the-way places. Sometimes I found it too scary.' She looked down gloomily. 'Now I wish I had gone with her.'

Melanie leaned over to touch her hand. She let a moment pass before asking, 'Was there no one else she could ask to come?'

Estelle thought about it. 'Yes. Sometimes Adalie would come with us. She was as fearless as Julia. When I couldn't come, they would explore deserted islands together.'

Melanie thought about it for a minute or two. *Adalie.* The name didn't ring a bell. Melanie took a blind gamble by asking, 'Who's Adalie?'

Estelle turned around to look at her. 'You don't *know* her?'

Melanie was afraid she had made a serious gaffe.

'She's Jason's girlfriend!' said Estelle, before quickly correcting herself. '*Was.*'

'I don't know Jason quite well,' Melanie remarked.

'Who does?' answered Estelle, then she seemed to remember something. She ran back to the wheelhouse for her purse. She quickly returned with her cell phone.

'Here they were in happier times,' she said sitting back down. She flicked through some pictures and handed the phone to Melanie: 'There's Julia, me, Jason and Adalie.' Estelle added meaningfully, 'Before they became sworn enemies.'

'Who became sworn enemies?'

'Jason and his girlfriend, of course.'

'Why did they become sworn enemies?'

Estelle was clearly enjoying the chance to gossip about Julia's stepbrother. 'Let's just say, Jason has a way of letting a girl down none too gently.'

197

'I noticed.'

Again, Estelle gave her a probing look.

'I just sensed he's that kind of guy,' Melanie shrugged by way of explanation.

Estelle nodded approvingly. 'You've got good instincts. Listen to them.'

Melanie looked at the photos on Estelle's phone, taken on the Sea Tiger or at various night clubs, parties, or weekend outings. Julia and Jason appeared to be like any two siblings with reasonably happy relations.

Estelle looked seductive as always, with that equivocal, indefinable air. Julia, Melanie's double, looked serious and preoccupied, while her step brother was visibly enjoying himself, with no hint of what he was thinking, his arm around the girl he was supposed to be in love with at the time.

Melanie noticed that Julia never mixed friends. In the shots with Adalie and Estelle, for instance, there were never the Waldens or anyone connected to her work. Estelle was clearly not in the same orbit as Rosie, because the images never included Julia's stepmother. Estelle seemed to belong to that compartment of Julia's life she kept hidden from everyone else.

'What was she like?' Melanie asked. 'Adalie, I mean.'

Estelle made a face. 'Typical Hong Kong girl. Always short of money.'

'Hence, Jason.'

'Exactly.'

'Did she and Julia get along?'

'Oh, wonderfully! They were like two halves of a pod. Jason hated it when they got together.'

'Why?'

'They loved nothing more than to gang up on him. You know how siblings can be.'

'I know.'

'Speaking of siblings, Adalie probably had more in common with Julia than I did,' grinned Estelle.

'What do you mean?'

'Adalie's brother is one of the few men who make Jason seem tame by comparison.'

Melanie leaned closer. 'How?'

'Well he's a boy who grew up in the bowels of Kowloon, so he's been in all sorts of scrapes. He's worked as a debt collector for the Triads, was detained on suspicion of forgery. He was once questioned over the death of a man who was attacked with meat cleavers outside a Karaoke bar in Wan Chai.'

Melanie laughed. 'That's probably what made Adalie so attractive to Jason.'

Estelle nodded emphatically. 'Yes. The dark side he couldn't have.'

'Or at least the dark side he couldn't openly indulge,' added Melanie.

She had just glimpsed that dark side. But she didn't want to tell Estelle about it. She didn't think the time was right. A long silence passed.

'Where's Adalie now?' Melanie asked.

Estelle's answer made Melanie's heart sink. 'I've no idea.'

'What a shame,' Melanie lamented, seeing a great opportunity slip from her grasp.

'Oh wait!' Estelle jerked up in her seat. She reached for her phone.

Melanie's heart filled with hope as Estelle punched the keys of her phone. Then she held it out to Melanie, 'This was her address,' she said. 'Why don't you go pay her a visit?'

The thought appealed to Melanie. She thought about it all night. She came to work plotting when to do it. But what she found waiting for her that morning changed all her plans.

The fax sheet laid out on her desk looked innocuous. She picked it up casually, and walked to the window before fixing here eyes on the text.

The title "Double Criminal" jumped out at her. It was a photocopy of an article cut out of a Chinese language daily from several years before. It told the story of the wife of a high-ranking official in the Chinese Communist Party. The wife had been tried and found guilty of various crimes that included embezzlement and attempted murder. She was sentenced to twenty years in prison.

The news item wasn't about her trial, however. It described, instead, the scandal that broke out when authorities made a stunning discovery: that the woman serving the sentence was not in fact the official's wife. It was a double hired by the Party official to take the place of his wife in prison. The article went into lurid detail about the injustice that happened right under the noses of the penal system.

Melanie summoned her secretary.

'Did you leave this on my desk?' she held up the fax.

Miss Lin nodded. 'It was on your machine when I came in this morning.'

'And you were here at six?' Melanie asked.

'Yes, Miss Tang.'

That meant the fax had probably come overnight. She looked at the number at the bottom of the page. It didn't ring a bell.

Chapter XV

The faxed article lay before her as she had breakfast the next morning. She wondered if it had been sent to her by mistake. The story it told seemed far removed from her lavish surroundings at the moment. Yet she couldn't help but sense hidden parallels it hinted at. Was it a warning? Did someone know the truth about her and was goading her?
She didn't feel safe going out into the open. Whoever had sent it must be watching her for a reaction.

Her instincts told her to stay away from places where she was too visible. So she called her secretary to say she wasn't coming in that day.

She looked through her agenda and found one entry she had marked urgent. It was to call Jennifer Maynard, Julia's secret lawyer. She focused all her attention on preparing for the encounter.

For a start, she looked through Julia's papers from Bernadette. Added to that now were the unfinished forms Julia had left with the Waldens in the weeks before she vanished.

Their partially filled boxes hinted at the interrupted plans of the heiress, and their implications for her fortune. No wonder she had chosen to work with someone who had no connections whatsoever to her father's company.

Next she combed through the emails Julia had saved in her PDA. Those from Maynard detailed Julia's involvement with a the non-profit organizations administered by Jennifer. Entries in Julia's Agenda revealed that their last meeting had been on the 2nd of February, 2004. They had dinner at the Spring Moon restaurant at the Peninsula hotel.

She wanted her own rendezvous with Maynard to be as close to that original meeting as possible. She was hoping the similarity in setting might rub off on her.

She phoned Jennifer and suggested meeting that night.

'I'd love to,' said Jennifer. 'Where?'

'I'm hoping you're not tired of the Spring Moon?' Melanie replied.

'Why of course, the Spring Moon! ' Jennifer answered with a slight laugh, as if recognizing a quirk she had come across before.

'Shall we say 7:00?' said Melanie.

'Fabulous.'

Hours before her appointment she went into Julia's walk-in closet. She tried on different outfits, thinking back on all the images of Julia she had committed to memory. She could see why many people had been fooled. She looked different even to herself now. Like someone putting on a uniform, she was taking on the whole aura of the person she was impersonating.

She knew that one's facial expressions outweighed the actual features in people's minds. A living, dynamic face in front of them was always more compelling than a memory. Slowly, they gave up the wispy reminiscence of the person they had known, and accepted the one before them as perhaps being more real. And with the passage of time, associates and distant acquaintances were more likely to question their own recollections, more likely to wonder if the traits they recalled would have remained the same.

She tried on a range of bags and jewellery, all the time going over every kind of question Jennifer might ask her.

She arrived at the Peninsula Hotel half an hour before her reservation. The maitre d' took a look at the name in his register and made a deep bow. All at once her worries about being too early were dispelled.

'This way, Miss Tang,' he said and led her through the tastefully wrought recreation of 1920's Shanghainese splendour. He led her to a window table, which she didn't remember asking for, but which she knew must have been encoded in the hotel's logs on Julia Tang.

She positioned herself facing away from the light, partly to keep her face in shadow, and partly in keeping with Julia's compulsion for privacy. She had brought Julia's calf-leather portfolio, and was wearing the ruby brooch she had seen in the missing woman's last photos.

She ordered some tea and watched other diners arrive, as waiters bearing oversized trays moved briskly between the tables.

Shortly after 7:00, a slim brunette was led to her table. She was of medium height, with hazel eyes that settled on Melanie. There was a blank pause when Melanie feared all her preparation might suddenly unravel.

'Julia! I'm sorry!'

Melanie got up and waved her apologies away. It was as she had intended, hoping the other woman would be flustered at being late, with less time to scrutinize her. Melanie let Jennifer take in her clothes, her face, the garnet earrings from Spain, and the blue lapis lazuli pendant that matched her blue evening dress. They were all accoutrements that were meant to evoke her predecessor.

'How wonderful to see you!' the Englishwoman stepped forward to give her a hug. As she returned the embrace, Melanie felt like someone who had cleared a chasm. She took a moment to catch her breath.

They sat down.

'My God It's been *ages!'* uttered Jennifer, looking around at their surroundings.

'A bit longer than I perhaps intended,' said Melanie, tilting her head the way she knew Julia often did.

Jennifer glanced around. 'The place looks the same.'

'Though you somehow know it's not,' Melanie remarked. She deliberately prolonged the pause, waiting for Jennifer to react.

'I know,' she reached out sympathetically to touch Melanie's hand. 'So much has happened. I'm so sorry to hear about your father.'

Melanie relaxed. Jennifer had read precisely the meaning into her words she had hoped she would. It meant Jennifer was filling in the blanks about what had happened since she had last seen Julia.

While they studied the menu Melanie found opportunities to insinuate various expressions of Julia's into the conversation, as well as details she had gleaned from Maynard's emails.

'I really appreciate your taking the time to see me,' Jennifer uttered after they had had their first drinks. 'I understand things have been a little rough.'

Melanie could sense that Jennifer was also feeling her way forward.

Melanie remembered the string of anxious emails from Maynard that went unanswered in Julia's PDA.

'I'm sorry I haven't been able to reply to any of your messages,' she said.

Jennifer looked up a little. 'I understand. With the complications involving your father. And all that trouble about that Party official's trial in China.'

Melanie took a gamble. 'So you heard?

'Biyu told me,' Jennifer disclosed. 'But for a long time she was really worried. Then she called me a few weeks ago to tell me the good news....I thought hurrah. At last we can get on with our unfinished business!'

By then they had worked their way through the meal and Melanie picked up her portfolio.

'Speaking of unfinished business,' she laid down the forms on the table.

Whatever doubts Jennifer Maynard may have had about her, the appearance of Julia's half-done forms swept it all away. Better than any identification, it placed Melanie firmly in the stalled negotiations Maynard and Julia were in the middle of six years before.

Jennifer scanned the documents. After several minutes, she seemed satisfied, and she put them in her bag. Then she took out her own set of papers and placed them before Melanie. 'And these are for you.'

While Melanie perused them, Jennifer explained, 'Everything's been set up. All that needs to be done, as you told me, is for you to go to Geneva and finalize the accounts.'

'I hope the six year delay hasn't derailed everything,' ventured Melanie.

'You said all they needed was for you to sign the final forms. In fact the last time we talked, you said your father was going to Geneva. You were afraid he would stop the process.'

A lingering question had been answered in Melanie's mind. So Arthur's last trip had some connection to whatever his daughter was planning with Jennifer.

Melanie looked at the papers. *Child Outreach Initiative.*
Green Globe. Traffic Stop. They were names Melanie had come
across in Julia's archived emails. But the documents now in her
hands detailed how each organization worked, and how they
were to be financed.

They showed that Julia's involvement with the charities
were not just superficial gestures of philanthropy, or an effort to
protect her fortune from the authorities. Her intention to
support them was real. In the bureaucratic language of the forms
she found hints of Julia's good heart.

They showed Arthur Tang's daughter to be a woman
with a noble sense of purpose. She had defied her powerful
father to pursue her goals. And perhaps she paid the price for it.

Once their business was concluded, the two women sat
back and had a relaxed chat. Melanie was glad for the dim
lighting of the place and the noise from the other diners. They
helped cover up what slight disparities there might between her
voice and Julia's, between her features and that of the heiress.

At last Melanie put away the documents. Now she had a
good idea what had happened in Julia's last days. She understood
why she had been given a chance to impersonate an heiress.

Julia Tang had left some important tasks unfinished. It
was an endeavour worthy of completion. Someone like Julia did
not deserve to vanish without a trace.

She deserved to be resurrected.

Chapter XVI

Melanie was roused from her deep sleep by an early morning call.

After profuse apologies, Kin Ho blurted out, 'Did you go to China?'

She tried to glean if it was his attempt at humour. It was not.

'Why in heavens would I do that?'

Kin Ho clucked his tongue. 'Remember those papers you were looking for?' he said.

The papers that had been missing from Arthur's safe, thought Melanie. 'What about them?'

'Well, they've somehow turned up in China,' Kin told her. 'Now Li Kun Ming's links to your father will be proven beyond any doubt.'

Melanie gripped the phone hard. 'How on earth did it get to China?'

'I don't know.' After a long pause, the old bookkeeper added, 'I'm sure you know what this means.'

By now Melanie was pacing nervously by the her window. 'No. What does it mean?'

Kin cleared his throat. 'Your father is gone. So the Chinese authorities will summon you instead.'

Suddenly Melanie felt cold all over. This was the day Mason had prayed would never come. This was the moment it would all come crashing down.

She peeked out the window at the sun casting its first fringe of gilt on the nearby hills. Behind that rosy picture, the bear lurking just outside the colony was about to reach out towards her.

Suddenly she understood everything. This was why they had let her take Julia's place. Belatedly she grasped the significance of the article faxed to her office just two days before. The story called "Double Criminal." It really was a reference to her.

She was exactly like that hapless woman duped into going to prison in place of the Party official's wife. Finally it all made sense.

She looked at her lavish surroundings. How enticing they had made it for her.

She got dressed quickly and packed as many clothes as she could into an overnight bag. She searched through the drawers, scooping up everything that might be useful, including any scraps that might help them piece together her real identity.

Then she hurried downstairs before any of the maids came in, putting the bag and Julia's portfolio by the door. Then, after wolfing down the barest breakfast, she ordered the chauffeur to bring her the keys to her car.

He came back with four sets of keys jangling in his hand, one for each of Julia's luxury cars.

'I don't want them,' she waved them away.

He lowered them timidly, worried he had made a mistake.

'Tell me,' said Melanie, 'what car does your wife drive?'

The chauffeur cringed visibly at the unexpected question. 'Why, a Volkswagen, ma'am.'

'Bring me her car,' ordered Melanie. 'She can use any of mine for the moment.'

He stood smiling uncertainly for some moments. But when he saw she was serious, he ran off to do her bidding.

She heard him making phone calls in one of the rooms down the hall. She walked through the house while she waited, making sure she had left nothing crucial behind. She knew this was probably the last time she would be here.

She stepped out to the balcony and looked out on the city below. It gave her a twinge to leave all this behind. Which made her sure Julia hadn't done so of her own accord.

When she came back in the living room, the chauffeur was already standing there, holding a key.

'My wife brought her car, ma'am,' he held it out with a smile.

'Put my bags in it,' she said. He picked up her things and went downstairs.

When she came down to the driveway he was standing next to the Volkswagen.

'Give me the keys,' she said.

He looked at her with barely disguised shock as she opened the door and got behind the wheel.

''Let your wife take the Audi,' she instructed. 'Ad if I'm not back by this evening, take the Rover and park it at this address.'

She gave him Kin Ho's calling card. He scrutinized the address, but for several moments couldn't make heads or tails of it. Things were happening too fast for his mind to absorb. It said *Room 814 , Evergreen Building, 7609 Tonkin Street.* He had never even heard of the building, let alone go there on the instructions of his celestial masters.

He knew it to be in one of the poorer districts of the former colony, and he couldn't imagine why the young lady would want to leave one of her cars there. But he accepted it without question and stepped away from the car.

Melanie had one last order. 'Leave the Rover's keys with Mr. Ho in Room 814.'

Then she pulled out of the drive and sped down Severn Road, leaving the chauffeur looking after her quizzically, wondering what strange thing would happen next.

She raced down the hill with her thoughts in a jumble. She almost welcomed the thought of another crash as she steered the car around the sharp bend. The blaring horn of a bus coming out of a blind curve brought her to her senses. Her hands were shaking. The blood was roaring in her ears.

Her first instinct was to get on a plane and leave. All of the Tang's riches would be useless to her from a Chinese prison. She saw the black column of 2FC ahead of her, and veered away from her usual route.

When she reached Central, she slowed down to find a quiet spot. She found one off Gresson Street and pulled into a side street behind York Place. The first thing she did was to walk to the skip between the buildings and throw in her hairbrush. It contained enough material to establish who she really was.

Then she went back to the car and checked the contents of her overnight bag. She looked at Julia's passport with her own picture in it now. At the moment no one but Mason knew her real name. There was no record of Melanie Brooks ever entering the territory. Melanie Brooks had disappeared, just like the heiress.

She thought of her options. If she went to the authorities and owned up to her ruse, she might be able to prove that she wasn't the woman they were looking for, the one being sought for various crimes. She could be charged with fraud, but that was probably less serious than any of the offences Julia Tang was wanted for. It added up to quite a dilemma. It was enough to make anyone want to disappear.

She got back into the car and called Stanley Wang.

'Julia! Yes!' his voice was a taut mix of dread and control. He was evidently well aware what had happened, and understood perfectly why she wouldn't tell him where she was.

'Do you know if they're already looking for me?' she said.

There was a long pause, then Stanley came back on. 'No one knows for sure,' he said. 'But I think we can expect it.'

'Good. Let me know if they come to Severn Road.'

'Yes, of course.' After a thoughtful interval he added, 'Will you be needing the jet?'

For the briefest instant, Melanie was tempted to say yes. But she felt a momentary surge of hope. 'Not quite yet. It might not come to that. We'll see.'

Her own assurance seemed to boost Stanley's confidence. She hung up and turned off her phone. She left it off for the rest of the day.

That simple act: turning off Julia's phone, coupled with driving a car that belonged to the chauffeur's wife, brought an incalculable sense of liberation. She felt almost like a kid playing an outlandish game of make believe as she drove to her next destination, an address in Tong Chau Street in Kowloon.

She navigated the tight, sporadic traffic on *Apliu* Street and parked in front of a low, rundown building. She had to search her memory to recognize the large characters spelling out the name *Wah Fu Court* across the top of the public housing estate.

She walked down the uneven path and entered the foyer of the improbably named Wah Fu Court. The place was deserted at that hour. She could hear the creak of old cables as the lift made its way down the shaft towards her. The doors opened, revealing the bare steel interior which exuded strong smells of urine and eucalyptus. She stepped in with some trepidation, and the box began its unsteady ascent.

The doors opened again on the ninth floor. She walked into corridor, following the directions Estelle had given her. She stopped at the door that was painted green, protected by an outer grating of thick, unpainted iron. Melanie rang the bell a few times. At first it seemed there was no one home. Then she heard the sound of bolts being slid back and the green panel flew open.

A young woman peered out at her. She recognized the face she had committed to memory from the photo Estelle had given her.

Adalie was slim and about the same height as Melanie, wearing a sleeveless top and a tight pair of jeans.

'Adalie?' Melanie said uncertainly. 'Remember me?'

Jason's former girlfriend squinted through the iron bars before her face lit up in shock. 'Julia?'

More locks were unfastened and Adalie stepped out to embrace her.

'When did you get back?' she said, pulling Melanie through the doorway.

'I can't believe it,' Adalie kept saying. 'You've never visited me before! I'm so glad you came.'

So was Melanie. If Julia had never been to this place, then Melanie didn't have to feign a familiarity she didn't have. She was groping in the dark and hoping it didn't show. Adalie belonged to Julia's secret world that few people had known about.

She let Adalie lead her through the narrow hall of the cramped apartment, is if it were some rabbit hole by which she would get to another realm of wonders or horrors.

They sat down on hard chairs placed so close together they could hardly stretch out their legs. Melanie noticed the toys on the floor. She tried to think back on everything Estelle had told her. She ventured a remark, 'How's the little one?'

Adalie smiled. 'Not so little anymore.' She gave a laugh. 'But he's staying with my sister now. So it's just me and my mother for a while.'

Adalie got up and disappeared into the rear of the apartment. She came back carrying a small tea set and a tray of biscuits.

'You shouldn't have,' Melanie protested.

Adalie lay it on the table. Then she started pouring out the steaming liquid into the tiny cups. Melanie gratefully sniffed the warm jasmine vapours. It briefly gave her a feeling of normality.

Adalie picked up her cup and smiled at her. Melanie tried to disguise her unease at hearing people passing on the corridor outside. The time she had spent on Severn Road had made her unused to being in such close quarters with strangers. She nervously took little sips of the strong hot drink. She was surprised that it soothed her.

When she had drained her cup Adalie poured her another one. The slow, repetitive ritual hypnotized her into a temporary sense of safety. She looked around the room and realized she was probably safer here than anywhere else in the whole territory. This was the last place anyone would think to look for her.

At last Adalie put down her cup and said, 'So how's you're wonderful brother?'

Melanie smiled at the sarcasm in her voice.

'As wonderful as always' answered Melanie. 'How's yours?'

Adalie threw her head back in laughter. She touched Melanie's hand. 'We're the same.'

At that an old camaraderie was renewed, and Adalie got up again. I'm so glad you came,' she said. 'I still have a few things of Jason's.'

She took a few steps into the space between the rooms. 'I've been wanting to give them back. *But.*'

Melanie stood up and joined her. 'I know. I understand.'

Adalie opened one of the doors. Melanie followed her in. The room was barely more than eight feet square, and, right next to a single bed, a chest of drawers stood flush against the wall. A TV and a diminutive stereo were piled on top of each other over it.

One corner was taken up by a tall dark wood cabinet. The gap between its top and the ceiling was jammed with boxes of varying sizes and colours.

It was a daunting mass. Adalie scratched her head with an exasperated sigh, deciding where to start.

'It all happened so quickly,' she carried on a chatter as she rummaged through the various boxes, emptying some and laying others side by side on the bed. When the bed was full, she started spreading the containers out on the floor.

Melanie stepped back through the doorway to make way. At last Adalie yanked out a small silk pouch from the jumble. She gave a triumphant cry, 'Aha!'

She came out of the room shaking the pouch in front of Melanie. Something jingled inside.

'I knew it was here somewhere,' she said, untying the pouch. 'Now he can have it back.'

Melanie held out her hand, and Adalie emptied the pouch into her palm. 'So now I can get on with *my* life.'

Melanie looked at the keys in her hand. She gave Adalie a puzzled look.

'From *his* apartment,' Adalie told her.

Melanie thought hard. 'The one in Repulse Bay?'

Adalie looked a little confused. '*No!* He'd never let me near his real one. The *other* one.'

Melanie had a feeling that at last she was getting even with Jason. 'The other one?'

Adalie shook her head and laughed. 'Of course! He never told you. No one in your family was supposed to know.'

Melanie let out a nervous laugh.

'One of Jason's naughty little secrets,' Adalie gave her a conspiring glance.

'Well, now I know.'

'Too bad I can't be there when you tell Rosie,' Adalie giggled. 'Wouldn't mommy be so shocked to know her little boy has been soiling his hands on a dirty girl from Sham Shui Po!'

'Rosie doesn't like to be reminded where she came from,' said Melanie. Adalie snickered and they walked out to the front of the apartment again.

Melanie felt it was time to divulge the real reason she had come. 'There's been some problems at home,' she started. 'I don't really feel like going home tonight.'

Adalie understood right away. 'You need a place to stay?'

Melanie nodded. 'Nothing fancy. Just an empty apartment. Or even a pension house if possible.'

Adalie sucked on a tooth for a few moments. Then she gestured at the keys in Melanie's hand. 'That's perfect then. You might as well put it to good use.'

Melanie looked at Jason's keys. 'Not if Jason's there.'

'He hasn't been there in months,' Adalie said. 'It's been vacant since I left.'

Melanie thought about it. But she didn't want to be back within the family's reach. That was precisely why she had left.

'I'd really rather find a hotel,' she said.

Adalie went to the corner and pulled out a phone book. She flipped through the pages, weighing a number of luxury options she thought befitted someone in Julia's position. But Melanie turned all of them down.

'Those are places people are likely to recognize me,' she said. 'I'd like to keep this private. I don't want my family squabbles to end up in the gossip columns.'

'Okay,' smiled Adalie. 'I know exactly what you mean.'

Adalie made several phone calls until she thought she found a suitable place.

She got off the phone and turned to Melanie. 'There's a hotel not far from here,' she said. 'It has about eight rooms.'

'That sounds perfect!'

They went down to get into Melanie's car. Adalie reacted with disbelief at the sight of the modest vehicle.

'What happened to your car?' She stood a distance away.

'I'm just borrowing it,' Melanie opened the passenger door for her. 'Until mine gets fixed.'

Adalie got in with a mystified look, not certain what to expect.

They drove the five miles to the Tea House Hotel. It was a two-star establishment that catered to undemanding transients. They didn't ask too many questions or keep too many records. Which was exactly what Melanie wanted.

As she was checking in, Melanie did something that didn't surprise Jason's ex-lover. She asked Adalie to register the room under her own name.

Adalie winked. 'Why should your life be anyone else's business?'

They went up to leave Melanie's bags in her room, then they went for a bite in the restaurant next door. Adalie kept asking if Melanie was sure about her decision. 'Are you sure you'll be comfortable?'

Melanie assured her again and again that it was fine. Then she remembered what Estelle had said about Adalie's persistent money problems. She took some money from her purse and put it in one of the hotel envelopes.

When they had finished their tea, Melanie slipped the envelope across the table to Adalie, 'I understand Jason hasn't been very helpful to you lately,' she said.

Adalie opened the packet and peeked inside. She put it down with a shake of the head.

'It's the least I can do,' Melanie pressed. Estelle had assured her it was something Julia had often done for Jason's girlfriends.

'You've been so helpful to me today,' she said. 'Please.'

Adalie relented. She looked into the envelope again and laughed. 'Your credit card is in here, silly!'

Melanie feigned surprise. 'Is it? Oh well,' she said with a wave of the hand. 'I've got another one.'

Adalie turned the card over in her hand, wondering if this was happening for real.

'But I don't know your signature,' she said.

Melanie took a hotel pad and inscribed Julia's signature three times, exactly as she had practiced it with Mason, exactly as it was on the card she had just given Adalie.

Adalie slipped the pad quickly into her purse and got up. Jason's stepsister was acting a little stranger than usual.

But Adalie was used to strange situations, and she had grown to expect nothing normal from Jason's family. She wasn't sure exactly what was going on, but like the intrepid girl she was, she would ride it for what it was worth. She gave Melanie a peck on the cheek and left.

Chapter XVII

Rosie had the entire staff of Severn Road lined up in front of her, from the head housekeeper, to the four maids, the six kitchen staff and the gardener, all cowering at her shrill eruptions of rage.

She made them pore over every detail of what had seemed a very ordinary day. Pacing like an incensed tigress in her cage, she coaxed out very particular of Melanie's last movements, including any scraps of paper she might have left in her room, scribbled telephone numbers, receipts, letterheads or calling cards. She made them riffle through the rubbish bins in the room, trying to turn up anything unusual.

But Melanie had been more thorough than any of them could suspect, wiping her prints off every surface she had touched, taking with her every item of clothing she had ever worn from Julia's wardrobe.

The only things the servants found missing were those clothes Melanie had taken, along with some of the purses and accessories from Julia's collection that was so vast and ever-changing they'd never completely kept track of it.

The new girl from Shanxi province had found a torn half of a fax page under the bed, but she had no idea if it had any significance, and didn't want to go over the heads of her superiors by mentioning it to Rosie.

None of them knew of any calls the young lady might have received, or anyone she might have met the day before. All they could say was that the young woman had been a little more hurried than usual as she took her breakfast, going up to her room several times before driving off by herself.

'Which car did she take?' Rosie barked.

All eyes turned to the chauffeur, who, like a condemned man, suddenly straightened up from his slouch. He lowered his eyes to the floor and muttered, 'I'll go check, ma'am.'

He already knew the answer, but he ran all the same to the wall where the car keys were hung. He came back to report to Rosie, 'The Rover's keys are gone, ma'am.'

That way he didn't actually tell a lie, but he also avoided involving his wife in the complication.

'Good,' Rosie stepped back, muttering under her breath: 'The Rover, then.'

The chauffeur was relieved that she seemed happy with his answer. For the moment she didn't ask any more questions.

He didn't know how long it would be before Rosie learned that her rebellious stepdaughter was driving a car lent to her by the chauffeur's wife. He understood families, and he knew that when a child defied her parent, the results were often explosive. He had seen, however, how this family he worked for could turn normal domestic spats into catastrophic clashes.

He regretted getting caught up in it, but he knew he didn't have a choice. It would have been unthinkable to refuse a request from Arthur Tang's daughter, even if it meant the destruction of the chauffeur's own loved ones. In his culture, servants were often buried with their dead masters, to continue their servitude even into the next world, Old Chin didn't understand the intricacies of the Tangs' larger affairs, but he had a clear understanding of his own humble duties.

If they did find the Rover, he reflected belatedly, they would also know that he was the one who had driven it to the address on Tonkin Street. He didn't know what any of it meant. They were like pieces of a puzzle so gigantic no one had ever glimpsed its whole.

He himself was only a small part of that conundrum, and he hoped his own insignificance would save him from whatever calamity was threatening the great household.

Rosie walked off to make some phone calls, while the servants remained standing where they were. No one dared move a muscle as Rosie planted herself on the sofa, and repeated the facts as she had just extracted to a series of people on the other end.

At last she got up and rustled past the assembled staff. She marched to the door and bellowed out one last missive, 'Call me if she comes back!'

Downstairs she climbed into the Maybach and sat across from Jason.

As the heavy car coasted down Mount Austin Road, she took out her phone to call Stanley Wang.

She asked him if he had heard from "Julia."

'Yes, of course,' Stanley replied. 'She called me early yesterday.'

His nonchalance was an affront to her.

'And you didn't tell me?' Rosie said with an edge to her voice. It infuriated her that Stanley would get a call before her.

'Was everything all right?' she demanded. 'When is she coming home?'

'She said she just had some things to take care of,' Stanley continued calmly. 'She might not come to the office for a while.'

'You didn't *ask* her *where* she was?' Rosie's voice rose again.

There was a slight pause, and Stanley said, 'No. Maybe she thought it was better if we didn't know. Under the circumstances.'

Rosie knew exactly what those circumstances were.

She hung up and turned to Jason. 'The bitch has gone underground.'

Jason gave a laugh. 'She's even more like Julia than we thought.'

The driver veered left to go into Stubbs Road. Rosie glanced at the glass towers already catching the morning sun on either side of them.

'Yes,' she said. 'Julia and the old disappearing act. You think she'd get tired of it.'

Jason jerked away from the window with a worried look. 'You don't think she's left Hong Kong, do you?'

For a moment Rosie looked confused. She wasn't sure if he meant the real Julia or the impostor. She looked out the window. They had reached the bottom of the slope.

Jason clucked his tongue. 'I told you we should have taken her passport.'

'We had to show some faith, dear,' Rosie patted his hand. 'Make her think we were all taken in.'

'Why?'

Rosie raised her shoulder in a coquettish pose. 'Look how well it's worked? If we hadn't played along, no one in the company would have believed it. Then where would we be?'

Jason nodded slowly, finally understanding. 'So you never believed she was Julia?'

'What does it matter what I believe?' shrugged Rosie. 'The market believes she's Julia. That's why this whole Midas deal is pushing through.' She leaned forward with a triumphant grin. 'And it's just about to turn everything to gold.'

222

At that very moment a bright light shone on her face and blinded her.

To their right, the rising sun was framed between the impossibly slim towers known as the Chop Sticks. Its blaze was magnified by the dazzling landscape of glass around them.

'Unless she slips out of our hands,' Jason said.

'She *won't*,' Rosie pouted with certainty. 'She didn't put on such a good show just to bow out before the finale.'

After a thoughtful interval Jason said, 'I'm not sure leaking those papers was such a good idea, though.'

'Well we had to jump start the Midas deal,' said Rosie. She stroked her son's cheek. 'Don't worry, honey. It's her neck not ours.'

'The question is,' said Jason, 'will the Chinese government believe she's Julia?'

'All they need is someone to throw into prison,' Rosie blithely replied. 'Make everyone believe they're serious about corruption. About stamping out the bad apples. Even if it means going across the border to snare anyone they think is helping to plunder their country.'

She put the phone back in her purse. For a moment, she fondly caressed its gold clasp. 'They're not going to look too closely if they've got the right person or not.'

Jason chuckled and looked out the window again. 'You're right, mother,' he said. 'The world runs on illusions. I didn't believe you before. But now I do.'

They rode in silence until they took the exit towards Shouson Hill. After five minutes or so they reached the second roundabout. The driver took the second exit and Repulse Bay came into view.

'It's a good thing Julia's disappearance was kept so quiet,' Rosie said. 'It's true what they've always said. Silence is golden.'

At Tang Worldwide Stanley was having a crazy day. Rosie had been right. The Midas deal was reaping its handsome rewards, and in the first half hour of trading that morning, the conglomerate's stock price had risen six times.

The rumours about papers proving Arthur's collusion with Li Kun Ming didn't produce the slump Stanley had feared. Instead there was almost a desperation, a kind of free-for-all that was engulfing everyone.

Stanley was one of the few people left in the company old enough to remember the war. He recalled the time news came that the unstoppable Japanese advance had finally reached Shanghai. Back then there was also an unlikely surge of activity everywhere.

It had been like this euphoric frenzy he was seeing. A kind of wild abandon that Stanley knew was driven by denial.

He called Brad Walden into his office.

The young man came in shaking his head. 'Another percentage point! If this goes on, we'll all be millionaires by the end of the day.'

He sat down and gave Stanley a rundown of what was going on across the company. 'Our lawyers have put together a motion in the event Miss Tang chooses to turn herself in.'

'She has no reason to do that,' insisted Stanley.

'It might be the only way out. Don't be fooled by this rally you're seeing. It'll all fizzle out as soon as Beijing issues the order to shut us down.'

Stanley was adamant. 'It won't come to that.'

'We can't be seen to be harbouring a fugitive.'

'Julia *isn't* a fugitive. No order has been given for her arrest.'

Brad gave him a sideways look. 'We both know it's only a matter of time.'

'I keep telling you, Brad,' seethed Stanley. 'There is no reason to arrest Julia. She had nothing to do with Li Kun Ming.'

'Her father evidently did.'

'It was an indirect involvement at best.'

'But she's benefiting from that involvement,' pointed out Brad. 'As are we, incidentally.'

Stanley struggled to keep his emotions under control. 'Stop this!' he slammed a fist on his desk. 'Stop this speculation!'

'Stanley,' pleaded Brad. 'I'm trying to make you see reason. What's going to happen if Julia is suddenly arrested?'

Stanley sat back and contemplated the awful prospect.

'We might be forced to accept Rosie as the new Director,' Brad kept up the pressure. 'Do you know what that would mean?'

A defeated look came over Stanley's face. 'That would really be the end.'

'Don't you see it?' Brad pressed. 'Arthur had foreseen this. That's why he designed things this way.'

Stanley raised his head slowly. 'What do you mean?'

Brad leaned his elbow on Stanley's desk. 'Arthur structured it so that only his *direct descendant* or someone from his late *wife's family* could take over from him.' Brad raised two fingers to emphasize his points.

Something suddenly dawned on Stanley. 'I see what you mean!'

'Yes,' said Brad. 'I think it's time we involved Linda's sister Bernadette.'

Stanley seemed enlivened by the idea. 'Rosie will fight it tooth and nail.'

'But at least it we'll have a chance.'

'Yes, yes,' smiled Stanley at last. 'It might just work.'

He pulled some papers together and stuffed them into a folder in his drawer.

Brad got up to leave. Stanley picked up his phone and dialled a number.

Chapter XVIII

While all the speculation was going on about her whereabouts, Melanie was settling into her small hotel. It was only a few miles across Kowloon Bay from the room she had vacated on Severn Road. But it felt like a world away.

It was a modest family-run establishment, and the occupants and the staff had gotten used to seeing her quietly going about her business, giving no hint that she had any connection to the large events playing out across the former colony.

To all intents she looked just like any prospective migrant scoping out opportunities for herself in the prosperous city, leaving behind some dead-end life on the mainland.

At night she could hear the noises from the street, listening to the clatter of other tenants in the other rooms. It was a long way from the velvet cocoon inhabited by Julia Tang. But oddly enough, it was here that she felt her first breath of freedom since arriving in Hong Kong.

Lost in the teeming threshold of China, without any of the accoutrements of wealth, staying in a room registered under the name of Jason's former girlfriend, she felt free.

Mason's charade had been more of a prison than she had realized. She wondered if that was how Julia Tang had felt most of her life. Could that be why some people weren't surprised she had disappeared?

Melanie relished being able to follow the most ordinary routines, going down for tea in the mornings, walking around the streets when she wanted to, without having to think of the role she had to play, and the costs of making a mistake.

From her humble hideaway she was able to watch the repercussions of Li Kun Ming's conviction in China, and its ominous implications for Hong Kong and Tang Worldwide. There were scattered rumours of a search for Arthur Tang's daughter.

Hearing them made her glad she was here in the crowded backstreets of Kowloon, where no one would even think to look for her.

She made as few phone calls as possible, turning on her computer for short periods to log onto her company files. Thus she was able to check how Stanley and his fellow managers were carrying out her instructions, keeping the company going despite this new crisis.

The conglomerate had gone into autopilot, just like it had when Arthur suddenly died, and when his daughter disappeared. The same automatic mechanisms had ensured the company's survival before, and now Melanie knew that she just had to let them do their work while she tried to find a way to extricate herself.

Sometime before the evening, she got the call she had been dreading. It was Rosie.

'We're in the house right now,' she chirped.

Melanie happened to be walking on a busy street, and she quickly looked for a quiet corner to talk.

'Why is it so noisy?' Rosie demanded over the din at Melanie's end.

Melanie turned away from the dense stream of passers-by to avoid giving Rosie a hint of where she was. She found a narrow passage, which she followed past several delivery bays stacked with crates, until she found herself at the back of a restaurant.

There, she stood between the piles of refuse and the hot window of the busy kitchen.

'Where are you?' asked Rosie. ' Is everything okay? I hear you haven't come home for several nights.'

Just then she sounded like someone trying to entice an escaped bird back into its cage.

'I'm okay,' Melanie answered softly. 'I just needed to get away for a while.'

'I know,' Rosie said with surprising sympathy. 'It gets crazy doesn't it? I feel like doing that myself sometimes.'

Melanie didn't respond. She listened out for any signs of who was with Rosie and what they might be up to.

As if reading her mind, Rosie said, "Jason is with me. We're all very worried. Even Stanley has no idea where you are.'

'Listen,' Melanie said. 'I just need to think things through. I need to be alone for a while.'

Rosie jumped in with a suggestion. 'Why don't you go to Dijon? No one's using the villa. You can be there by yourself. You can go to all those vineyards you like. Bring along a friend.'

Melanie knew exactly what Rosie was doing. *Keeping me within her reach.*

'That's nice of you,' she demurred. 'But I might just…she closed her eyes and thought of home. Her real home. 'I might just…drift around for a few days,' she murmured into the phone. 'I promise I won't take too long.'

Rosie's voice brightened. 'Oh, is that what you're doing? That makes sense.' She let out a laugh. ' 'Just like the old days.'

Melanie realized she had planted an idea in Rosie's mind she had never intended to.

'Don't sail off too far,' Rosie said with a little humour now. 'Just don't be as long as the last time.'

Melanie had the eerie feeling that Rose was talking to her as if she really was Julia.

'I won't,' Melanie said. 'I promise you. It won't be anything like the last time.'

She hung up. After the call, she turned off the phone and stood at the end of the passage, trying to read into everything Rosie had said.

She looked up and saw the small square of sky framed by the building tops above her. It made her feel like she was in the bottom of a well, with no chance of jumping out.

She came out to the front of the street again. Back among the mass of humanity moving in all directions, she was a creature hiding in the midst of a large herd, protected by sheer numbers.

I'm in the sprawl of China, she thought. *The Land of a Hundred Names.*

The kingdom that had culled all the names from its vast history into just a hundred names that its enormous population now had to make do with. Melanie had appropriated one of those names. An illustrious one with all its baggage, and shedding it now might be the last thing she ever did.

It felt strange being here, back in the place where she was abandoned long ago. Gambling with her life and freedom, against an enemy she couldn't possibly beat. Her only protection was not being known, being invisible among the thousands of ordinary people that Julia Tang and her family had never mingled with.

She hurried back to her hotel and got in the Volkswagen. She knew it wouldn't be long before the chauffeur revealed that she had left driving his wife's car. So she made her way to Tonkin Street to retrieve the Rover.

When she got there, she drove past Kin Ho's building until she was at a construction site. She parked the Volkswagen behind some unused equipment, where she hoped it would take some days to be found.

Then she walked back the two blocks to Kin Ho's office.

When the got there, she traded the Volkswagen's keys for the Rover's, telling the old accountant where the chauffeur could pick up his wife's car. Kin Ho nodded without asking any questions.

Melanie left his office and rode the lift down to the basement.

She got in the vehicle and rummaged in her purse for her phone. Her hand touched something. She took it out with some puzzlement.

It was the keys to Jason's secret apartment.

She smiled. It was time to go deeper into the rabbit hole.

She made her way to Tai Po at around 10:00 o' clock. It was late enough to avoid any unwanted encounters.

When she passed the Old Market, she slowed to a crawl. She prepared to turn off near Tolo Harbour, expecting Jason's secret apartment to be somewhere among the luxury waterfront properties.

But the GPS told her to go further. The device took her past all the likely places, until she arrived at a bleak public housing estate.

It stood right next to a vast industrial park. She couldn't imagine Jason keeping a residence somewhere like this.

On the other hand, it was perfect. Jason could indulge in his double life here without anyone being the wiser. The location was so out of character no one would link it to him.

She drove around the crowded lot until she found a place to park. She walked under poles of drying laundry hanging over tiny front balconies high above her.

She reflected that it was one thing Julia shared with her stepbrother: this need to conceal one part of her life from another. It was only thanks to this that Melanie and Mason were able to perpetrate their deception. Now she was using the family's propensity for secrets to save herself.

As soon as she entered the dingy looking lobby, she wondered if she had come to the wrong place. The walls and the floor were plastered with the same cheap varnished tiles that reeked of urine and spoiled food.

The lift arrived with surprising peed. But she had to steel herself to step into the claustrophobic enclosure and punch the button. She heard ominous creaks in the shaft above her as the pulleys engaged to hoist her up.

When the doors opened, she stepped out and strode past the doors, checking the numbers until she got to the last one.

She listened out for any noises from inside before taking out the keys.

It was completely silent.

When she opened the door she was dumbfounded. The interior was as plush as the exterior was drab.

Outside, it was perfectly disguised to blend in with all the other units in the building, but inside it brimmed with all the luxury Melanie knew Jason and his mother never denied themselves.

It consisted of two apartments, joined together through arched passages knocked out of the walls. Being there was like

232

peering into Jason's mind, the way his feelings and intentions contrasted sharply with his seemingly nonchalant veneer.

The dwelling was surprisingly tidy for one that wasn't occupied. Melanie wondered if there was a cleaner. In which case Melanie knew she would have be out before daylight.

Her watch said it was nearly 11:00. That gave her two or three hours at most.

She couldn't decide where to start.

Jason must have been so sure no one would find his little lair. None of the drawers were locked. Either he trusted his girlfriend implicitly, or he was very confident she wouldn't glean the import of the things he left lying around.

In two spots Melanie found items she wouldn't have considered significant. Like Adalie, she would have dismissed them as random things. But their presence in a location Jason kept secret made them quite intriguing.

One of them was an old Marine GPS which, to her chagrin, it wouldn't turn on. It showed heavy wear but seemed well taken care of. There was no way of knowing how long it had been there, if it was broken or just out of charge.

It surprised her that Jason would have such a thing. Melanie knew he had no interest in sailing whatsoever. She surmised it might have belonged to Adalie or another friend.

In the next drawer, concealed under a jumble of objects, she found an envelope. In it were a few pages folded neatly to fit in one tight packet. She took out the sheets and gave them a quick scan.

They were photocopies from some book, finely printed text that contained a mix of English and Chinese characters. She had no idea what it related to, but sensed it could be important. She glanced quickly at her watch.

She had less than an half an hour left. The search had taken longer than she had thought.

She had only covered half the territory. She had to hurry.

In the time she left, she ransacked every space she still hadn't searched. She squeezed into the space under the bed, poked in the cupboards, probed even inside the fuse panel and under the kitchen sink.

She dug out something from the bottom of a night stand.

It was a piece of metal with a rough edge on one side. It was smooth and rounded, made of aluminium or some other light metal. Its odd shape made it almost impossible to deduce its function.

But the rough edge hinted it may have been broken off from some larger piece.

Aware of the clock ticking, she hurriedly went through the rest of the rooms, careful to put everything back as she had found it.

At last, satisfied that she had erased all trace of her visit, she stuffed the objects she had found into her purse.

Then she went out, locking the front door and walking as silently as she could towards the lift.

It was almost 2:00 a.m. when she got back to the hotel.

Exhausted but exhilarated, she couldn't resist opening the envelope from Jason's apartment.

She didn't know exactly what she was looking for, but perhaps there could be numbers, a name, a phone or an address. What she found instead were sheets of dense text organized into columns. She recognized some Chinese ideograms: characters for "water," "gorge," and "mountain."

She had no inkling what they could mean.

Chapter XIX

She was awake long before daylight, sitting anxiously by the window, waiting for someone to knock or kick in her door. Her small room felt even smaller, and the world outside seemed about to crash in on her.

She laid out the things she had found in Jason's apartment. She picked up the marine GPS and studied it. Nothing could make it come to life.

It was a tantalizing dead-end lying inert on her table, its secrets draining away by the minute.

She went downstairs and stopped at the front desk.

'I've lost my charger,' she said holding up the GPS. 'Could you find me a replacement?'

The sleepy, overworked clerk took the gadget and turned it over in his hand. He seemed uncertain, but he said, 'We'll find one and send it up to your room.'

She went out to get her breakfast, crossing the deserted corner in the early morning stillness.

She was the first customer in the tiny restaurant, and she had her pick of the empty tables.

She took one by the window and watched the street slowly come to life, as the faint whiff of jasmine wafted in the still-cool air. A tradesman rode by on an ancient bicycle, balancing a large box of flour on his bike. From the opposite direction, an old woman was pushing a cart of flowers through the still empty road.

Gradually, those shadowy relics of Hong Kong's old village life gave way to the thickening stream of cars, and the place went back to its noisy urban pace.

Melanie spread out the papers she had brought with her from Severn Road. Among them were the photocopies from Arthur Tang's book that Kin Ho had made for her. It all seemed so long ago now.

She scanned the entries, not looking for anything specific, but hoping for some nugget to jump out at her. She saw a name she had never come across before. *Laurent Courbin.*

It stood out only because it was completely unfamiliar. Yet it was in a cluster of entries which included the number of Arthur's life insurance policies, and accounts he held in various banks. The name was written next to a ten-digit number. It had to be significant.

She dialled Kin Ho's number. It was only 7:20.

The phone rang a third time before it was picked up. Kin Ho's voice came on.

'Do you have Laurent Courbin's number?' she asked, staring at the unfamiliar name. She could hear the rustling of papers as the accountant checked his records.

'Yes,' Kin Ho came back on. 'I've got his direct number in Geneva.'

It was all the confirmation Melanie needed.

'Wait for me,' she said. 'I'll be right there.'

She went back to the hotel. One of the clerks stopped her at the Reception.

'We found it,' she said, holding up an adapter. Melanie stared at it for a moment, then remembered the Marine GPS.

'Why, thank you!' she beamed at the girl who had already gone back behind the counter. She dashed into the lift and went upstairs.

In the room she plugged in the device to charge, then hurried out again.

In about twenty minutes she had reached Kin Ho's office.

The old accountant was having tea with his subordinates when she arrived. He quickly got up and followed her into his office.

'Will Mr. Courbin be in now?' she asked.

Kin looked up at the wall clock. 'It'll be in the evening,' he said. 'But I'm sure he'll still be available.'

He went to the safe to retrieve his file of confidential information. After a meticulous search he located the private numbers he had refused to share with Rosie or anyone else.

He sat down at his desk to make the call.

'Mr. Courbin,' he said when he got connected. 'I have Miss Tang here for you.'

He handed the receiver to Melanie.

'Well, how are you, Miss Tang?' said the Frenchman with his practiced familiarity.

Melanie composed herself for one of the most important requests she was ever going to make. Her heart was beating fast. She knew the private banker wouldn't give her any information if she slipped up.

She said she was calling about her account.

'Why, yes, of course.' She heard him tapping energetically on a keyboard, humming to himself. After a few moments he was back.

'And may I have the account number, please?'

She felt the moment had come, and she uttered the 10-digit number she had found in Arthur's papers.

The Frenchman gave an embarrassed cough. 'I'm sorry about the little formality,' Miss Tang. But could you please give me your access code?'

The rush Melanie had been expecting came to a sudden halt. 'Access code?'

'Yes, ma'am. We agreed that you would not use a password. You wanted to use an access code. A sixteen digit one as you specified.'

Melanie didn't know of any access code. Worse, she had no idea where to find it.

'I don't have it with me right now,' she murmured to the banker. 'I'll call you again once I have it.'

Uncertain whether she would be able to keep that promise, she hung up.

She took the long way back to the Teahouse, trying to get over her disappointment. It was the first real wall she had come up against. One Mason hadn't been able to prepare her for.

Now it was up to her. She had to improvise as best she could.

She parked the Rover and walked dejectedly into the hotel.

But when she trudged into her room, there was something waiting for her that rekindled her hope. The marine GPS lay on her beside table was showing a green light.

The device lit up in her hands, charting out the previous owner's unknown world.

One door had closed on her, but another one just opened.

She still didn't know who the device belonged to, or what its significance was to her search.

As she flicked absently through the menus, she found several saved locations. The first was called "Double Haven 1." Another was called "Quarry 1."

She had no idea what each set of coordinates represented, and she needed someone to guide her.

Calling Mason now was out of the question. So, taking a random pick of anyone else she could phone, she ended up ringing Estelle.

There were several rings before Estelle's voice came on. She sounded faint and far away.

'Estelle, it's Melanie.'

'Why, hello!'

'I was wondering if you were free for lunch today,' Melanie said.

The pause was filled with static, and Estelle's reply came with a delay. 'Why, I'd love to. But unfortunately, I'm in Tokyo right now.'

'Oh. When will you be back?'

'In a week or so. I'm just leasing out my apartment here.'

''That's a shame. I hope I get a chance to see you.'

'Why, are you leaving?'

'Yes, I might have to.'

That is a shame,' said Estelle clucked her tongue. 'Anyway I should be able to bring back what I promised you.'

Melanie searched her mind. 'What did you promise me?'

'You know, the report from Wolverton Services,' answered Estelle. 'The agency Julia hired.'

'Why, yes,' Melanie said.

The pieces of Julia Tang's puzzle were flung across several parts of the world. Melanie didn't know if she still had time to hunt them all down.

Its massive sweep tantalized her, and made her despair of ever solving it.

She said goodbye to Estelle and hung up.

She sat for a few moments thinking, looking through her phone's contacts list.

When she came to Chad's number, she paused for a moment.

Obviously, to learn about the locations on the GPS, she needed the yacht. But she knew she would never be able to take out *Sea Tiger* without alerting Rosie. Word that "Julia" had shown up at the yacht club was sure to reach Rosie or anyone else who was looking for her.

That made Chad her best option. She dialled his number.

After two rings Chad's voice came on.

Fortunately he didn't seem to find it strange that she would ask him to take out the *Sea Tiger* and pick her up from somewhere.

'Where do you want me to meet you?' he asked.

Melanie hesitated. She looked down on the marine GPS. She clicked down to the first saved location. 'Do you know Double Haven?'

'Why, of course.'

Melanie checked her watch. 'Shall we say two o'clock?'

'Fine.'

She drove back to the hotel to pack a few clothes. She put them in a small backpack and sauntered through the lobby as though she were just going out for a bit of shopping.

Then she used the Marine GPS to find her way by road to Double Haven.

But the device was old, and hadn't been updated in years. She lost her way a few times, and once ended up at an intersection that brought her straight onto oncoming traffic.

She proceeded with more caution, ready to compensate for the ageing device.

At last she found her way into the Marine Reserve, which was completely deserted on a weekday.

She drove around slowly, trying to glean why Julia would save the location on her GPS.

After half an hour, there was still no sign of Chad.

She waited in the car until she caught sight of the yacht coming in. It seemed almost stationary at times as it crept towards the dock. She ran out to meet it.

Chad jumped down on the jetty to give her a hug. He looked very tanned and laid back.

They bantered while he got the vessel ready. He regaled her with anecdotes about his recent cruise, while she improvised a casual account of her own activities that did not include leaving Severn Road and hiding from the authorities.

Finally, when they were untied, he turned on the motor and said, So where are we going today?'

She took out the marine GPS. 'Let's go down memory lane.'

His eyes lit up in recognition. 'You still have that old thing?' he laughed. He fingered the gadget thoughtfully and put it on the mount by the wheel.

'Which location are we headed for today?' he turned to her.

'Try Quarry 1,' she said. 'It's one of the first saved locations.'

He looked a little puzzled at first, and looked uncertainly through the GPS menu.

At length he found it. 'There!' he pressed a button. 'Done!'

In Melanie's mind, Chad had just confirmed that the GPS was Julia's. They had obviously used it together before and Chad might be familiar with some of the saved locations.

She pushed her suspicions to the back of her mind, sitting back and relinquishing all responsibility as the vessel left port and glided out into the open water.

Chad took them on a big arc until the cluster of islands that made up Double Haven were just shimmering dots behind them.

After about twenty minutes Melanie looked around doubtfully. The coordinates Chad was following seemed to be taking them well outside the territory. He looked a bit confused, too, and cast her a dubious glance. 'I don't remember coming out this way very often.'

'It's fine,' she reassured him.

'We'll have the Marine Police upon us at any minute now,' he fretted, slowing down. 'They'll want to know what we're doing.'

'We're not doing anything illegal,' insisted Melanie. 'They can come aboard if they like.'

The device beeped. Melanie jumped up to peer at the screen.

'There. See? 'she tapped the illuminated arrow on the gadget's face. ' We're just a couple of hundred feet away.'

Chad scanned the horizon. 'But I don't see anything.'
Melanie shielded her eyes from the haze.

There was nothing. Even she began to have her own misgivings. What if the outdated maps had taken then in the wrong direction?

242

'Maybe we should turn back,' urged Chad.

'No. It's there!'

At last it appeared, a deserted rock jutting out of the water, jagged and unwelcoming. It looked slightly eerie in its isolation.

She remembered Estelle's words. How Julia liked to explore deserted places, lonely spots off the beaten track. The kinds of places Estelle was too scared to accompany her to.

What was it in Julia's character that attracted her to such places? Was she looking for an escape from her stifling position? Or was there a more practical reason?

Why would she save this position on her device?

As they drew closer they saw the signs warning against approaching or disembarking. The water around it was slick with oil. The shore that she could see was rocky and unkempt, with only a few ledges from which to clamber onto the rest of the islet.

'It's only used to quarry building materials now,' commented Chad. 'There's nothing there. And it would be dangerous to go anywhere on foot.'

He circled a few times and couldn't find a suitable place to land.

Melanie went out on the railings to examine the barren atoll

'There!' she pointed. 'That's close enough. And you can tie up at one of those rigs!'

He gave her a horrified look. 'Surely you're not thinking of getting off?'

'Please.'

He gave a resigned shrug and turned the wheel in the direction she wanted. Melanie thanked God for Estelle's warning. Julia's stubbornness seemed well-known to those around her.

Once they rounded the point, they found the rusty capstans on the cargo dock.

'I could lose my licence for coming here,' he groaned.

'Just drop me off here and berth back there,' said Melanie.

Chad reluctantly moved the craft forward. They swung back and forth until they were almost at the edge of the quay.

Then Melanie took the GPS off the bracket and put it in her bag.

Chad watched her with disbelief as she climbed onto the deck.

When he saw there was no stopping her, he left the wheel to join her. He helped her over the precarious gap between the vessel and the quay.

He watched her pick her way to end of the wharf.

'I'll be no more than half an hour,' she called out through cupped hands. 'I promise.'

Chad got down on one knee to peer into the water below the craft.

After a thoughtful pause, he seemed satisfied.

He dropped anchor into the oil-slicked sea.

At last he killed the engine and rode anchor in the lee of the rock.

Melanie followed a rough trail that stretched over the shale, and found a stark landscape opening up before her. The arid flatness was relieved only by a few patches of vegetation here and there. Everything else had been levelled by massive earth-moving machines.

The arrow on her GPS pointed up the hill. Her heart sank at the sight of the long, ragged climb. But she forced herself to make the hard, hot trudge until the device beeped again.

A flashing sign told her she was less than fifty feet from the saved location called "Quarry 1."

The ascent had taken longer than she had expected. She had only ten minutes left of the half hour she had promised to Chad. She found herself at the edge of a mammoth pit.

It looked like a large dried-out lake, the remnants of hills around it blasted into dust and carted away to feed Hong Kong's outsize greed for land and construction.

It gave her vertigo just to look over the edge into the darkness far below. It went so deep into the earth it seemed to be reaching towards the ocean floor. She glimpsed the sheen of water at the bottom, as if the sea were already seeping in.

The scale of the hole dwarfed her. It gave her butterflies in her stomach just to come too close. Why would Julia keep coming back to such a place?

She checked the GPS again. The next saved position was labelled simply "qbx."

Melanie set it as her next destination. The device pointed her towards the middle of the chasm.

She worried about the outdated maps on the device again. She wondered if she was letting it take her into her own doom. But the prize of finding out Julia's secrets was too great to ignore.

She took a deep breath and inched towards the rim.

She made out a kind of walkway below her. To reach it she had to go down a steep narrow stairway, blocked by an orange metal barrier that was chained and padlocked, plastered with more of the official warnings.

She leaned out and saw, across the yawning width of the pit, a mirror image of the walkway below her. The route seemed newer and safer, but she had no time to go all that way around.

So she clambered over the barrier and lowered herself on the vertical ladder. The rungs were rough from rust, and she felt flakes of steel and paint come off on her hands.

There was still enough light from the sky to see the passage. She lowered herself carefully and dusted off her hands.

She felt her way gingerly along the salt-eaten walkway that snaked in and out of the shadows, sometimes taking her under unstable protrusions of mud and rock.

Tufts of grass had grown on the escarpment, and fronds of wild fern dangled from above her, like hairy tentacles of some hideous subterranean monster.

She was in a totally different world, a dimension of skewed scale that she found oppressive.

She picked her way along the limestone until the GPS beeped one more time. She had reached the saved location called "qbx."

She was near the end of the path. Just a few feet ahead, the rail bent around the side of rock face and disappeared into the darkness. To go further without a light would have been madness.

So she stayed where she was and studied the spot that Julia had stored in her GPS for some reason.

It was a kind of natural recess in the crag. There were cavities where the electrical conduits had been attached before they were moved to another site. Two electrical boxes remained in the lowest niche, both in varying states of corrosion.

One was so badly damaged she couldn't get it to open. The other one had more slack, and little by little she managed to increase the gap.

Steeling herself, she put her hand into the opening. A tiny swarm immediately engulfed her arm. She jumped back with a cry.

Her shout briefly echoed on the walls above her, before being absorbed in the stone.

She looked up at the rim of rock above her. That's what a scream for help would be like, she thought. A fleeting, feeble noise muffled by the distance.

Glancing up at the weakening daylight in the sky, she used all her strength to get the damaged box to open. Fighting a powerful wave of revulsion, she put her hand further in. She felt around until her fingertips closed on something solid.

She remembered Julia was left-handed, and she would have chosen that side if she wanted to hide anything.

Melanie brought the object out into the light.

It was some kind of metal container, heavy and tightly sealed. She gave it a gentle shake. There were tiny clinks from inside.

She looked at her watch. She had less then two minutes left.

She hurriedly put the container in her bag and scurried back up the walkway. The rest of the pit's secrets would have to wait.

When she was directly under the ferns again, she stumbled and got one foot caught between two metal slats.

For a moment an overpowering sense of desperation came over her. She was down here alone, deep in an atoll where she wasn't supposed to be. In a territory where no one even knew her real name.

If anything happened to her now, it would be as if she had never existed. Her whole life would have been like a charade, swept away like an unfinished child's puzzle.

She pulled her foot free and staggered up to the sheer flight of steps. At the end, she hoisted herself up until she was over the barrier again.

Then, seeing the distance she had yet to cover, a new terror assailed her. What if Chad had left?

She stumbled down the stony slope, ignoring the pain in her ankle, fearing the worst. If Chad *had* left, there would be no way for her to get help. She didn't even know whom to call.

She looked around at the emptiness around her and felt that dread of abandonment again. It was the long-buried feeling of desertion that came back now and again. It stemmed from those days long ago, when a stranger had found her crying under the *sakura* tree, to be taken into an orphanage with other abandoned children, to be offered up for adoption by anyone who cared to take her.

Ignoring the agony in her foot, she limped down three hundred meters or so. The stony incline below her was still impossibly far from the shore.

Finally, she spotted the yacht.

Relief washed over her. She waved towards the yacht. Chad sent out a blast on the vessel's horn.

Now that she knew he was still there, Melanie was tempted to linger. She looked across to one of the few patches of greenery with one tree still standing. Everything else on the atoll looked dead.

There was something familiar about that green spot, a peculiar oasis in this man-made desert. She felt as if she'd seen it before. But how? She hadn't even had an inkling this atoll existed before.

Far away beyond that patch she could see some kind of landmark. She wondered where she had seen it before, then an urgent blast from *Sea Tiger*'s horn intruded on her thoughts.

Chad was standing on the yacht's deck, waving both arms.

Her speculations about the place would have to wait.

She stepped away from the area and started making her way down.

Chad must have noticed how she was limping. He jumped ashore to help her.

'What happened?' he asked as they struggled back onto the vessel. He practically carried her over the gap.

When they were on the vessel, he helped her onto a chair and surveyed her foot worriedly. 'We might need to go straight to the hospital.'

'No!' Melanie almost shouted. Going back to the hospital now was the last thing she wanted. Chad seemed shocked by her vehemence.

She tried to soften her tone.

'I know you warned me,' she said sheepishly. 'But you know how I am with abandoned places. I just can't leave them alone.'

The tension remained on Chad's face. Then a memory seemed to click in place. 'I might have known,' he shook his head.

'You want me to drive you home at least?' he insisted.

'It's nothing a bit of sea air won't cure,' she waved off his concern. 'In fact, I'm thinking of keeping the yacht for a while. I might squeeze in a couple of days' sailing while the weather's good.'

He looked at her dubiously for several moments.

At last he gave a resigned shrug, 'Ok.'

He went out to weigh anchor. Melanie closed her eyes to picture the pit she had just left. Why Julia would come to such a place still perplexed her. She heard Chad coming back.

She opened here eyes to see him at the wheelhouse.
'Ready?'

She nodded and the engine came alive.

Melanie lay back and raised her leg on the other deck chair as Chad pulled away from the rock. She kept her gaze on the ceiling as they traversed the empty stretch. Soon they were back in familiar waters.

A loud hoot from the horn of a passing ferry made her sit up. There were more vessels around them. She recognized Sulphur Channel, and knew they were just a few miles from land.

Kennedy Town came into view on their right, then she got up to join Chad. 'I can take over from here,' she said.

He stepped away from the wheel and loped towards one of the chairs.

She reduced speed to make the round past Green Island lighthouse. Then she asked,

'Shall I drop you off at the Yacht Club?'

He seemed taken aback by the question, but he gave her a reluctant nod.

So she made her way through the busy cross-harbour traffic to make a detour at Causeway Bay.

She glided to a stop alongside the jetty.

'Let me know how it goes,' said Chad and jumped onto the quayside.

She turned around to continue on to Double Haven, where she had left the Rover.

Chapter XX

Melanie woke up in the calm of the Teahouse, a world away from the intrigues she knew were going on across the border, building up to engulf her. As she moved around and got ready for her day, news came on the radio about Li Kun Ming's execution in China. It brought home the seriousness of her situation.

The report concluded with a few lines about the possible arrest of Arthur Tang's daughter, who was now being sought.

To anyone in the small hotel, those momentous events seemed like distant rumours that had little to do with the unassuming woman moving quietly amongst them. Only Melanie knew better.

She was right in the heart of the matter. She was the eye driving the storm that was about to swallow up the territory.

It made her miss being an innocent bystander. She longed for the simplicity of her life before Mason came into the picture. Before she glimpsed the audacious alternative to her own humdrum existence.

Now she wondered if she would ever be able to return to that former life.

She walked around the room and stopped at the sideboard. She opened the drawer to take out the box she had found on the atoll.

It was made of heavy matte aluminium, with solid latches. It seemed too attractive to be spirited away in the place where he had found it.

The catch was plated with white gold, and didn't show any signs of corrosion. She pressed it and the lid sprang open.

She felt around the velvet-lined interior, expecting a key of some kind, a pouch of diamonds, or perhaps even a scrap of paper with a number.

Instead she found a delicate gold necklace. She held it up to the light from the window. There were tiny jade pendants dangling along its entire length.

On closer inspection, she found that each pendant had a tiny gold character embedded in the stone.

She recognized the characters for "field", then "obstacle". Then there was the ideogram that meant "grouping."

Was that supposed to refer to the conglomerate?

It wasn't a very long necklace, and the next ideogram in the sequence was the one that stood for "contemplation."

The ornament seemed to simply be an expression of its owner's mystical or philosophical preoccupations. It was not the key to weighty secrets she had been hoping to find.

In fact, it didn't at all seem to be the kind of object one would go to the trouble of concealing in a place like the desert island. Julia Tang was striking her more and more as a woman of many riddles.

Melanie sat thinking for a long time. It didn't make sense. She picked up the box again and felt more thoroughly inside.

She fished out a faded slip of paper. It appeared to be the receipt from the jeweller. She squinted at the faint imprints and read the name: *Double Fortune Jewellers*. The date of the invoice told her that it was bought a few months before Julia was last seen.

Why would she go to the expense of buying a costly piece of jewellery, only to hide it in a place no one was likely to find it?

It was sheer luck that Melanie had stumbled upon it. If not for the GPS, she would never have found it.

The GPS. Her gaze fell upon the device on her night stand. It was a connection to Julia, the best one yet that tied Jason to his missing stepsister.

What exactly had happened? How did the instrument end up in Jason's little hideaway?

The thought of Jason made her freeze. Did he know by now that someone had been to his secret apartment? That his treasure trove of trophies had been found?

Suddenly her cell phone rang. It vibrated against the wood of the side table like a startling presence in the room.

'Hello?' she answered.

'Miss Tang!'

Melanie paused before confirming her identity.

'Julia?' the caller inquired hesitantly. 'Is that you?'

She recognized Kin Ho.

'Why hello,' she said at length.

'Those pictures you asked me to get,' said the bookkeeper. 'They're in my office now.'

'Pictures?'

'The ones from the police. The ones they took of your boat.' Kin added with a hint of self congratulation, 'They were sealed before. But I managed to convince them.'

Melanie remembered. 'Good. Keep them there. I'm on my way.'

She scooped up several items into her bag and dashed out of the hotel.

Kin met her at the door and led her through the narrow corridor. They passed two empty offices and stopped at the conference table. Kin Ho proudly pointed to the packet lying right in the middle, 'That's it.'

She sat down and tore the packet open. She spread out the contents in front of her.

A quick glance told her that the craft was a Sabre class dinghy, small and light enough to be sailed single-handed.

After several minutes she questioned why the images had been sealed at all. None of them showed the slightest hint of anything untoward. It looked like any boat that had seen steady use over the years.

She tried rearranging the photos according to which part of the vessel they showed. Only then did she find it.

There it was, on the boom, lost in the mass of clew hooks and rigging. A small steel bar with a slight gap. It was a quirk of this particular design. Most people would have missed it. Only her long experience with boats alerted her: the opening seemed bigger than it should be.

The detail would have been clear to anyone looking for signs of seaworthiness, but not to someone looking for signs of a crime.

She turned to Kin bent over his desk. 'Do you have a magnifying glass?'

He got up and rifled through one of the cabinets. He peeked out from behind the door, holding up a magnifier with a smile.

'Thank you,' Melanie crossed the room to take it. Then she picked up the photos and went into one of the empty offices. She locked the door and took out the items she had brought from the hotel.

One of them was the piece of metal she had found in Jason's apartment. She studied the fragment under the glass and compared it with close-ups of the boat's fittings. She tried to imagine how and where the hunk of iron might fit in.

Then she went back to the gap she had first noticed on the dinghy's outhaul rail. She looked at several angles, but in the end she was sure: the metallic part she had found was from the rail on Julia's craft. The flaw was very subtle, and it wasn't in one of the most obvious sections of the craft.

Anyone who didn't know what they were looking for would have easily overlooked it. The tear marks matched perfectly. That sliver of iron was the detail the investigators hadn't known about.

Because all this time it had been hidden in a place no one knew existed. A place Melanie would never have found if not for Jason's vindictive ex-girlfriend.

Melanie gathered her things. She thanked Arthur's old accountant and left.

She parked the Rover in its usual place, then walked back to the hotel without thinking, following the routine of the past few days. But this time there was something different.

She heard someone pounding on a door. The noise seemed irrelevant to her until she was only a few feet from her own door.

She saw the three men standing in the hallway. They were banging on *her* door. 'Miss Tang! Please come out!'

She went cold all over. The men had clearly been there for some time, waiting for a response that would never come. She took in the two men in plain clothes, the third man in uniform.

To her horror, she realized that the people at the front desk must have seen her come in. They might be sending up someone right now.

She changed course without raising her head, pivoting towards the service door to her right.

Her steps seemed to echo too loudly in the deserted stairwell, and the three flights of stairs seemed to take forever before she reached the ground floor.

She slowed down to a seemingly casual gait and sidled past the new arrivals at the front, her mind racing.

How did they find her? Did someone in the hotel learn who she was?

This was the moment she had been dreading. The long arm of China had reached her little refuge.

She remembered what Mason had said about mounting the tiger. Indeed Arthur's life was proof that those who rode the wild cat never found a way to dismount. Perhaps, like Arthur and his daughter Julia, Melanie was about to find out the same thing.

She burst out onto the street in a daze of panic. The noise of the crowded street oppressed her.

She only found relief when she arrived at the Rover. She jumped inside. The silence in the plush interior momentarily shut out the chaos around her.

She needed time to think. With numb fingers, she fumbled on her phone to call Estelle. But there was no answer. The dull, repeating tone receded into a cold silence on the other end.

She looked at her bag on the seat beside her. In it were Arthur's papers, along with the items she had found in Jason's apartment.

Now, there was the box she had found in the quarry. They were the only things that had value to her now. All those possessions she had amassed as "Julia Tang" were quickly losing their worth, like the imaginary treasures in a dream that was quickly dissipating.

Her other things lay scattered around her room upstairs, a vague promise that she was coming back.

How long would it be before they forced her door open?

She tried to single out something that she might have missed. Some minor detail which, like the lump of titanium in Jason's apartment, might be her downfall.

She forced herself to take stock. She vividly recalled the exact moment she had found the marine GPS in Jason's apartment. It was the first thing to link Jason to Julia's disappearance.

That and the scrap of metal that turned out to be a missing part from her boat. They made a very powerful case against Rosie's precious son.

But despite all that proof, there was one thing that worked against her.

How could she come forward and claim Jason had murdered his stepsister? When she was here, alive, pretending to be that stepsister?

Her mind was still absorbed in the quandary when she turned on the engine and drove away.

She was cruising past the Mong Kok Stadium when she heard the news that "Julia Tang" had been detained. She nearly screeched to a halt.

She felt the confusion of someone in a hall of mirrors. How could they say she had been captured when she was here, trying desperately to save herself?

Or could they mean someone else masquerading as Julia Tang?

Or even, God forbid, the real heiress that everyone thought was missing?

She listened tensely to the rest of the report, waiting for the moment they would announce the make and model of the vehicle "Julia Tang" was driving.

Again the questions assailed her. How had they defeated her precautions? Right down to the fact that Adalie had registered the room in her own name? Had Adalie betrayed her? Had she been caught and forced to talk?

She felt bad about dragging Jason's former girlfriend into all this. In a sudden fit of guilt, she decided she would pay Adalie a visit.

She reached the next intersection and turned off from the main road, heading for Tong Chau Street.

When she got to *Wah Fu* Court, she jumped out of the car, rode the lift to the ninth floor.

She sprinted towards the green door, reaching out to ring the bell before something stopped her. What would be awaiting her inside?

The memory of the men pounding on her door at the hotel flashed through her mind. She fought her own misgivings and rang the bell.

There was no answer. She reached in through the bars and gave the door a loud rap. 'Adalie? Adalie, it's me!'

She stopped short of calling herself Julia in the deserted passage.

But there was only silence from inside.

She was about to leave when she heard footsteps coming up from the stairwell.

'I see you've made a new friend,' said a familiar voice behind her. She spun around.

It was Jason.

'I got to hand it to you,' he grinned. 'I never expected you to ferret her out.'

'Where is Adalie?' she demanded. 'What have you done to her?'

'Don't you worry about her,' he replied. 'You should worry more about yourself.'

He took a few steps towards her. She moved back.

'I'm warning you, Jason,' she hissed. 'You'll only make it worse for yourself.'

'What are you going to do?' he scoffed. 'Call the police? That would be very helpful. I'm sure they'd love to know where you are.'

She folded her arms and said, 'I know what happened to Julia.'

He gave her his lop-sided smile. 'Do you, now?'

'And you do, too,' she said. 'That's why you could never believe I was her. That she could possibly come back.'

He gave a defiant toss of the head. 'Prove it.'

'I can,' she said. 'I have the GPS from her boat. And the missing part from one of the rails. I found them in your secret apartment.'

When he looked up, his face was dark. 'Go ahead. Walk into any police station. Tell them you're my half-sister come back from the dead. Then tell them how you're going to serve time for Julia's crimes.'

He had just described her exact dilemma.

'That's why you and I are going to keep quiet about it,' Jason uttered smugly. 'We're going to pretend we don't know what we know.'

259

He crossed his arms and leaned back against the wall. 'And who knows? Things just might go on the way they always have.'

'As though nothing ever happened,' said Melanie.

'Exactly.'

Chapter XXI

She spent the night on the *Sea Tiger*. When she woke up in the morning, the deserted harbour was peaceful, the water glassy. She came out to the stern, and the slap of the water against her hull was the only sound she could hear for miles around.

The few other craft docked nearby were empty, but she was careful not to be seen.

She was grateful for Arthur Tang's insistence that his yacht be always kept ready for use. That order remained in force even after his death. So she had come back to the preserve and found a comfortable bed waiting for her in the vessel's stateroom, all the equipment ready for service.

The yacht had provided a handy alternative to the Teahouse, which was now known to the police, and perhaps to whoever else that wanted to find her. She couldn't quite work out how they had made the connection to her. It was worrying.

She turned on the TV in the main compartment. The first images that flickered on brought in the turmoil of the outside world.

One of the leading news stories was about a woman arrested just the day before. She was said to be masquerading as Julia Tang. It shocked Melanie to hear the words "masquerading as Julia Tang."

For a surreal moment she wondered if the story was about her, detailing her subterfuge and how it had been discovered. She focused on the small screen until the footage appeared of a handcuffed woman being led into a police car.

Adalie. She had been caught using Julia Tang's credit cards and was brought in for questioning.

All at once Melanie understood: the police coming to her hotel, the news of "Julia Tang" being detained. It was all Adalie.

Melanie had set off deception upon deception, so that the mirages she had created were taking on a life of their own.

She pictured the entire Tang family squirming at this very public intrusion into their private affairs, threatening to expose things they wanted to remain concealed. Now, more than ever, they would be moving heaven and earth to find her.

Make her pay for the damage she was causing. Feed her to the hungry dragon that was threatening to devour them all.

She got up, too restless to stay in the vessel, eager to get back to the real world.

She came out on deck and jumped onto the jetty. Her footsteps on the wood sounded loud in the stillness.

There was a dewy coolness from the trees as he crossed the empty parking lot. The Rover's leather seats still held the previous night's chill.

She turned on the engine and drove towards the exit.

Suddenly her phone rang. She stopped the vehicle and composed herself for the call, fixing in her mind what the situation was and what Julia would be likely to say. The habit had become even more ingrained as this deadly game of chess reached its final stages.

At last she answered.

'Guess who's back!' chimed Estelle. She chattered excitedly and seemed eager to meet up. 'I brought you back something from Japan.'

Melanie explained that she was trying to avoid being in the city, and proposed a sail instead.

'Sounds wonderful,' Estelle replied. 'Why don't you pick me up from Sai Kung? I'll be at Club Marina Cove in an hour or so.'

Melanie pulled over to consider her options. She knew this might be her last chance to see Estelle. And Julia's old friend might offer new insights into the riddles that still lay before her. Like the access code the Swiss banker Laurent Courbin had asked for.

'Alright,' she said into the phone. 'I'll be at Marina Cove in an hour.'

She hung up and turned the vehicle around. She parked in a more isolated spot, then walked back towards the yacht.

She encountered no more than three other craft as she sailed the eight miles to Sai Kung, maintaining a leisurely pace until she sighted the harbour. A hundred feet from land, she slowed down even more so she could glide into the tricky mouth of Marina Cove.

Estelle was already there. She jumped up and waved as soon as Melanie had manoeuvred around the breakwater.

Melanie eased the yacht alongside the quay.

Estelle ran down the jetty, dressed in shorts and a sleeveless black top for the warmer weather, swinging a muslin bag from her elbow. Melanie left the engine to idle and leaned out to help Estelle on board.

Estelle settled in one of the chairs as Melanie steered them out of the wharf.

They kept up an easy chatter as they motored out towards Hebe Haven, Melanie feeling less constrained to keep up her role.

When they got to their destination, a few other vessels were already there, bobbing on the water like doves spread out on a shimmering blue cloth.

Estelle was full of news about her trip to Japan. It reminded Melanie of the first time they had gone out on the *Sea Tiger* together. Everything had seemed so perfect then, and Melanie was still buoyed by the sense that she had passed the most difficult tests she could ever take.

Now she looked at the sea around her and wondered how much longer this dream would last. She felt like a sinner about to be kicked out of Paradise, and wanted to make the most of the time she had left.

Estelle took something out of her bag and laid it on the counter.

'This is that thing I promised you last time.' She sat back with an expectant smile.

It was an official looking folder. Melanie lifted the cover and saw the words: *Wolverton Services.*

She arched an eyebrow at Estelle.

'Read it,' Estelle urged, eager to see her reaction.

Melanie turned her attention to the file. The word that first sprang out at her was: *surveillance.* The focus of the investigation were referred to merely as *Subject A* and *Subject B.*

Julia had evidently feared having the document fall into the wrong hands, and asked the agency not to identify the subjects directly.

But the addresses mentioned, as well as the vehicles and locations, had a ring of familiarity to Melanie.

The account seemed to describe the daily movements of an ordinary American couple, and it wasn't easy to see why an heiress like Julia Tang would go to such lengths to find out about their activities.

The surveillance was commissioned by Julia two years before her disappearance. Reading it now gave Melanie an odd feeling. There were hints that that the heiress wasn't quite as oblivious to Melanie's existence as one would have expected. Perhaps Mason hadn't stumbled into Melanie's life quite by accident after all.

Almost as if the tycoon's daughter knew what lay ahead, and had somehow conceived a role for her unsuspecting look-alike, living out her mundane existence a continent away.

It was that existence which was detailed in the report Melanie was reading now: details about her parents' routines, financial affairs, and travels to China.

Had this all been part of Julia's plan? Had she conceived it so that Mason would find Melanie and entice her to stand in for Julia Tang? So that the heiress could go off and do whatever her soul longed to do, and leave her hapless substitute to pay the price for her misdeeds?

The notion made Melanie feel as if she were in an inescapable maze. As if everything had been pre-programmed. As if every move had been anticipated by the master puppeteer who was somehow controlling Melanie's every step, even from beyond the grave. That is, if she really was in the grave.

She became aware of Estelle looking at her.

'Does it make sense to you?' she said with that playful half-smile.

Melanie shook her head. Suddenly it occurred to her, *Was Estelle, too, part of the plan?* Had she been placed there to pull Melanie into an entanglement she never meant to enter? Was Melanie just following a trail of bread crumbs left by Julia herself?

Had she been meant to stumble upon Jason's secrets, which would make her set out to prove a crime that may or may not have happened?

Melanie was afraid to consider the possibilities. It gave her the sensation of coming too close to a cliff's edge and looking down at the abyss.

She fingered the folder and looked at Estelle. 'Did Julia ever talk about this?'

Estelle looked inward for a moment. Then she gave a shrug, 'All I know is it had something to do with what her mother had told her on her deathbed.'

There it was again. Something revealed by Julia's mother as she lay dying. Melanie suddenly remembered Bernadette:

It couldn't have been easy, Julia's aunt had said. *Trying to find someone you've never known.*

Melanie closed her eyes. She could almost glimpse Julia's shadow there, moving in the half light, revealing more of herself, but never quite coming out.

Melanie slid the folder back towards Estelle.

'But that's yours,' Estelle said. 'You need it more than I do.'

Melanie got up to put it into her bag. As she did so her hand touched a metal object. It was Julia's box.

She opened it and plucked out the necklace. She dangled it in front of Estelle. 'Does this look familiar?'

Estelle stared at it for several moments. 'I've been wondering what happened to that,' she said softly. 'Where on earth did you find it?'

'Where on earth indeed,' Melanie smiled, handing it to her. Estelle fingered the pendant with a hint of sadness, caressing each link tenderly.

Melanie pulled her chair closer, and they sat with their heads close together, poring over the chain.

'The characters don't seem to mean much of anything,' said Melanie, lifting up one of the gold-on-jade ornaments.

'Usually you'd expect to find a name, a word, or even a number. A date perhaps?'

'They're not particularly attractive either,' sneered Estelle.

Melanie agreed. 'Funny that anyone would spend an obviously great amount of money on something that doesn't seem to have much significance.'

'Or beauty.'

'Yes.'

Estelle gazed seaward for a moment, lost in thought. 'It's a bit unlike Julia. I never really knew her to have much interest in the *I Ching*.'

'The *I Ching*?'

Estelle looked at her with surprise. 'That's what these characters are. They're hexagrams from the *I Ching*.'

Melanie raised the choker and tried to read the gilded ideograms. 'But words like *field, obstacle,*' she said. 'What could they be referring to?'

'Julia made me learn this,' Estelle turned her chair around towards Melanie. ' She had found a way to use the *I Ching* to make a code.'

Melanie was dumbfounded. '*How?*'

'Each hexagram has a number, right?' said Estelle.

Melanie nodded. 'So?'

'So there are only 64 hexagrams in the *I Ching*. But the way Julia developed it, if a character was upside down, its number was reversed. '

Estelle ran her fingers along the length of the band until she found a particular ideogram. 'Here, for instance,' she indicated, 'is the symbol is for *yi*, meaning *swallowing*. But it's upside down.'

Melanie waited for her to explain.

'It's the 27th hexagram,' divulged Estelle. 'But because it's inverted it should be read as 72.'

It began to make sense to Melanie. With the unexpected guidance of Estelle, she began to see how Julia had disguised the function of the seemingly ordinary ornament. Now she understood why the missing woman had gone to great lengths to make sure the necklace was found by no one else.

It was just one more layer in the Chinese box of riddles Julia had woven around herself. Melanie hoped it would be the last.

She held up the delicate gold hoop with renewed admiration. She recognized the central locket as hexagram 56, which meant *wanderer*. Melanie wondered if Julia had wanted this to mean herself.

Her thoughts were rudely interrupted by a loud speedboat that suddenly appeared to their starboard. It thundered across the space in front of them, leaving a white gash in the blue surface. The water around them bobbed up and down for several moments.

The bay was getting busy.

Estelle made an irritated noise, starting to fidget. 'Maybe it's time we went somewhere else.'

Melanie got up and turned the engine on. A glance at the sky told her they had a good two to three hours of daylight left.

'Shall I take the long way round?' she asked Estelle.

Estelle nodded enthusiastically. 'The longest possible!'

They made a large arc around Clearwater Bay and bore South past Ma Wan island. Soon they were back in the open waters Melanie had explored with Chad before.

'Jason hated this place,' Estelle remarked.

'He did?' said Melanie. 'But I thought he didn't sail at all.'

'He doesn't,' said Estelle. 'But almost everyone around him did.' She leaned over the railing. 'Julia did. Adalie and Feng did. Jason would only come along because of them.'

'Feng?' Melanie repeated the name. 'I think I've heard that name before. Who is she?'

Estelle gave her a meaningful smile. 'It's a he.'

'Oh.'

'He's Jason's best friend.'

'Funny. I wonder where I've met him.'

They sailed on in silence for a while. Privately, Melanie recalled her encounter with Jason the night before. She went over everything he had told her.

He seemed to be offering her some kind of compromise. If she kept quiet about what she knew, he would stop trying to expose her. They would be bound by a covenant of silence.

The whole world would accept that she was Julia Tang, and she could continue this sumptuous existence. In exchange she would grant him whatever he wished, and pretend she didn't know what she did.

Tang Worldwide would keep reaping its millions, and everyone would be happy. Everything could go on as they had before.

As the *Sea Tiger* bore them in its velvet capsule, Melanie realized that this was the price of going on with this dream She could throw Julia's box overboard and pretend she had never found it. She could turn a blind eye to what she was almost sure was Jason's crime.

He, in turn, would tacitly accept her ruse, and their truce would be sealed by an unimaginable fortune.

'That place is so spooky!' she heard Estelle say. Melanie turned to where she was pointing.

In the distance Melanie made out a shape. It was faint, like a ghost in the haze. Then the arid contours became more defined. She recognized the deserted island where she had found Julia's necklace.

'That place gives me the creeps,' said Estelle. 'Please don't go anywhere near it.'

Melanie agreed. She started to turn the vessel around. But something made her hesitate. She didn't complete the turn, but slowed down to study the lonely rock a few hundred feet to their stern.

'What's the matter?' said Estelle.

Melanie remained transfixed for a few moments. Suddenly she knew how Jason had done it. Melanie turned her gaze back to the expanse in front of them.

'Nothing,' she said. 'I just thought I saw something.'

She straightened the vessel and headed back towards the city. The rock receded in the waning light behind them, and Melanie made up her mind. She would pay it one last visit. She would find out what else that forlorn atoll was hiding.

After a half hour or so, Victoria Harbour loomed in front of them. As they eased back closer to the shoreline Melanie remembered where she had heard the name *Feng*.

It had stuck in her memory for some reason.

It was the name of the man driving the other car on the night she had her accident!

Chapter XXII

Since four that morning she had been listening out for the vehicle that patrolled the preserve overnight. After the last one had passed, she knew she had to wait just another hour before the gates opened.

It was still dim when she walked out to the parking lot. The car windows were still frosted from the previous night's chill. She got in the vehicle and shut the door quietly. The touch of the cold leather made her shiver, and her breath came out in a wisp of vapour.

She sat quietly for a moment, watching the light slowly spread in the woods around her. She knew she had come to the end. Her wild ride on the tiger would soon be over. She felt the urge to say goodbye, or at least close something.

She reached over to the back for her purse. She took out her phone and wondered who to call at such a time. Estelle? But she certainly intended to see the Frenchwoman one last time before it was all done.

Who then? Kin Ho? She still had some unfinished business with him, and it was too early to get to that.

A sudden thought flashed in her mind. It made her smile. *Why not Rosie?*

That would be quite fitting, she thought. It would be the extravagant finale that this adventure deserved.

She felt an impish pleasure as she dialled Rosie's number. Her heart beat a little faster when she heard the first ring. She tried to imagine what Julia's stepmother would say to say to her. Then she heard the faint tinkle from somewhere. She turned around, listening out for the sound.

It rang a few more times before she finally confirmed it. Rosie's phone was somewhere in the Rover! It made her laugh out loud. Rosie had outfoxed her yet again. *Just as I had hoped,* she thought.

No wonder she had always felt Rose was never far away. Now it all made perfect sense. They had known where she was all along.

They had probably used Rosie's phone to track her. Yet they hadn't come to get her. That was the puzzling part.

Perhaps they wanted to know how far she would go. Or they were hoping she would lead them to a place they had no hope of finding.

She would oblige. She put Rosie's phone in her bag. It would go with her every step of the way.

She drove out of the reserve to get to the town.

She stopped at a chandlery and picked up supplies she would need for an extended journey. She brought everything back and loaded them onto the vessel.

Around mid-afternoon she did a final check of the equipment. In the lazarette she found old ropes, life vests and flares. Some of the vests had harnesses.

She was satisfied she had enough food and necessities to last for even a month at sea. Then she turned on the computer and downloaded the latest weather reports.

At last she untied the vessel, then, with one final look at the deserted reserve, she sailed out of the harbour. She made a slight detour at a fuel dock to load 30,000 litres of fuel. At last she was ready.

The breeze was picking up as she motored out towards the open sea. She bore west, away from the main island. As

Double Haven receded behind her, she felt some trepidation, as if she were deliberately repeating Julia Tang's journey into tragedy.

Just little over a half hour later she was at the fringe of the territory. She slowed down and veered slightly from her true course. She tacked from one side to the other until she was sure there was no Marine Police in the vicinity.

Then she glided past the warning signs towards the solitary rock, steering away from the side where Chad had tied up before. The multi-coloured stripes of oil led her back around to the cargo dock.

As she came out of the atoll's lee, the wind hit her full in the face, and a sudden surge took her by surprise. For a moment the vessel swung between the islet and the open sea. She turned the boat around and picked her way carefully between the buoys warning of hidden outcrops.

She made a pendulum-like progress until she reached the jagged quay, almost invisible behind the rusting carcass of an abandoned barge. She nosed the craft right up against the pile.

As the waves buffeted the hull, she stepped back in the lazarette and grabbed a torch. On an impulse she snatched one of the vests, along with a coil of rope.

Then she went out on deck. She teetered momentarily over the rainbow-streaked gap of water as she tied up the craft. Then with some effort she managed to pull herself up onto land.

The stench of rotting molluscs assailed her as she made her way over the stony ground. The remnants of an old shed provided temporary shelter as she surveyed the disintegrating pier.

It didn't look like it would last much longer. She hoped this would be her last visit.

She struggled up the uneven ground, past transport sheds and truck bays, motionless except for the shreds of old tarp and plastic flying in the wind.

The absence of any other landmarks disoriented her. The old structures were far below her now, and all she saw ahead of her was the sweep of waste rock and earth. It was an unsettling landscape. But there was one spot that drew her.

It was the one with the lone tree that set it off from the aridness all around it. She remembered being drawn to it the last time she had come with Chad.

It was one of the reasons she had come back. Now a handful of seabirds pecked at the little food they could find around it. They scattered with piercing shrieks as she came near.

She took out her phone and searched for the photo Estelle had given her. She held it up against the tree. She could see part of the same trail that had been captured in the image.

Now in the fading light, Melanie could see the tall structure in the distance, some kind of edifice far away.

It was hard to tell what kind of building it was exactly, but there was no doubt in her mind. The picture was taken here, in the very location where she was standing.

Julia had stood here and taken the last image she would ever send to anyone. Perhaps there was something symbolic in her choice.

Melanie wondered if that image of a green patch somehow reflected what Julia felt about her own life. A life of holding onto the fragile things she valued amidst the arid world created by her father's fortune.

She had sent the image to Estelle, then she went off, never to be seen again.

Did Julia end her own life? Did she find some other means of escape? Or did something worse happen to her? This was what Melanie had come to find out.

She turned back towards the shoreline below. The sea around her was empty for miles around. She was satisfied that the *Sea Tiger* was well concealed.

She set off towards the pit. As she made her way over the huge scars in the earth, trying to retrace the steps Julia must have taken. There seemed no other reasons for anyone to come here.

Only the most drastic possibility kept recurring in her mind.

But somewhere there was a lingering doubt. Why would Julia bother to hide the necklace if she had meant to kill herself? Why bother creating such a complex code?

By the time she reached the top of the knoll she stopped to look out over the water.

Some distance away, a small speck of white caught her eye. It was making impossibly slow progress across the stretch of blue. At the distance, it was hard to tell what kind of vessel it was.

But she was sure it was coming towards her. Like an accusing finger pointed straight at her, coming to expose her misdeeds.

She ran through possible ways she could justify her presence on the island.

But soon the craft had come close enough for her to make out its shape. It was some kind of pleasure boat, not a Marine patrol.

She relaxed. Just some weekend sailors looking for the best place to watch the sunset.

She turned around and resumed her route towards the pit. She slogged over the pebbly earth until she reached the barrier.

She rattled it a few times, checking the stability of the frame. She was grateful for the light that still cast its waning glow around her. But in most of the quarry below her, it was already dark. In that blackness lay the rest of Julia Tang's puzzle.

A glimpse of the chasm below made her knees go weak. Now she was glad she had brought the coil of rope.

She took one deep breath and raised herself up over the fence.

Her shoe almost got snagged at the sharp edge of the top bar.

When she climbed down on the other side, she let her light sweep a small area around her, afraid of seeing something that would stop her now.

Then she felt her way down the sheer staircase that pointed straight down into the blackness. She fought the fluttering in her stomach as her foot found each rung.

Further down, her torch carved out a pallid hole in the thick shadows. Every instinct told her to turn back and leave. But she willed herself to move forward.

With each step, a small portion of the quarry revealed itself under her light. It seemed a long way down to the sheen of water she could see below.

She noticed gaps in the corroded steel. The lattice that was holding her up from the abyss wasn't as solid as it had seemed to her before. She listened out for creaks in the metal, thuds that rang through the entire frame at her feet.

At last she reached the recess where she had found Julia's necklace. She pulled out her phone and took a picture of the recess. This was the spot Julia had marked as "qbx" in her GPS. It suggested she intended to come back to it at some later time.

From here she would have had to go back up the narrow steps and over that fence before she got out into the light.

Unless her way was blocked.

It's possible she thought. Perhaps *Julia had come by herself. Not knowing she had been followed.*

Melanie looked up at the way she had to go to get back to the surface. *Perhaps that's what happened.*

It would explain why Julia had never been found. Why her GPS ended up in Jason's apartment. Why Jason had never believed Julia could ever come back alive.

Now she knew how to use the knowledge. She knew how to redress the wrong. It would mean exposing her own deception. But perhaps this was how it was all meant to end.

She started walking back towards the exit.

She had taken more than twenty paces when a pain suddenly spread over her arm. The torch was knocked from her hand and fell clattering to the blackness below. She was thrown back against the rock, her face smarting from the blow.

She was now in complete darkness, and she felt around her on the ground for the light.

'What a nosy little bitch you are,' said Jason's voice from somewhere above her.

She struggled to get up, holding onto the wall for support.

'I could say the same about you,' she managed to respond, still struggling for breath. 'You're the one who listens in on other people's phone conversations. You're the one who keeps track of your stepsister's movements.'

'You're not my stepsister!' came his voice in the dark.

'I don't mean me. I meant Julia.'

Slowly and quietly, she got up and inched away from where she thought he was. She still couldn't see where her light had fallen. But she knew the ladder leading out was somewhere behind Jason

'I'm warning you,' she said. 'Julia took a picture the last time she was here.'

'So?' he laughed. 'A lot of good that did her.'

'She sent it to a friend,' countered Melanie. 'That friend has the picture on her phone. She knows this was the last place Julia visited.'

There was a pause as Jason tried to absorb what she had said. She listened out for his movements as she manoeuvred to get past him. If she stayed close to the ground, he would have to bend down to stop her.

'What friend?' His voice startled her in the gloom.

It was her turn to be silent. Estelle would never know she was in danger. That was perhaps why she had never mentioned receiving that last picture from Julia.

'What friend?' Jason's voice boomed again, closer this time. She tried to move away.

'You're lying,' he scoffed at length. 'There's no friend. And there's no picture.'

'Of course there is!' Melanie cried. 'That friend knows Julia's GPS was in your apartment. Along with a piece missing from Julia's boat. The apartment you've been keeping secret all this time.'

There was a scraping on the ground near her. She flinched at the thought he was just a foot or so away.

'A lot of good that will do you,' he snickered.

Then he suddenly grabbed her. She tried to wriggle free and they both ended up on the ground, Melanie's cheek pressing hard against the rusty steel that smelled of oil and seawater. He kept trying to loop his arm around her neck. Their struggle resounded on the metal scaffolding as their knees and elbows thumped against the metal.

'No!' she screamed. 'You won't do it a second time!'

She writhed under his weight until she was face up again. In the confusion she felt something getting entangled in her legs. Then she remembered. The coil of rope was twisted around them both.

She tried to push him away but he kept pressing down on her.

Finally she pushed head against his neck and buried her teeth into the skin.

He fell back from her with a howl of pain.

It gave her time to scramble back to her feet. She ran towards the stairs.

She could hear him pounding breathlessly behind her. She managed to scamper up several steps, groping in the dark, bruising her hands and her face against the rungs.

Then she felt his tight grip around her ankles. She kicked hopelessly against his hold. She grabbed onto the handrail, fighting to keep him from pulling her back down.

She tried to pull herself up on the handrail, cutting her hands on the rough metal. He increased the pressure to drag her down. She groped above her for anything to throw down at him. Her hand got tangled in one of the cords dangling from her knee.

'You want to be Julia?' he shouted from below her. 'Go ahead. You can join her down there!'

She grabbed anything from her pockets to fling down at him. She reached up over he ledge, grabbing dirt, clumps of grass or rocks, anything to pitch.

She heard him cry out in pain.

'Bitch!' he yelled. 'That's the last thing you ever did!'

It was completely dark above them now. She could feel him trying to pull himself up by her leg, and she twisted her whole body to slip out of his grasp.

He pulled even harder. The pain on her ankle was excruciating, her nails broke against the ledge as she slipped down a few inches.

With a desperate whimper, she bent her knee and kicked back wildly. She felt her heel hitting something.

Jason's grip on her legs seemed to go slack.

She felt an upward rush as the rope went taut in her hand and she felt herself being pulled down towards the abyss.

Chapter XXIII

It was only thanks to Feng that Jason's absence became known. He had waited on his boat as Jason had instructed. But when the delay had stretched out to over four hours, he finally took the vessel's emergency light and came ashore.

He picked his way gingerly over the unkempt quay. Then, seeing no other way, he started lumbering up the hill.

The desert island was doubly forbidding at night. The uphill ground was dotted with massive mounds of gravel as it stretched out into the darkness above him. The risk of injury was a greater deterrent than any threat of fines for unauthorized visits.

Feng's light only hinted at the hidden perils up ahead, a total blackness with only the sound of the ocean coming from the other side.

He forced himself to trudge up the pockmarked terrain. Jason could have easily lost his footing and injured himself.

Feng was sure he had seen another craft just on the other side of the atoll as they approached.

'Who could that be?' Feng had asked. But Jason was in one of those moods and didn't bother to reply.

Feng couldn't stifle his curiosity, however, and steered around the islet to get a closer look.

'What're you doing?' Jason had suddenly snapped. "We don't have time to mess about! Just tie up where we did before and let me off.'

Feng knew better than to argue with his friend, or to question why he had insisted on coming to the old quarry at exactly that time. So Feng looked for a protected spot as best he could. When he did, he dropped anchor and watched Jason scramble ashore and disappear up the rocky trail.

That was the same direction Feng would follow hours later, studying the otherworldly landscape in the faint light. The howling wind made him even more jittery, and then he was confronted with the gigantic crater.

The monstrous hole in the earth was as deep and black as the night above him. It was a greater menace than Feng had ever imagined. He lost his nerve.

He knew he had no hope of saving his friend. He had to call for help, even at the risk of being fined for the unauthorized visit. He fumbled for his phone and dialled Emergency Services.

But as soon as he heard the number ringing he began to have doubts. He knew Jason's family well enough never to respond in the usual manner. So he hung up and phoned Rosie instead.

'What?' her fury was almost as bad as the rebuke Feng was expecting from the rescue services. He struggled to explain the situation to her, telling her what little he knew of Jason's secretive mission.

The impulsive trip was typical of Jason's spur-of-the-moment whims. And just as typically, he had expected Feng to comply with his wishes without asking for any explanation.

'All right then,' Rosie said with exasperation, 'call 999. But get out of there!'

That was exactly what Feng had been intending. He was in enough trouble with his father as it was. With the drag racing and the multiple citations for speeding, now adding this could be the last straw.

He punched in the triple 9 number with shaking hands, and waited breathlessly for a response.

'*Wei?*' the emergency dispatcher's voice came on.

Feng was afraid to say that he was actually at the site of the emergency. For several moments he could only stammer that his friend had not returned.

'Returned from where?' asked the operator.

'He was going to the quarry,' blurted out Feng. 'He was supposed to be back hours ago. But he's not.'

'What time did he leave?'

Feng gave the time he and Jason had set off from the marina.

'How did he intend to get to the quarry?' demanded the operator.

Feng provided a vague description of his own movements with Jason, omitting any mention of his own part in it.

'Can you give a description of the vessel he was sailing on?' the operator posed further.

'No,' lied Feng. 'I didn't see it. I just dropped him off at the marina.'

He hung up before the operator could ask any more questions, then staggered down towards the wharf.

He was in such a rush to get back in his boat that he dropped the light into the water.

He hastily weighed anchor, turned on his motor and blasted away from the rock.

When he was about fifty feet away from the rock he turned around and saw the plastic torch bobbing in the water, flailing its beam crazily into the gloom all around. Feng muttered under his breath and turned the bow lights on.

He steered past the warning buoys until the rock had disappeared behind him.

He took the long way around, avoiding the brightly lit channel where he knew the Marine Police might already be steaming in the opposite direction.

It was nearly midnight by the time he got back to Hong Kong Island. He tied up at his berth and decided to call Rosie again.

She answered after the second ring.

'Are you back?' she demanded. 'Come see me at once!'

The hour didn't matter to Rosie. Normal time and distances were irrelevant to her. She expected her wishes to be fulfilled instantly, without her having to leave her seat.

Somehow they always were, as if by magic.

So Feng forgot about going home and drove to Rosie's penthouse instead.

He knocked softly on the door.

Rosie threw it open and Feng stood there, pale with worry.

'What happened?' she inquired in a shrill voice. He stumbled in and slumped into a chair.

'Jason asked me to take him to the quarry.'

'What on earth for?'

Feng looked at the floor. 'I don't know.'

'And?'

'When we got there, he told me to wait on the boat. He walked up the hill.'

'Where was he going?'

'He didn't tell me.'

Rosie got up and marched back and forth in her silk slippers.

'He didn't ask you to come?'

Feng shook his head. 'You know him. He just said there was something he needed to do.'

'In the quarry?

Feng nodded in a way that showed his own disbelief.

'What could he possibly need to do there?'

Feng held out his hands helplessly. 'He wouldn't say.'

Rosie turned quickly and crossed the room. She opened the glass cabinet and poured herself a drink. She had already downed a gulp before she remembered to ask Feng, 'You want one?'

He nodded and got up to fetch it himself. He poured himself a large Courvoisier.

When he sat down again Rosie resumed the pressure. 'Who have you told?'

'Apart from 999?' said Feng, staring into his brandy. 'Nobody.'

For a moment, Rosie also seemed transfixed by the golden liquid in her own glass. It caught the light from the red lantern behind her, and the pretty little reflection danced in her eyes.

Feng saw an amused look flit across her face now and then, as if remembering the various other mischiefs her son had perpetrated before. Then the features tightened again into a vexed expression.

'Well!' she stood up.

Feng knew to knock back his drink and get to his feet. Rosie walked with him to the door. 'That's all we can do for now.'

'You did right,' she reassured him. He turned around to face her in the hall.

'Let's see what they say in the morning,' Rosie said and shut the door.

Once again Tang Worldwide's culture of silence paid off. Despite the distraught phone calls from early in the morning to late at night, the hushed impromptu gatherings of executives behind closed doors, Stanley Wang managed to direct the mammoth company operations while autonomous mechanisms did their job in secret.

Those mechanisms had been put in place long before he came along. And he knew they would most likely outlive him, carrying on their functions long after he was gone.

The company had proved more enduring than its creator Arthur Tang. It had survived his demise and had weathered the vagaries surrounding his chosen successor, Julia Tang.

Now the company was carrying them through another turbulent patch.

It was like a huge humming machine, an intelligent ship bearing them through space, taking care of all their needs. It nurtured them like a caring mother, protected them like a father. It replaced any deity or kinship in their lives, becoming the one uniting entity in their existence. And though at times it demanded sacrifices of them, on the whole it rewarded them with security and plenty.

Stanley kept close watch on the market figures, and was gratified to see that there were no sudden dips or spikes that might hint at something going awry behind his company's gleaming granite façade. He was glad for the faith he had kept in forces greater than him. Thanks to them he felt cushioned from the drastic changes suddenly taking place all around him again.

The unwitting hero of this part of the story was Feng. Thanks to him a large-scale search of the quarry ensued. So desperate was Rosie to find her son that she didn't even try to interfere.

But when at last his body was found, no one could prevent the wild, uncontrollable publicity that erupted.

Thankfully, the tragedy was one step removed from the conglomerate by Arthur's death. The fatality was simply identified as the stepson of the company's late founder.

Perhaps stunned by the speed of events, Rosie didn't act until it was too late. Drunk with grief, she staggered from one place to another, looking for someone to tear apart. She made scenes in the boardroom, the company headquarters or anywhere else she could find an audience.

But all her desperate venom couldn't stop the genie from coming out of the bottle. Her son's presence on the banned island gave rise to a host of other questions. Including many that had been buried long ago.

A more thorough examination of the pit was ordered.

And after many weeks of upheaval, another set of remains was found. They had been there longer, and would perhaps have stayed hidden forever if not for Jason's accident.

Forensic tests took another month, but they confirmed that the bones were those of a young female who died in her early thirties. Perhaps only then, was the mystery of Julia Tang finally laid to rest.

Anywhere else, the quandary would have ended there. But if the remains of the missing heiress had at last been found, then who was the young woman who had suddenly appeared on the scene and set this denouement in motion?

Hundreds of miles away, that same young woman was leaving 33 Boulevard Georges-Favon in Geneva, closely clutching Julia Tang's monogrammed calf leather portfolio. In it were copies of bank documents she had just signed, along with two envelopes from the safety deposit box that had been maintained under the heiress' name until its closure that day.

As she walked to the corner, the sun shone down on her. She raised her face to feel its warmth: *at last she had gotten off the tiger.*

She caught a taxi back to her hotel.

In her room, she laid out the portfolio's contents on her bed. In one of the envelopes she found something more important than all of Julia Tang's stock certificates. It was the elusive letter Bernadette had mentioned long before.

In it Julia's dying mother made her most important last confession. She recounted how she had abandoned a child two years before Julia was born. Linda's last behest was that Julia find that forsaken child.

And that explained why the heiress spent her last years tracking down the sibling she had never known. It also explained to Melanie how Bernard Mason had found her, and why there were so many parallels between her and the missing heiress.

Back in Hong Kong, the papers were abuzz with news of the Tang's great philanthropy, and the unveiling of charities created from the most generous endowment the former colony had ever seen.

For years thereafter, the territory would remain transfixed with the Tangs. Most baffling of all was the story of the heiress who was said to return from the grave to solve her own murder.

Only to vanish again.

END

ABOUT THE AUTHOR

Jose Sevilla Ho was born in the Philippines in 1961. He went to study film directing at the Moscow Film Institute and lived in Russia for seven years. He has since worked as a university lecturer in the Philippines, Hong Kong, and Singapore, teaching film theory and screenwriting.

In 2002 he moved briefly to China, from where his grandfather Ho Xu Yang had emigrated in 1928. His daughter was born in Beijing.

He now lives in the United States with his wife and daughter. This is his third novel.

www.ingramcontent.com/pod-product-compliance
Lightning Source LLC
Chambersburg PA
CBHW020241180626
46810CB00006B/2302